A Stranger in Mayfair

**Center Point
Large Print**

*Also by Charles Finch and available from
Center Point Large Print:*

The Fleet Street Murders
The September Society

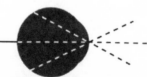

**This Large Print Book carries the
Seal of Approval of N.A.V.H.**

A
Stranger in
Mayfair

CHARLES
FINCH

CENTER POINT LARGE PRINT
THORNDIKE, MAINE

This Center Point Large Print edition is
published in the year 2011 by arrangement with
St. Martin's Press.

The text of this Large Print edition is unabridged.
In other aspects, this book may vary
from the original edition.
Printed in the United States of America.
Set in 16-point Times New Roman type.

ISBN: 978-1-61173-080-7

Library of Congress Cataloging-in-Publication Data

Finch, Charles (Charles B.)
A stranger in Mayfair / Charles Finch.
 p. cm.
ISBN 978-1-61173-080-7 (library binding : alk. paper)
1. Lenox, Charles (Fictitious character)—Fiction.
  2. Private investigators—England—London—Fiction.
  3. Murder—Investigation—Fiction. 4. London (England)—Fiction.
  5. Large type books. I. Title.
PS3606.I526S77 2011
813′.6—dc22

2011001260

To Emily, with love

acknowledgments

In the course of writing this series of books I have thanked my friends and family so comprehensively and doggedly that they must be exhausted. So I'll give them a break, except to mention the keen eyes and ongoing support of Charlie Spicer, Kate Lee, Yaniv Soha, Sarah Melnyk, Andy Martin, and Kaitlyn Flynn. The rest of you know who you are and how deep my gratitude is.

Oh, and thanks to Lucy!

prologue

"Clara, who is that gentleman? He looks familiar."

The question startled Clara Woodward, a slender, light-haired girl, out of her deep reverie. They had been sitting silently for ten minutes, and she had used most of the time to ponder the limitless wonders of her friend Harold Webb: his gentle good looks, his kind smile, his intelligent eyes, the dashing cut of his clothes.

It was hopeless. He was in London, and here she was in the entrance hall of a hotel in Paris. While to another girl this might have seemed wonderful (it was quite a grand, ancient hotel, the Crillon, situated handsomely on the place de la Concorde, and the hall itself was opulent, gilded and hung with old tapestries), to Clara it seemed a tragedy. With an inward sigh she turned her attention to her Aunt Bess.

"Which one do you mean?"

"There, the rather tall and thin one, with the brown hair."

Clara turned her gaze across the hotel's lobby. "And the short beard? That's Charles Lenox, I believe." In fact she knew it perfectly well. Two or three people had pointed him out to her, and she had once met him at a party in Belgravia. "I know he just recently married Lady—"

"Lady Jane Grey, yes, yes, I remember him now. They do let *anybody* into this hotel! It's shocking, most shocking."

"What's wrong with him, Aunt?"

"From everything I hear he's a fearfully low sort—consorts with common criminals. I know he calls himself a detective—Of all things!"

"I think she's very beautiful. I saw her in the restaurant."

"Lady Jane Grey?" Doubt clouded the older woman's brow. "I always heard she was of good stock, of course. Your late uncle once rode to hounds with her father, the Earl of Houghton, about ten years ago I think—yes, in 1854 or '5, I feel quite sure. I never heard a single good thing of Charles Lenox, though, you may be certain of that. For one thing, his closest friend is Thomas McConnell."

Clara looked blank. "Is that so bad?"

"My dear! He married far above himself, and he drinks like a fish. What do you say to a man who has a drunk for a near friend?"

"There was ever so much fuss when Mr. Lenox stopped that man at the Mint from stealing all that money—do you remember? The murdered journalists?"

"He probably murdered them himself," said Bess in a complacent tone. Whether it wanted to or not, she was determined to watch the world slide into iniquity.

The amateur detective—for such he was, and would own it much more proudly than someone like Bess, who thought it a betrayal of his birth, would prefer—paced across the marble floor of the hall. It was otherwise empty, too early in the afternoon for people to be at their tea. Clara thought gloomily of all the hotel's other residents, out buying lovely dresses and drinking lovely wine and seeing lovely gardens.

In truth, she knew far more of London and its society than her aunt ever could, and now she pulled out her trump card. She rather liked the look of Lenox, and adored the style and beauty of his new wife. "Wasn't he just elected to Parliament, Aunt?" she said sweetly.

Bess dismissed this with a scowl. "Oh, anyone is in Parliament these days, Clara, it's a disgrace. No, what matters is that for all his adult life he has been a detective. It's the lowest thing I ever heard, I swear."

Clara was only half listening, however, because her own mention of Parliament had recalled Harold to her again. Parliament was his ambition, and whatever he wanted she did, too, passionately.

It was hopeless, she repeated to herself. Utterly hopeless.

And for the silliest reason! It wasn't because

he didn't reciprocate her affection. He did, which made her heart flutter to contemplate. Unfortunately, he hadn't any money, and though it didn't matter a whit to her, her parents, who controlled her own marriage portion, had forbidden the match. Thus she was in Paris, out of London, her home city, and with her tedious, countrified aunt, who lived primarily in Kent and spent only a month of the year in town. "It will be nice for her and nice for you," her parents had said. They weren't cruel people—but oh, how cruelly they were behaving!

"I remember now," said her aunt. "George Barnard was the Master of the Mint, and he was trying to steal from it. But surely it was Scotland Yard who solved that mystery, wasn't it? Yes, I remember very definitely that it was Scotland Yard."

"But everyone in London knows that it was really Charlie Lenox," said Clara. "He never takes the credit. And he goes to the best places, I promise you."

"What the world's coming to!" said Bess, rolling her eyes heavenward. "Of course it's only because he's taking advantage of poor Lady Jane—charmed her, I'm sure, with his slick ways, and now she's burdened with him for good. Oh, dear, the thought of it!" Bess fanned herself fretfully.

"They're lifelong friends, I believe. They lived

in houses side by side for years before he proposed. I think it's wonderfully romantic."

"Clara Woodward, you're determined to vex me, aren't you? Why won't girls listen to *sense* these days. A detective, no matter what society he sees or how many Parliaments he's in, is the least savory, vilest, most evil-minded—"

But here she broke off, because the unsavory, vile, evil-minded man himself was walking toward them from across the hall.

It was a wide room, dotted with tables and sofas, with gold leaf everywhere and vast trees dimming the noise—or at any rate Bess prayed they dimmed the noise. The man's face was friendly enough. Perhaps he hadn't heard her.

"How do you do? I'm afraid that I must presume on very slight acquaintance to reintroduce myself to your niece. I'm Charles Lenox."

"How do you do, Mr. Lenox. My name is Bess Telford. You've met my niece?"

"Once, yes, but only very briefly, as I recall, and I'm ashamed to say I don't remember her name. Your name, ma'am?" he said, turning to Clara.

"This is Clara Woodward," said Bess, simpering a little. The Earls of Houghton, after all. And now she seemed to recall something about an older brother, too. Was it Edward Lenox? Edmund Lenox? A leading man in Parliament.

"As I say, I must apologize for presuming upon

our very brief first meeting, but I was wondering whether either of you had seen my wife here. I was five minutes late to meet her, and now it's been fifteen minutes. The clerks didn't spy her, but I thought you might have."

"Oh! How worrisome! I haven't seen her, I'm sorry to say, and in this city what might happen to an honest Englishwoman is anybody's—"

"I haven't seen her either," said Clara to save her aunt's solecism. For her efforts she earned a reproving look from her relation. "Did you see the Robinsons before you left London?"

This was their mutual acquaintance. "I did, yes, they—"

Determined not to be superseded by her niece, however, Bess said, "Remind me, Mr. Lenox, about the affair at the Mint—wasn't it you who sent that wicked man Barnard away to prison, and saved all of our money?"

Lenox turned red, and Clara felt she could have sunk into the ground. "Ah—I remember— I recall the incident to which I believe you're referring, ma'am, but it was not I, it was Scotland Yard, that apprehended the criminal."

"And that September Society—"

Thankfully for Lenox, at that moment Lady Jane Grey burst into the lobby, trailed by a small French girl in a dressmaker's uniform, some sort of apprentice, carrying a parcel under her arm.

"Charles!" cried out Lady Jane. "There you are! Whatever punctuality I ever could claim has been stolen from me by this city. I'm so sorry. But do introduce me, please, to your friends."

She was a lovely woman, though not immediately striking. She was plainly dressed, in a simple blue gown with a gray ribbon at the waist, and her dark curls looked natural, not affected. What Clara noticed, however, was the tremendous poise and wisdom of her eyes—and the faint lattice of wrinkles around them. She must have been thirty-five or thirty-six. Lenox himself was forty or just past.

After all the proper introductions had been effected and Bess had regaled the company at length with the story of that day hunting with Lady Jane's father in 1854 or 1855, Lenox invited the pair to dine with them the next night. When this plan was agreed he and his wife left, looking, Clara thought with a feeling of melancholy, as pink-faced and happy and thrilled as all newlyweds should.

She listened to her aunt expatiate on Lady Jane's virtues, and then heard her conclude, "And really he doesn't seem all that bad—for a detective, I mean. For a detective."

chapter one

For an Englishman it was a strange time to be in France. During much of the century a strong enmity had existed between the countries' two governments, first because of Napoleon's rather uncouth attempt to conquer Europe, then because of the lingering hostility born of that time. Now, though, the emperor's nephew ruled France and had shown himself more liberal than his uncle —he had freed the press and the government from many of their previous restrictions—and an uneasy peace had sprung up across the Channel.

Even during the worst of times, just after Waterloo, for instance, there had been civility among open-minded French and English men, and now a man like Lenox, who loved so much about France—its coffee, its food, its wine, its architecture, its countryside, its literature—could visit the place with open admiration. There were republican rumblings in the capitol, however, and many Frenchmen, whose grandfathers had survived the revolution, felt fearful of what the next years might bring. Both Lenox and Lady Jane were happy that they had come when they did. Who knew what changes another shift in regime might bring? Who knew whether they would ever be able to visit again? And since that was the case, they had done all they could. Lady Jane had ordered dresses by the dozen (the seamstresses here being so infinitely preferable to English dressmakers—even at the height of the war fashion had been smuggled from one country to the other), while Lenox had spent his days closeted with a dozen different politicians, all of them sympathetic.

For he was in fact the newly minted Member of Parliament for Stirrington—had been elected not six months since. In that time he had barely entered the great chamber, however. He and Lady Jane had married in the Whitsun Recess, and now, in the Summer Recess, they were on their honeymoon. Paris was their final destination. They had spent three weeks traveling through the beautiful lake towns of the Alps, then another two in the French countryside.

In truth, as wonderful as it had been, both longed to be home. They missed London, missed their friends, and missed the little street off Grosvenor Square, Hampden Lane, where they had lived in side-by-side town houses for the better part of two decades. When they returned the two houses would be one: Over the past months an architect had supervised the demolition of the walls between them and seamlessly joined the buildings' rooms to create one large house. It gave Lenox a good deal of private pleasure to contemplate this physical symbol of their union. For long years Jane had been his closest friend, and he could scarcely believe that he was lucky enough now to be married to her. Their births were close enough (hers slightly higher), and they had grown up together, but within London society she was one of the brightest stars, and while he was welcome everywhere and had a great variety of friends, he was viewed as idiosyncratic because of his career. Perhaps his marriage and his admission to Parliament would change that. He hated to admit it, but he wouldn't mind. It had been hard to go it alone for so long in the face of everyone's polite disapproval of his vocation.

That evening they were in their sitting room at the Crillon. She was at a small carved desk, writing her correspondence, and he was sitting in an armchair, reading. A cool summer breeze blew in through the window.

As if she were reading his mind, she looked up and said, "To think—in three days we'll be home!"

"I can't wait," he said quietly and ardently.

"I've had a letter from Toto. She's simply enormous, she says, and she and Thomas seem to be quite content together—what does she say? Here it is: *Thomas and I sit together in the evenings. I knit and he reads, except when we both stop and talk about baby names and what room to give the child and, oh, everything.* That sounds like Toto, doesn't it? She writes just the way she speaks."

Bess Telford's facts had been mingled with rumors—Thomas McConnell was a doctor and occasionally did drink too much. A talented surgeon from a family of minor nobility in Scotland, he had come to London to practice in Harley Street and shortly thereafter, almost to his surprise, married one of the most admired young women in the city. Lady Victoria Phillips was born with beauty and immense fortune, and in personality she was entirely winning—effervescent, affectionate, gossiping, and slightly silly—but she was also young. While their marriage had been happy for three years, after that it had become first an acrimonious and then a terrible one, full of fights and cold silences. For a period of two years the couple barely spoke, and Toto spent much of her time at her parents' house in the country. It was during this time that Thomas had begun to drink. Shamed by his wife's family into selling his practice for a song to a Phillips cousin (it wasn't considered fitting that the husband of Toto Phillips should be a professional man) his subsequent aimlessness had been cruel to his spirit. It was only within the last year or two that Toto and Thomas's relationship had healed, and her pregnancy—which was why, eight months in, she could describe herself as enormous—was just the final bond they needed to restore them to happiness.

The trouble between them had been terrible to Lenox and Lady Jane. Thomas was Charles's medical assistant when a case demanded it, and besides that a close friend, and as for Jane, Toto was a cousin of hers, and more like a niece than any of Jane's actual nieces. The couple's renewed closeness was a massive relief. Toto's series of letters had been more and more happy with each one, as the birth of her baby came closer and closer.

"Where will she go for the birth?" asked Lenox.

"I believe they intend to stay in London."

"I would have thought they might go to her father's house."

"In a way I'm glad they won't. It's always been too easy for Toto to flee to her family. Perhaps it's a sign that she's growing up."

Lenox stood. "Shall we go to dinner soon?" he asked.

"I'd rather just stay in, if you don't mind?"

He smiled. "Of course."

The next morning was August 25, the day in France of the Feast of St. Louis. By more than a century's tradition it was also the day the famous Salon opened at the Louvre palace, and the greatest artists of France and indeed the world displayed their year's work. Lenox and Lady Jane went early, heard Napoleon III speak, and spent a long day looking around. People surrounded a painting by Manet and another by Whistler, and while Lenox admired these profoundly he soon found himself steering away from the crowds and toward the back rooms. Here he found in one dim corner a series of three extremely blurred, thick-painted canvases of sunrise, even less distinct than Manet's. They seemed to be little more than evocations of figure and light. He stared at them for half an hour and, after consulting his new wife, bought one, the littlest one, which was blue and orange.

That evening they dined with Bess and Clara, and the next day they took a trip to the country and toured a small town with one of the politicians Lenox had met, who represented the district the town belonged to.

Then, just like that, it was all over. They had to wake very early the next morning to finish the packing their servants had begun and send their luggage off. By nine o'clock they were in a carriage on the way to Calais, and by noon they were aboard their ferry.

It was summer, but for some reason the Channel was extremely foggy, and as they stood on deck a wet, gray wind swirled around them.

"It seems like a dream, doesn't it?" said Lady Jane. "I feel as if we left yesterday. But think of all those beautiful Swiss villages, Charles! Think of that hundred-foot waterfall!"

"We ate in that restaurant on the mountain-side."

"And our guide when we went up there!"

"It was a wonderful trip," he said, leaning on the rail, "but I'm glad we're going home. I'm ready to be married in London now."

She laughed her clear, low laugh and said, "I am, too."

He hadn't been quite joking. He stole a glance at Jane, and his heart filled with happiness. For years he had thought himself a happy man—indeed had been happy and fortunate in his friendships, his work, his interests, his family—but now he understood that in that entire time something vital had been missing. It was she. This was a new kind of happiness. It wasn't only the mawkish love of penny fiction, though that was there. It was also a feeling of deep security in the universe, which derived from the knowledge of an equal soul and spirit going through life together with you. From time to time he thought his heart would break, it made him so glad, and felt so precarious, so new, so unsure.

A mild, wispy rain started to fall when they were nearly across the water. Jane went inside, but Lenox said he thought he might stay out and look.

And he was lucky to have done so. At certain

times in our lives we all feel grateful for one outworn idea or another, and now was one of those times for Lenox: As the fog cleared he saw much closer and bigger than he had expected the vast, pristine white face of the cliffs of Dover come into view. It made him feel he was home. Just like Jane did.

chapter two

It was fortunate that the man who had designed and built the ten houses along Hampden Lane in 1788 had built them to the same scale, albeit in different configurations. Lenox's and Lady Jane's houses both had twelve-foot-deep basements where the staff could work and live, eight-step front stairs that led to broad front doors (his was red, hers white), four floors of rooms, and a narrow back garden. It meant they fit together.

Still, to join them had taken a great deal of ingenuity on the part of a young builder named, aptly enough, Stackhouse. On the first floor he had knocked down the wall between their two dining rooms, creating a single long hall, which could now entertain fifty people or so. More importantly, it had left intact the two most important rooms in the house: Lady Jane's sitting room, a rose colored square where she entertained her friends and took her tea, and Lenox's study, a long, lived-in chamber full of overstuffed armchairs, with books lining every surface and a desk piled under hundreds of papers and trinkets. Its high windows looked over the street, and on the opposite end its fireplace was where Lenox sat with his friends.

Upstairs there was a large new bedroom for them, and on the third floor two small parlors became a very nice billiard room for Lenox. In the basement the builders only made a slim hallway between the houses, firstly so as not to tamper with the foundation and secondly because the couple didn't need as much space down there. They were reducing their staff. They only required one coachman now, two footmen, one cook (Lenox's, Ellie, was foul-mouthed but talented), and one bootboy. Lady Jane's cook gave notice, explaining that it was excellent timing, since she and her husband had always hoped to open a pub and now had the money. Still, it would leave four people out of work. Fortunately Lady Jane's brother always needed servants, and those who wanted to move from London to the country received their new billets happily. Three of them took this offer, and the fourth, a bright young lad who had been Lenox's coachman, took two months' pay and set out for South Africa to make his fortune, with a letter of introduction from his now former employer.

All of this still left one enormous problem: the butlers. Both Lenox and Lady Jane had long-serving butlers who seemed half part of the family. In fact it was unusual for a woman to have a butler rather than a housekeeper, but Jane had insisted on it when she first came to London, and now Kirk, an extremely fat, extremely dignified Yorkshireman, had been with her for nearly twenty years. More seriously, there was Graham. For all of Lenox's adult life, Graham had been his butler, and more importantly his confidant and companion. They had met when Lenox was a student and Graham a scout at Balliol College; special circumstances had bound them there, and when Lenox left for London he had taken Graham with him. He had fetched Lenox his morning coffee, yes, but Graham had also helped him in a dozen of his cases, campaigned for him in Stirrington, and traveled with him across Europe and to Russia. Now all that might change.

So when Lenox returned to London, he went over the new house with an awed, pleased eye—it was just as he had imagined it being—but with the consciousness as well that he had to confront the problem of Graham. The next morning he had a rather radical idea.

He rang the bell, and soon Graham appeared with a breakfast tray laden with eggs, ham, kippers, and toast, a pot of fragrant black coffee to the side. He was a compact, sandy-haired, and intelligent-looking man.

"Good morning, Graham."

"Good morning, sir. May I welcome you back less formally to London?" The previous night the servants had lined the hall and curtsied and bowed in turn to the newlyweds, then presented them with the wedding present of a silver teapot.

"Thanks. That's awfully kind of you—it's a wonderful pot. Graham, would you sit down and keep me company for a moment? You don't mind if I eat, do you? Fetch yourself a cup to have some of this coffee if you like."

Graham shook his head at the offer but sat down in the armchair across from Lenox, an act that would have drawn gasps from many of Lenox's acquaintances for its familiarity. They made idle chat about Switzerland as Lenox gulped down coffee and eggs, until at last, sated, he pushed his plate away and sat happily back, patting the crimson dressing gown over his stomach.

"How long have we known each other, Graham?" asked Lenox.

"Twenty-one years, sir."

"Is it really that long? Yes, I suppose I was eighteen. It scarcely seems credible. Twenty-one years. We've grown middle-aged together, haven't we?"

"Indeed, sir."

"I just got married, Graham."

The butler, who had been at the wedding, allowed himself the ghost of a smile. "I heard something of it, sir."

"Did you never consider it?"

"Once, sir, but the lady's affections were otherwise engaged."

"I'm sorry to hear it."

"It was many years ago, sir, when we still lived in Oxford."

"Have you been happy in your employment?"

"Yes, sir." Graham was an understated man, but he said this emphatically. "Both in my daily duties and in the less usual ones you have asked me to perform, Mr. Lenox."

"I'm glad to hear it. You don't fancy a change of work?"

"No, sir. Not in the slightest."

"You mustn't look so stony-faced, Graham. I'm not firing you—not by a long shot. Remind me, what papers do you read?"

"Excuse me?"

"What newspapers do you read?"

"The house subscribes to—"

"No, Graham, not the house—*you*."

"Below stairs we take the *Times* and the *Manchester Guardian*, sir. In my spare hours I usually read both."

"Does anyone else read them downstairs?"

Graham looked discomfited. "Well—no, sir."

"You know as much about politics as I do, or very nearly," murmured Lenox, more to himself than his companion.

"Sir?"

"May I shock you, Graham?"

"Yes, sir."

"I want you to come work for me."

The butler very nearly laughed. "Sir?"

Lenox sighed, stood up, and began pacing the study. "I've been troubled during all my time on the Continent about the business of a secretary. I interviewed eight candidates, all young men just up from Cambridge or Oxford, all of them of excellent family and eager to be personal secretary to a gentleman in Parliament. The trouble was that I felt that each one of them was sizing me up to decide when he could have my seat. They were all too ambitious, Graham. Or perhaps that's not it—perhaps it's simply that I didn't know them, and I didn't want to risk getting to know them as they worked for me."

"You cannot be suggesting, sir—"

"You read more than half the men sitting in Parliament, Graham. More importantly, I trust you." Lenox walked up to the study's row of high windows, his slippers softly padding the thick rug. He stared into the bright, summery street for a few moments. "I want you to come be my secretary."

Graham stood up too now, quite clearly agitated. "If I may speak freely, sir—"

"Yes?"

"It is an utterly impossible request. As gratified as I am at your consideration, Mr. Lenox, I am in no way suited to such a role—a role that belongs to someone—someone from the great universities, someone with far more education than I possess, and . . . if I may speak frankly, sir, someone of your own class."

"I'm not trying to change the world. I simply want someone I can trust."

Graham swallowed. "As a solution to a simple staffing problem, sir, I must say I find it exceedingly inelegant."

Lenox waved an irritated hand. "No, no. I want both you and Kirk to be happy, of course, but it's more than that. For one thing, you've been overqualified by your natural merits for years. More to the point—more selfishly—I'm new at this. I need help."

At last Graham was silent. Finally, he said, "I'm honored, sir."

"Will you do it?"

"I cannot say, sir. May I have time to consider the proposal?"

"Yes, of course."

"Would I still live here?"

"If you liked, yes. You shall always have lodging while I draw breath, as you well know."

"And if I say no, sir? What will become of me then?"

Grumpily, Lenox said, "Well, we'd keep both of you, of course—and we'd hire five more butlers, just to make sure we had one in every room."

Now Graham did laugh. "Thank you, sir."

"Before you get above your old station, would you mind helping me with this painting?"

It was the one from the Salon, the blurry one. The two men pried its crate open, took its wrappings off, and then walked it down to the dining hall. There they hung it, tilting it imperceptibly back and forth until it was just level.

"May I ask who painted it?" Graham asked.

"A chap named Monet," said Lenox. "Rhymes with bonnet, I think. I never heard of him myself. Funny, the picture looked better over in Paris."

"Such is often the case with these flashy Continental objects, sir," said Graham with evident disapproval.

As they got the picture hung just right, there was a knock at the door. Through the troubling weeks that followed, Lenox sometimes wished he and Graham had ignored that knock and the ominous events it portended.

chapter three

The gentleman's name was Ludovic Starling. Lenox had known him for a decade. Nevertheless it was a surprise to find him at the door, for there was little acquaintance between the two men.

Ludo was through and through a son of Wiltshire, with a family that had sat obstinately on the same plot of land there since the Restoration, when one of Ludo's progenitors had remained covertly loyal to the King. This man, Cheshire Starling, a blacksmith, had received six hundred prime acres in thanks for printing twelve copies of a single handbill that denounced (with dazzlingly poor syntax) Oliver Cromwell and his people. With a grant of three hundred pounds Cheshire had erected a tidy L-shaped hall, and the generations that had succeeded him in it had been filled with dull, pasty, and, despite their fanciful surname, heavy-footed men. The Starling women had just as little enterprise, and in all the family had been content to remain just as they were, year after year and decade after decade. Century after century. No Starling was ever too dismal a failure or too great a success, and the little parcel of family money never dipped or rose too high in value. The cousins were all looked after. They were a comfortable, pointless clan.

Until Ludovic, that is. About Lenox's age, he had gone up to university as a willowy, handsome, ambitious lad of seventeen. From there he had moved to London and by the age of thirty had through his marriage attained a seat in Parliament; his father-in-law was a Scottish lord with land in Kintyre and a district in pocket. Since then Ludo had been a reliable backbencher and more recently had assumed a prominent position in his party's hierarchy. He had also gained weight and was now a red-faced, sturdy, and social creature, who loved to drink and play cards. A year before he had inherited Starling Hall—an only child—but hadn't visited it since his father's funeral. All this Lenox knew by the way, just as well as he knew a thousand other short biographies of his London acquaintanceship.

"Why, Ludo, what can I do for you?" asked Lenox, who had come down the hall and watched Graham open the door.

"There you are, Charles. I'm sorry to pop up unannounced like this."

Graham left, and Lenox shepherded Ludo into the study to sit. "You're very welcome, of course. How is Elizabeth?"

"Quite well, thanks. A bit unsure of what to do

with herself, with Alfred at Cambridge and Paul following him in the fall. They're both here for the summer holidays at the moment, at least."

"Following in their father's footsteps at Downing, I take it? Here, come into my study. Have you come about Parliament? I'm to meet with a group of gentlemen this afternoon to discuss our position in the colonies. I expressed an interest on the subject, and James Hilary was kind enough to include me."

Ludo shook his head. "No, not that at all. Congratulations, by the way."

"Thanks."

"In fact I've come for another reason. A lad in my house has been killed."

"My God!"

"Not in my house," Ludo hastened to add. He was restless, anxious. In Lenox's study he stood up and paced back and forth. "A lad *of* my house, I should have said. In fact his actual demise took place in an alley just behind us, off of South Audley."

"Who was it?"

"Not anyone I knew well—a young man named Clarke, Frederick Clarke, who worked for me. He was only nineteen."

"How was he killed?"

"Bludgeoned to death. There was no weapon at the scene apparently."

"The Yard is in?"

"Oh yes—it happened last night. Two constables are there now, keeping people clear of the area. I came to see you because—well, because I know you've worked as a detective in the past. Kept your cases very quiet, too."

"This young man, Frederick Clarke, worked for you?"

"Yes, as a footman. His mother, Marie, was our housekeeper briefly, about fifteen years ago. Almost as soon as she came into our service she inherited something from her family and moved back to her hometown to open a pub. Apparently her son wanted to come to London, and she wrote asking if we might take him on, so of course we said yes."

"Decent of you."

"Elizabeth has a long memory for these things —you know how kind she is. He's been with us for four years now, but I spend so much time at the House and at the Turf"—this was his club, whose membership consisted largely of sportsmen and cardplayers—"that I don't know all the faces."

Four years! thought Lenox. It seemed impossible to live under the same roof as a person for so long without knowing him through and through. "You didn't know him, or you didn't know him well?"

"Didn't know him well, I should have said. Of course I knew his face and exchanged a few words with him here and there. But Eliza is very upset, and I promised her that I would ask for your help. She's the reason I'm here, in fact. Although we were both relieved when we remembered you had just gotten back into town."

"Oh?"

Ludo's face flushed, and his tone became confidential. "In truth I wouldn't mind it quietly handled, and I know I can count on your discretion. Quite between you and me, there has been some talk of a title."

"A title for you?" asked Lenox, surprised. A title usually capped a career. Ludo was still young, or at least middle-aged.

"I've been a guest at the palace quite often recently, and play whist with one of the royals almost every night. I won't say his name. But apparently my service in Parliament has been observed and may be commended."

"I congratulate you."

"It would please me immensely, I don't mind saying. It always rather rankled in our family that the old King didn't hand us something in that line. God bless him," he added as an afterthought.

This was puzzlingly intimate, thought Lenox, and then asked, "Why must it be quiet? Surely there's no implication that you killed the boy?"

"I? Never!" Ludo laughed. "Besides having no reason on earth to do it, I was sat firmly at the card table for ten hours last night, with Frank Derbyshire and a whole host of others."

"Of course. I didn't mean—"

"It's only that the slightest breath of scandal or infelicity can shake this sort of thing. It's all so fragile, you know."

"The title?"

"Yes, exactly. Also, as I say, Eliza is quite upset—most upset—and asked me to come."

Lenox was puzzled by Ludo's behavior. Did he care about this lad, Frederick Clarke? Why not let the Yard handle it? And why was he bursting with all this information about his prospects for an elevation to the House of Lords? It seemed in awfully poor taste. Then it occurred to Lenox that perhaps Ludo couldn't share any of this potential good fortune with his friends, or even his family, lest it fall through and make him look like a liar or a fool. It might be that he needed an audience, someone who would listen with appropriate gravity to the news but who would keep it to himself. Yes, Lenox decided, it was because the man had run over the tantalizing facts so often in his mind and needed to blurt them out to stay sane. Had been bursting with the news. Strange indeed, though, to deliver it as he simultaneously delivered news of a murder.

He was terribly restless. "Here, sit," said Lenox. At last Ludo settled into the armchair

Graham had only recently occupied, opposite Lenox and in front of the cold hearth.

"Thanks, thanks," he said. "Now—may I bring you back with me? My carriage is outside."

"I'm honored that you came to me, but it's the worst possible moment for me to take on any new responsibilities."

"You mean you can't come look?"

"I wish I could, but I cannot. The leaders of our party have made allowances because of my marriage, but as you well know the House reconvenes in a little more than a week's time, and there are meetings for me to attend hour after hour before then."

"If it's about money . . . ?"

Shocked, Lenox drew himself up in his chair and said, "No, it isn't."

Ludo saw straightaway that he had made a blunder. "I'm so terribly sorry. Of course it isn't about money. Forgive me."

"As I say, my responsibilities at the moment scarcely permit me any return to my old field. You of all people can understand how daunting it is to be a new Member."

"Yes, of course."

"The Yard is competent in these matters, I promise."

Ludo, still agitated, said, "Are you sure you couldn't come and have a quick look?"

In fact Lenox was sorely tempted to do it. He

missed his old work and, excited though he was about his new career, contemplated with mute dread the idea of giving detection up forever. Even while he had been on the Continent, absorbed by Jane and the local life, his mind had often turned back to old cases. Still, he said, "No, I'm afraid—"

"Oh, please, Lenox—if only for my wife. She has no peace of mind at all just now."

"But—"

"We must look out for each other, Members of the Commons. I wouldn't ask if I weren't distressed."

Lenox relented. "Just a look. Then perhaps I'll pass it on to my student, John Dallington, and he can delve into the matter if he chooses. Come along, I must hurry. That meeting about the colonies is in two hours."

chapter four

As he had one foot hiked up into Starling's carriage (a massive black conveyance with the family crest worked into its doors—a slightly low thing to have if you weren't a duke, perhaps) Lenox had the novel realization that for the first time since he was a boy he had a duty to keep someone apprised of his whereabouts. Stepping back down, he grinned to himself. He was a married man now. How wonderful to contemplate.

Jane was on one of the thousand social visits that occupied weekday mornings, making the rounds in her own old, slightly battered, and extremely homey carriage. She would be back soon, however.

"Just one moment, Ludo," said Lenox and dashed inside. He found Graham and asked him to tell Lady Jane where he was going; between this and the meeting it would be nearly supper before he returned.

"Yes, sir," said Graham. "Here, sir, your—"

"Ah, my watch. Don't think I've forgotten our conversation, by the by. Will you think about it?"

"Of course, sir."

"Since you're still a butler for the moment, however, don't forget to tell Jane where I am." Lenox laughed and stepped quickly back out to join Ludo. He realized as he laughed that his spirits had lightened with the prospect of a new case.

They went through Mayfair at a rapid trot. It was Lenox's home neighborhood, the one in which he felt most comfortable, and much of his adult life had been spent inside this stretch of London from Piccadilly to Hyde Park. As it had been for the past century or so, it was a fashionable place, the most expensive part of the city, with faddish restaurants, white glove hotels, and a gentle, calm aspect: The boulevards were wide and uncrowded, the houses well kept, and the shops tidy and pleasant. In some parts of London one felt quite hemmed in on the narrow streets, with carriages brushing by each other and mongers shouting to sell their fruit or fish, but Mayfair seemed somehow more civilized. It certainly wasn't a quarter of London that Lenox associated with murder. Though the practice was all but dead, you'd still be more likely to see a duel between gentlemen in Green Park than any bloody-minded killing.

The carriage stopped a few hundred feet short of Curzon Street, where the Starling town house stood just off a corner. Ludo, who hadn't spoken during the trip, rapped the side of the carriage with his walking stick.

"Here it is," he said to Lenox as they stepped out. "The alley. Many of the servants on Curzon Street use it every day to do their errands. These constables have heard a fair bit of backchat from upset housemaids wanting to get by."

It was a narrow lane, the width of only two or three people, and slightly suffocating because the two brick walls that closed it off reached up five and six stories. South Audley Street, a busy thoroughfare, was bright and summery, full of people, but as Lenox peered down the lane it looked dim and sooty.

"What time of day did it happen?"

"In the evening, apparently. It's far busier during the day than at night. A young girl came across the body at half past eight and immediately fetched the officer at the end of the road."

Lenox nodded. It was an affluent neighborhood, of course, and as such would have been swarming with bobbies. The alley might have been the only place for blocks where an assailant could risk an assault without being immediately seized.

"Let's walk down and have a look."

The alley was fifty or sixty feet long, and halfway down that length a single constable stood. He was a tall, burly, and reassuring sort. It had been some time since Lenox had visited the site of a murder, and he had somehow forgotten, as one always did, the eerie feeling of it.

"Hello, Mr. Johnson," said Ludo. "Where did your Mr. Campbell go?"

"Back to his beat, sir. We had the inspector out, and he said only one person needed to stay here."

"To see if anyone returned to the scene?" Lenox asked.

"Yes, sir. Can't quite see the point myself, when there are thirty people clamoring to get in every minute or so."

"At any rate I'm glad you've kept the scene intact this long. Which inspector was it?"

"With all politeness and that, sir, I didn't catch your name?"

"I'm Charles Lenox, Constable Johnson."

The man's ruddy face lit up. "Lenox the detective!" he said brightly.

"That's right."

"You ought to have said so. We're all right grateful down the Yard that you caught that bastard Barnard. Excusing my language, sir," he added, nodding to Ludo.

"Not at all."

Barnard had killed—had ordered killed—a famous police inspector, a man by the name of Exeter. Lenox had uncovered the deed.

"Thank you," said Lenox, "although I must say that my role was extremely minor—the Yard did the vast majority of the work."

Johnson grinned and tapped his nose. "Our secret, sir," he said, "but I heard Inspector Jenkins tell about it all, sir. *All* of it," he added significantly.

Ludo looked at the pair slightly irritably, as if he suddenly suspected that Lenox might get a title now and there was only one to be had. "Would you mind if Mr. Lenox looked at the spot?" he asked.

"Not at all. Down this way, sir."

The genial tone of their conversation abruptly

changed as they came upon the scene of the murder. There was a large smear of dried blood along the brick walkway. *Only nineteen,* thought Lenox with a lurch in his heart. Just an hour before London had seemed like the most marvelous place in the world, but all at once it seemed like a midden of sorrows.

"As well as we can work it out, Mr. Clarke never saw the man who attacked him," said Johnson, now somber, business-like.

"Must it have been a man?" asked Lenox.

"Sir?"

"If this is a servants' lane, it's much more frequented by women then men, I would imagine. Was Clarke a large boy, Ludo?"

"Yes."

"Still, we mustn't exclude half of the population from our suspicion. Or slightly more than half, isn't it? Go on, Constable."

"The wound was on the back of the young man's head."

"Was he hit from above or below?"

"Sir?"

"Never mind. I'll ask—just a moment, I don't think you ever told me which inspector is looking at the case?"

"Old Fowler, sir."

"Grayson Fowler? Perhaps I'll ask him. Or it might be just as well to send for McConnell," muttered Lenox to himself.

He dropped to one knee and began to look very carefully at the vicinity of the attack on Frederick Clarke. Aside from the blood there was an unpleasantly evocative clump of hair on the ground.

"Did you remove anything from the area?" asked Lenox. "Or did Fowler?"

"Only the body, sir. All else is as it was."

"Which way was the body facing?"

"Toward the street you came from—South Audley Street, sir."

"And he was attacked from behind. Where does this alley lead?"

"To a small back lane with houses backed onto it, sir, including Mr. Starling's."

"I take it the servants use this lane to get between their houses and the street? If that's so it seems likely our attacker was either lying in wait or came from that direction. It makes me suspect one of your servants, Ludo."

"Oh?" said the man, who had been standing quietly off to the side.

"The men and women with whom Frederick Clarke spent nearly every hour of his life in quite close proximity—yes, our first thoughts must go to them. Still, it would be silly to draw any conclusions yet."

Rising from his crouched position, Lenox walked around the blood spill toward the side of the alley that led to the backs of the houses, away from the alley's busy end at South Audley Street. He ran his hands gingerly along the walls.

"Did Inspector Fowler say what kind of weapon it might have been?" he asked.

"No, sir."

"Ludo? To you?"

"He didn't say anything about it."

For the next ten minutes Lenox went up and down the alley, very carefully dragging his fingertips along each wall and walking gingerly, in short steps.

"What are you doing?" Starling eventually asked.

"Oh, just a suspicion," said Lenox quietly, still focusing intently on his fingertips and feet. "If the murderer was someone who came down this alley often . . . I've seen this kind of thing before."

"What?"

"Sometimes the murder weapon is whatever's at hand."

Suddenly Lenox felt his foot rock slightly. Without moving he bent down, then drew his foot back. The brick that had shifted when he trod on it now looked plainly disconnected from the ones that surrounded it. He gently pried it out and held it up for all three of them to look at.

"What is it?" asked Johnson.

"It's sticky," Lenox said.

"Cor!" said Johnson wonderingly.

On the bottom of the brick was a smudge of what was plainly fresh blood.

chapter five

For a moment the three men stood, staring mutely at the murder weapon.

"Does that mean it was a crime of passion?" asked Ludo.

"Why do you ask that?"

"A brick right at hand—an argument—it must have been the heat of the moment!"

"Impossible to say," Lenox said, shaking his head. "What it must confirm, I believe, is what I said earlier—that the murderer has come up and down this alley many times, and knew which loose brick would make for a decent weapon. Much simpler to replace the brick than bother hiding some blunt object, or throwing it away and risk it being found. Johnson, have you your whistle?"

"Yes, sir."

"Blow it for the nearest constable, and we'll have him fetch Fowler out for this fresh piece of evidence. Ludo, I need to leave, but as I said

I'll pass the case on to my assistant, John Dallington."

"Dallington?" said Ludo dubiously. "That boy of the Duke of Marchmain?"

Lenox laughed. "The very same. I assure you that he's quite a competent student of mine."

John Dallington had a firm reputation as the greatest rake, gambler, seducer, and libertine in all of London. Born to wealth and status, he had abjured the usual course (clergy or military) of most third sons of rank. It was to Lenox's very great surprise that this Dallington, who was perfectly charming, a small, dapper, handsome fellow, unmarked by his excesses, but without a reliable bone in his body, had asked to learn the art of detection. Against all odds he had since then picked up a great deal of Lenox's knowledge and even, in the business of the September Society, saved Lenox's life. He still drank and caroused now and then—it was troubling—but in the midst of their cases together his conduct had been largely faultless. More than that, it had been a balm to Lenox to have a colleague. For so long he had struggled alone to keep his head held high when people disdained his profession or pitied him—or, as that morning, offered him money. There had been Graham, of course, and even occasional help from his brother, but Dallington was different. He found Lenox's passion for detection not embarrassing, as many people seemed to, but fascinating. It was a comfort.

Still, Ludo's reaction to the name of John Dallington was scarcely surprising. If a century passed he wouldn't live down the character he had earned in three or four years during his early twenties.

"If you can vouch for his dependability," said Ludo with a doubtful grimace, "then I suppose that would be all right."

"I'll send Thomas McConnell to have a look at the body, too. I wouldn't mind seeing Frederick Clarke's clothes and possessions myself, either, but it will have to wait for another day."

There was then a footfall at the end of the alley, and all three men turned their heads to see who it was.

"Eliza!" said Ludo, glancing quickly at Lenox. "How are you, dear?"

"Hello, Ludovic. And who can this be—Charles Lenox?"

Lenox nodded. "How do you do, Mrs. Starling?"

Elizabeth Starling was a pretty, fragile, smallish woman, with a little bit of plumpness and big, soft brown eyes. She looked rather like Marie Antoinette playing a milkmaid at the Petit Trianon.

"Quite well, thank you. But I thought you were still on your—"

"Why have you come into the alley?" said Ludo.

46

"Don't interrupt, dear," she said good-naturedly. "Anyway, I might ask you the same thing. Mr. Lenox, I thought you were still on your honeymoon?"

Lenox looked at Ludo, who was beet red. "No, I told you Charles came back, dear. He was kind enough to come have a look at the scene of poor Frederick's death."

"You didn't tell me anything of the sort."

"And why *have* you come into the alley?"

"To see if Constable Johnson needs anything to drink or eat. Constable?"

"No, ma'am," said the bobby, touching a knuckle to his forehead.

"Well, come round if you do. Mr. Lenox, would you like a cup of tea?"

"I fear I already find myself late for an important meeting, thank you. Ludo, shall I be in touch?"

"Oh—yes, of course."

"Constable, your whistle?"

Reminded, Johnson whistled for help, and Lenox, doffing his hat, bade everyone goodbye.

As he walked down Curzon Street onto Half Moon Street (his meeting was in Whitehall, and he intended to cut through Green Park to get there) Lenox pondered Ludo Starling's bizarre behavior. For starters there was his strange, agitated manner throughout their encounter.

More significantly, why on earth had he claimed that his wife wanted Lenox on the case so badly when it was plain she had no idea he was in town?

But he put this out of his mind, ready for a different kind of challenge. He was going toward the Cabinet Office, a glorious old building erected on the site of the old Palace of Whitehall, where the Kings and Queens of England had lived until 1698, when they moved to St. James's Palace on Pall Mall. It now housed hundreds of government workers, but inside, strangely enough, you could still see what remained of Henry the Eighth's old tennis courts.

The meeting lasted several hours and was of intense interest to Lenox. He took copious notes (in fact he felt embarrassed to be without his personal secretary—all the rest of the dozen men in the room had bright young lads straight from Charterhouse and Cambridge seated just behind them) but never once spoke. At the break for tea he dispatched short notes to Dallington and McConnell, asking them to come by his house later, but otherwise his mind was wholly focused on his work for Parliament. They talked first about Hong Kong, which had been seized some thirty years before, then a sleepy town, now an expanding city; then they discussed the potential purchase from the ruler of Egypt of part of a great canal; and at last they talked at great length about

48

the recent consolidation of several disparate provinces into what was now called (Lenox still had trouble taking the name seriously) the Dominion of Canada. Victorialand had been perhaps too jingoistic a suggestion, but how infinitely preferable it would have been, Lenox thought, had they named it Anglia, as he had heard was proposed at the time.

Exhausted and pleased, he left the room six hours after he had first entered it, feeling firstly that he had a new understanding of the British colonial position (to think that in the last fifty years the empire had added two hundred million souls and five million square miles to its purview! What astonishing numbers, which none of the dustmen and bankers in the street thought about for more than a passing moment!) and secondly that he had a new collegiality with the men who ran the Colonial Office. Lenox had no intention of becoming a backbencher. He would wait his turn, to be sure, and could be patient—but what effort could win him in power and influence, it would.

It was understandable, therefore, that Frederick Clarke and Ludo Starling were far from his mind as he arrived in Hampden Lane. But no sooner had he turned the door handle than he remembered that McConnell and Dallington would likely be there. Supper with Jane would have to wait half an hour.

In fact it was only the younger of the two men who was there; Jane, according to Graham, was still out, but Lenox found John Dallington sitting in one of the comfortable armchairs in the study, feet propped up on the rail of the fireplace, a thin cigar in hand, and a huge smile on his face. This last because he was reading *Punch*.

"Mr. Punch's Book of Birthdays," Dallington said in response to Lenox's querying look. "But please!" He stood up. "Let me welcome you back from your honeymoon! It was the handsomest wedding I ever attended, I swear. I had to jostle with about a dozen cabinet ministers and fifteen dukes just to get a look at you. They were turning away mere viscounts at the door, the poor devils. Pretty hard on them."

Lenox grinned. "Was it as pompous as all that?"

"Pompous—never. Justly well attended, I would say. I swallowed two buckets of champagne at the breakfast and asked Lady Jane to elope with me. She said no, which was probably wise of her."

"She told me. You said something about letting the better detective win?" Lenox chuckled. "Have you surpassed me already?"

"Never. Still, I was intrigued by your note."

"Yes, thanks for coming. Drink?"

"Rum and soda if you've got it."

Lenox went to the drinks table and poured them each a tumbler. "It happened down by

Curzon Street. Did you ever hear of someone called Ludovic Starling?"

"I don't think so."

"He's in Parliament, a genial cove, quite sociable. One of his footmen went missing last night."

"I call that careless of Starling."

Lenox frowned. "It would be funnier if this unfortunate lad, Frederick Clarke, hadn't been found dead in a nearby alley."

"Oh, dear."

"Quite. I was just over at the scene."

"Oh?"

Lenox described Constable Johnson, Ludo's strange behavior, and finding the murder weapon.

"Well spotted," said Dallington at the conclusion of the story. "The brick, I mean. Does it really help us, though?"

"In a sense, yes. As I just said, I believe it means the murderer is local. Impatient, too—or in hot temper, though that's a debatable point. It also means that the Yard won't waste time searching for a weapon."

There was a knock at the door, and Graham entered, followed by Thomas McConnell.

"Hullo, Charles!" said the doctor. "Welcome back to England. And Dallington, excellent to see you."

"The baby is imminent?" Lenox asked.

"It's all very close," answered McConnell. He looked, as ever, slightly worn, with his battered heather coat and lined eyes, but he seemed happy as well. The two worst moods of his past —manic amiability and morose depression— were neither of them to be seen.

"Do you have time to look at something for me? It's why I wrote you."

"With all the pleasure in the world."

Lenox ran over the details of the case for McConnell's benefit, and then the three men sat and discussed how to handle things. In the end they concluded that Dallington would delve into matters on Curzon Street and McConnell would go have a look at the body. This left Lenox with the rather dry task of sending a note to Grayson Fowler and asking him to share information, always a tricky business. They agreed to recon-vene the next evening with their findings.

Though Lenox had a day full of meetings tomorrow to look forward to, he felt a slight pang. Was this as close as he would get, from now on? What about the midnight chase and the hot trail? Were they left to Dallington now?

Little did Lenox know how involved he would soon become, and how close to home danger would strike.

chapter six

Lady Jane returned that evening at half past
eight. At nearly the same time, so did her butler,
Kirk. He had been visiting a sister in York for
two weeks ("Who knew that butlers had sisters?"
Dallington had said when he heard the news) but
had come back by the evening train. With him
and Graham both below stairs, it was critical
that the issue of who would be the house's butler
be resolved once and for all. Doubly so, Lenox
felt, because of how unprotected he had felt at
the day's meeting without a personal secretary.

He and Lady Jane discussed this, and their
respective days, over lamb and preserves, and
afterward retired into the cozy sitting room in
what had been Jane's house before the merger.
It seemed funny to walk to it without leaving his
own house—but then, Charles realized even as he
thought that, it was all his own house now. How
strange.

"Do you find yourself still going to your own
door?" asked Lenox.

"Sometimes. I came to yours so often anyway
that the change isn't so great."

Despite the fusion, this room had retained

entirely Jane's personality, and he adored every part of it—the old letters tied with ribbon on the desk, the deep sofas, the rose-colored and white wallpaper (his own study had a brooding mahogany), the pretty curlicued mirror over the dainty bureau. Gradually, he knew, his own ways would suffuse her rooms, and hers would suffuse his. For the moment, it reminded him how special, how lucky, his new life was, and how intimate an act living together could be. In his fortieth year he was learning something entirely new.

They retired early, laughing lightly and holding hands, to bed. The next morning was bright and wet, with a big wind shifting all the trees on Hampden Lane. Lenox ventured out for another day of meetings (Graham was noncommittal all morning, and Lenox sensed he wanted some time) and arrived home late and soaked to the bone from the short walk.

Apparently McConnell and Dallington had been busy, too; freshly arrived, they had towels and were patting their faces dry.

"Hullo, both of you," said Lenox. "I bet you had a more exciting day than I did."

"What about corridors of power and all that nonsense?" asked Dallington, lighting his cigar. The usual neat carnation sat in his buttonhole, and despite the rain he looked well put together.

McConnell, on the other hand, looked weary

but had an unmistakable glow on his face—the pleasure of work.

"It *can* be exciting," said Lenox thoughtfully, "but at the moment all I want is to sit in the chamber itself, rather than listen to a long, haranguing lecture about taxes."

"Be a brick and make them lower, all right?" said Dallington.

Lenox laughed. "Yes, all right."

"Good chap."

There was a pause, and all three men waited expectantly. "Shall I go first?" asked McConnell after a moment.

"By all means," said Lenox. "No, wait! In all the activity of the day I plum forgot to write Inspector Fowler. He keeps late hours, though, so perhaps a note will still catch him. Just a moment."

The detective went to his desk and scribbled down a few lines, then rang the bell for Kirk.

"Take this down to Scotland Yard, would you?" he asked.

Kirk, looking taken aback, said, "Shall I leave it with the morning post?"

"I'm afraid I need it taken now."

"At this hour? If you please, of course."

Lenox had forgotten for a moment how used Graham was to all of his idiosyncrasies, and how different life would be without that luxury. "Wait a minute, though—perhaps Mr. Graham could take it."

"Certainly, sir," said Kirk, looking relieved.

Graham came and took the note, and in due course Dallington, Lenox, and McConnell were all seated again.

"Now, Thomas. I apologize."

"Not at all. There's not much to say, really. I went down and took a look at Frederick Clarke's body this afternoon, as we agreed. It wasn't a pretty sight. His wound was on the right side of the back of his head, and it was consistent with the corner of a brick as far as I could ascertain. I conferred with the coroner, and he agreed.

"I did notice one thing, however, that he hadn't picked up. There were barks and scrapes on both of his fists. I'm not entirely sure what that means. Perhaps it's unrelated to his death. At any rate they were a day old or so—scabbing up a little, not fresh."

"So he had been in a fight the day before he was killed?" Dallington asked.

"A day or two, yes."

Lenox made a note on the small pad he took from his jacket's breast pocket. "Dallington, if you go to the house on Curzon Street—hold on a moment, have you already?"

"Not yet."

"If you do, keep an eye out for anybody with similar markings. I should have told you before, by the way, always look at hands. It was Thomas who brought to my attention the importance of fingernails when we were working on a case together some years ago. The dead woman had pink soap under her fingernails, and from that fact we deduced her unfaithfulness to her husband."

"How?" asked Dallington.

McConnell chuckled bleakly. "She was a poor woman. Scented soap would have been well beyond her means. I should far more easily have believed it if she had lice. She worked in a tavern, quite a successful one in Ealing, and after we found the soap under her nails we began looking at every sink we could find in the owner's rooms over the pub. He had pink soap of the same scent on it. A bit of a dandy, I suppose. We couldn't prove anything based on that, but it was our first hint."

"After that it all came tumbling down around the man's head. Josiah Taylor. He hung for it, I'm afraid."

Dallington looked taken aback. "Goodness."

"It's something I try to avoid, but occasionally . . . at any rate, hands and fingers. A valuable tip."

The young lord took out his own notebook and jotted a few lines in it. "Thanks," he said. He was always on the lookout for these informal suggestions.

"What about you, then? You didn't go to the house?"

"Not yet, no. I didn't know whether Ludovic Starling would appreciate it."

"I told him you would come."

"Yes, but I thought it best to be forearmed. I compiled a list of all the house's inmates."

"Ah—excellent," said Lenox. "Let's hear it."

"Starling himself. He's forty-two and an MP. Spends much of his time at the Turf Club. Wife Eliza or Elizabeth, thirty-eight, son of a Scottish lord whose borough Ludovic sits for. So far none of this is new, of course. At the moment his children are home. There's Alfred, who is nineteen."

"The same age as Frederick Clarke," said McConnell.

"Alfred is at Downing College, Cambridge, doing Greats. A second year."

"It's just called classics there, you know, not Greats," said Lenox. "That's Oxford terminology."

"He's home for the summer holidays but leaving in two weeks to go back. Then there's his younger brother, Paul. He's seventeen, and he was at Westminster until two months ago. He's going up to Downing, too, at the same time as his brother.

"Rounding out this chummy household is an old man—Tiberius Starling, Ludo's great-uncle. He's eighty-eight and apparently deaf as a post. His best friend is a cat, which he apparently calls Tiberius Jr. From the sound of it he doesn't greatly esteem his niece-in-law, or even his nephew, really, but they keep him around because they want his money. They're afraid he'll leave it to the cat—no, really. I swear. No children, and he made a mint in the mines about a thousand years ago."

McConnell laughed. "How did you find all this out?"

"Asked acquaintances of mine, snooped around the neighborhood."

"What about below stairs?" asked Lenox.

"Five live in—it's quite a large house. There were two footmen, though now of course there's only the one. Aside from Frederick there's a chap named Foxley, Ben Foxley, a huge strapping fellow. I'll be sure to look at his hands."

"Could you tell anything about the assailant's height from Clarke's body?" asked Lenox of McConnell.

"Yes—we can identify him as being of roughly the same height as Clarke, give or take three or four inches in either direction. The blow didn't come from a sharp angle, up or down."

"So anyone of virtually any height," said Dallington wryly.

McConnell shrugged. "I wish it were more conclusive."

"Who else, John?"

"Sorry. Two footmen. One housemaid, Jenny

Rogers; one cook, Betsy Mints; and a butler, Jack Collingwood. I couldn't find out much about these three. In addition there are a scullery maid and a stableman who don't live in but are at the house most days."

"Seven in all, then. Six now."

"That's right."

"Plus five family members. That's eleven suspects," said McConnell.

"Old Tiberius couldn't lift a feather over his head, much less a brick," said Dallington.

"And Ludo was at cards at the time of the murder. The rest of them, Dallington?"

"All at home, strangely enough, except the scullery maid, who was at her own home in Liverpool Street."

"Then we can safely discount her. Still, that leaves eight. Without even mentioning the possibility that it's someone entirely outside of the Starling circle."

Just then Graham came in, trailed worriedly by Kirk, who looked ready either to stop him or announce him. Graham informed the group that Fowler had gone home for the evening. After a few minutes' further discussion, the three men stood up and parted, agreeing that they would meet again soon—or at least when Dallington had discovered anything worth looking into further.

chapter seven

The next morning Lenox woke feeling for the first time as if he were truly back in London. It put him in a happy mood, and he traipsed downstairs softly whistling. A little while later he sipped his morning coffee, standing with his cup by the second-floor windows and gazing out over the gray, blustery day, wearing his familiar old blue slippers and crimson dressing gown. For a fleeting moment his absence from home felt almost like a dream. Had it really been he who walked across Austrian heaths and Paris boulevards? Had it really been he who got married in that chapel three months ago? The displacement from his old life was jarring—and wonderful. He thought with a smile of Jane, still sleeping upstairs.

He was up earlier than she because it was an important day for him. In six days exactly he would attend his maiden session at the House of Commons, taking a seat for the first time along the green baize benches of that hallowed chamber. Today he had to move into his new offices, which were tucked into an obscure upper hallway of Parliament. He felt like a boy going to his new school.

It had always been his dream to sit in the Commons, though it was still, for all its modernizations, an exceedingly idiosyncratic institution. For one thing, different seats varied wildly in how they were won; most were fair and democratic, but some were almost insanely corrupt. Since the reforms of 1832 there was no longer any place as bad as Old Sarum (the town that had infamously elected two Members despite the notable handicap of having only eleven voters) or Dunwich (whose own two Members remained in the House for many years even after the town had literally fallen into the sea), but there were plenty of rotten and pocket boroughs that could be dispensed without so much as a single vote being cast. Ludo Starling held one of these, in fact.

Another strange thing about Parliament was that, though being an MP was one of the most prestigious and important jobs in the empire, it was entirely unpaid. Only men with cabinet assignments received any stipend, and as a result there was fierce competition for the under-secretaryships of obscure departments in government (Welsh affairs, municipal corporations). Lenox was fortunate, like many of the people who would be his colleagues now, in having private means, but there were also valuable and good gentlemen who were forced to quit Parliament when they couldn't pay for their own lodgings or food. Generally these men were found decent sinecures by the friends they had made, but what charm did supervising a distant Scottish county have compared to being in the House of Commons?

It was the scullery maid who had brought Lenox his coffee in the parlor, but now Graham entered.

"Good morning, sir," he said.

"Good morning. I say, you're dressed for a day in London. Why have you got your city togs on?"

"With your permission, I intend to go to your new office in Parliament shortly, sir."

For an instant Lenox was puzzled, and then with delight he cried out, "Graham! You'll do the job!"

"Yes, sir, with the provision that you understand my grave doubts ab—"

"Never mind that, never mind that! This is terrific news. Yes, head over there. Or would you rather wait for me?"

"I think it would be advisable were I to precede you there, sir, and begin cleaning and preparing the office."

"Cleaning? Leave that to someone else. I need you to take over my appointment book, for one thing. It's been driving me mad. You'll need to register with the guards. I believe you can go in through the Members' Entrance, or if not then you can get in through that garden to the west of the buildings. This is wonderful news, Graham."

"Shall we call it a probationary assignment, sir, pending our joint approval?"

"Call it whatever you like. Have you told Kirk?"

"Yes, sir."

"Excellent." Then Lenox's brow furrowed. "Mind you, he's not what I call an ideal butler. Still, the trade is more than worth it. I'm going upstairs to tell Jane that you've accepted. Are you pleased at least?"

The butler—former butler now—allowed himself a smile. "Yes, sir. Very," he said.

"Good. I'll see you at our new office, Graham."

An hour later, after Lenox had done a few chores, the two men stood in the empty office, looking at it. A tiny window in one corner provided a very little light, but it was a dim set of two rooms, one, slightly larger than the other, with a fireplace, bookshelves, and a large desk. This would be Lenox's. The outer room, through which all traffic would arrive, had two desks that faced each other. These would be for Graham and a new clerk, whom he would soon have to hire.

"Here we are," said Lenox. "Let's go over the appointment book."

For twenty minutes they sorted through various notes asking Lenox to attend meetings of business-men, railway chiefs, committees from the House of Lords (from which the Commons had truly begun to wrest power in the last thirty years), and a hundred other bodies of men. Graham promised to categorize the notes and respond to them, which lifted a weight off of Lenox's shoulders.

"But first you have your tour," said Graham.

"Have I?"

"A Mr. Bigham will be by shortly to give it to you, sir. He's the assistant to the parliamentary historian and generally guides new Members through the House when they arrive. Since you were elected at a by-election, however"—that is to say, a special, one-off election—"you will be the only person on the tour."

"We all have our trials."

There was a rap at the door, and a cheerful face, similar to Lenox's but slightly fatter and jollier, perhaps less pensive, popped through the crack. It was not the tour guide but Sir Edmund Chichester Lenox, 11th Baronet of Markethouse and Member of Parliament for the town of the same name. Charles's older brother.

Edmund was a genial soul, happier at Lenox House in the country than in town, but he was also an important and reliable member of his party, who took his duties seriously and refused credit for much of his work—to the extent that his importance in the House had been unknown to his own brother until two years before.

"Charles!" said Edmund. "I wondered whether you might be here. My God, they gave you the worst office in the entire place. Young Michaelson had it, but he traded out like a shot when he got the chance. I hope you don't die of a draft. But come: Has it really been ten weeks? Shake my hand. I stopped in earlier, and Graham told me you were to have a tour, but come have lunch at Bellamy's afterward, will you?"

This was the famous Members' restaurant at Parliament.

"Of course," said Lenox.

"Excellent. In that case, I'll take my leave and see you then." Edmund put on his hat, which had been in his hand, and left, whistling down the hallway.

Mr. Bigham, who arrived a few minutes later, proved to be a plump, small man, with big owlish glasses and a dry manner of speech. He sat in front of Lenox's desk for some twenty minutes and lectured him on various matters of protocol and procedure.

"As you know," he began, "the House meets at a quarter to four in the afternoon, except on Wednesdays, when we convene at noon. Each sitting begins with a religious service from which the public is barred, but as soon as that ends strangers come into the galleries. Here's a funny fact, Mr. Lenox: Although there are six hundred and seventy Members of Parliament, only about three hundred and fifty people can fit into the House of Commons! Remarkable, isn't it? For an important vote we might *just* cram four hundred in, but not more than that."

"I suppose many Members don't come to the sittings?"

"Oh, there are a hundred men who only come to London once a year but find it convenient or pleasurable to hold a seat. Another hundred live in London but still come to the House only once a year. In the end only two hundred or so attend regularly. There are always empty spots on the benches."

"I shall be part of that two hundred," said Lenox.

"Shall you?" Mr. Bigham smiled, his jowly face lit up. "I've heard that before, I can promise. Now, business. In any given session of the House, you'll first handle private business—anything of an essentially local nature and any vote pushed through by one of several important companies, including the railroads and the water works. Public business covers pretty much everything else you can imagine . . ."

Eventually the lecture was over and they were walking through a labyrinth of alternating small and vast hallways, some dim and low-ceilinged, others imposing and portrait-lined. Bigham kept up a steady prattle about the history of the building. A few times Lenox bumped into men he knew and stopped to say hello. It was all starting to feel real; he was here.

That feeling truly took hold of him when they entered the Commons. He had sat in the visitors' galleries, of course—had from them often watched his own father speak—but to be on the floor, so near the chair of the Speaker of the House . . . it was a remarkable thing. The room was tiny, ornate, and as hushed as a cathedral.

Mr. Bigham whispered reverently, "To think —from this chamber a group of six hundred and seventy men rule an empire of tens of millions of souls. Once you write your name in the Members' book, it will remain there forever as part of the history of this time. How lucky you are, Mr. Lenox!"

"I am," said Lenox. There was a strange hollow place in his chest. "I am," he repeated. "I know I am."

chapter eight

Still, he hadn't forgotten the murder. Lenox was particularly eager to see Ludo Starling again, if for no other reason than to further analyze the man's behavior, which had on their first encounter been so strange. The lie about his wife, for instance. The odd braggadocio of his claims about a palace-bestowed title.

Alas, between the meetings and the reading he had to do, there was no time for it. The task thus fell to Dallington and, of course, Scotland Yard. Inspector Fowler. He had replied to Lenox's inquiring note with a few perfunctory lines explaining that the Yard had the case well in hand and that outside interference could only hinder the course of the investigation. The note was distinctly unfriendly, if not hostile.

On the second evening after Lenox saw his new offices, Dallington came by with a report. Kirk announced him.

"Who's this new chappie buttling for you?" asked the young lord. "Surely Graham hasn't handed his notice in?"

"Not at all, no. He's become my political secretary. Kirk was Jane's butler for many years."

Dallington frowned. "My parents were always trying to make me be a political secretary to some sniveling politician. No offense, of course."

"Of course."

"I never saw the good in it. Parliament would burn to the ground before they made me a Member of it, and unless that was your goal it was just a job with long hours and no pay."

"We haven't spoken about your parents in some time."

"Oh?"

"Would it be intrusive of me to ask what their current mood is—on the subject of your new career, I mean?"

"Middling, I'd say. They haven't thrown themselves off a cliff yet, anyway. It helped when you spoke to Father."

"I'm glad."

"But leave that aside—how about Frederick Clarke?"

"Well?"

"What can you possibly mean by saying 'Well,' for God's sake?" asked Dallington with an irritable scowl. "I hope you don't think I've found the murderer or anything like that."

Lenox chuckled. "No. I only wondered what progress you had made."

"Too bloody little progress."

"What have you done?"

"Whatever I could. I was hoping to convince you to come speak to the family with me."

"Why?"

"Ludo Starling looks at me like I'm a leper."

"He judges you on outdated information, I fear."

"It's not as if I reeled in there on a bender. I was altogether respectful. But he simply said that it was up to the Yard now and turned me out. It was dashed uncomfortable, to be honest."

"What have you been doing instead, then?"

"Anything I could think of. I interviewed housekeepers and footmen up and down the street. None of them said anything interesting, unfortunately."

"They knew him? Clarke?"

"Oh, yes, from the shops and the alley—the one where he died. None of them had ever exchanged more than fifty words with him, though. Said he was extremely deferential and polite."

"That's a piece of information, at any rate. It makes it less likely that this was a crime of passion or anger."

"Yes, I hadn't thought of that."

"Anything else? Did you ask about the scabs and wounds on his hands?"

"Nobody knew a thing about them. Several people said how large he was, however. If he was in a fight it sounds as if he wouldn't have been easily overmatched."

"Which was perhaps one of the reasons an ambush was the murderer's soundest course. You've done quite well."

"Only that from two days! You could have solved the thing and been to Bath and back in that time."

Lenox laughed. "Not true. Still, it's important to speak to Ludo's family. What do you say to going now? I'm meant to be reading a blue book"—these were the dense parliamentary briefs all Members received for scrutiny—"but it's deathly boring."

"Just what I'd hoped for," said Dallington. "I have a cab outside. Is Lady Jane in?"

"She's with your mother, in fact." Jane and the Duchess of Marchmain were close friends. "Give me a moment to gather my things."

They pulled up to Ludo's large, rambling house not twenty minutes later and knocked on the door. The butler—Lenox remembered that his name was Jack Collingwood—opened the door and ushered them in. At odds with the majority of his profession's practitioners he was very young, perhaps thirty or a bit younger. While he went to fetch Ludo, Dallington whispered that he was the son of the Starlings' old butler. That accounted for his age.

Ludo looked much more composed now than the last time Lenox had seen him. "Hello, hello," he said. "How do you do, Charles?"

"Quite well, thank you. You've already met John Dallington?"

"Of course, yes. Good to see you again. Although as I said to him, the Yard can handle things from now on."

"Would you mind if we spoke to a few people in the house?" asked Lenox. "I have a spare evening."

"I really think—the Yard has been excellent. Mr. Fowler was here just this morning."

Then why did you ever come to me? Lenox thought. All he said was, "He's excellent, yes, but perhaps another set of eyes could see something new."

"Two more sets," said Dallington and grinned.

Ludo grimaced but relented. "Of course," he said. "With whom would you like to speak first?"

"Have you been through his room at all?"

"Oh, no. The maid stripped off the sheets but left everything else as it is. For his mother, you see. We thought she might want to look over his things before they're packed up."

"When does she arrive?"

"Today. She's traveling by post."

"What's the delay? It's been four days."

"I don't know," said Ludo. "Perhaps she had to find someone to look after her public house."

Lenox shrugged. "At any rate, it might be valuable to speak to her. But that's for tomorrow. Shall we have a look at the room? We need to know more about Frederick Clarke."

"By all means," said Ludo.

From the rather glum front parlor where they had been sitting, Ludo took them into the entry hall. There he led them through an unobtrusive door, painted the same color as the walls, and downstairs to the servants' quarters. The largest room downstairs, the kitchen, was bright and busy with cleaning up after supper. Down a slim hallway to the right was a row of doors.

"Which one was it again?" said Ludo to a pretty young girl. "Frederick's room?"

"It's the last on the right, sir."

The chamber when they reached it proved exceedingly modest, with only a bed and a small side table in it. There was one closet, too. On the side table were a stack of books and a candle that had burned down to a snub.

"Bring a lamp!" called Ludo down the hallway, and a moment later the same girl scurried down with it.

"Are you Jenny Rogers?" asked Dallington.

"Yes, sir," she said.

"How the devil did you know that?" asked Ludo.

"She doesn't look like Betsy Mints, aged forty, cook, to me," said Dallington.

"You've been looking into my household?"

"Yes."

"Quite routine," said Lenox.

"Still, I say, it's a bit awkward," said Ludo.

"We'll need to speak to you soon, Miss Rogers."

"You're not a suspect," added Dallington, still smiling. Lenox sighed. His apprentice couldn't resist a pretty woman.

chapter nine

After Jenny Rogers had blushed, offered a confused curtsy, and retreated down the hallway, Lenox and Dallington turned into the room to begin a proper examination. Ludo stayed in the hall, trying to peer over their shoulders and shifting nervously from foot to foot.

"He was reading rather heavy stuff," said Dallington, crouching down to look at the names on the spines of the books upon the side table.

"What?" said Lenox.

"There's something called *The Philosophy of Right* by a chap named Hegel, a pamphlet on universal suffrage, and a little quarto of George Crabbe's. He must have been the best-educated footman in London."

"Those are all from my library," said Ludo. "We encourage the staff to pluck what they will from it, but I'm afraid most of them read books from Mudie's—adventure stories and romances. Three-volume novels. You know the sort of trash."

"I rather like the triple-deckers myself," said Dallington. "They make the time go."

"To each his own," answered Ludo frostily.

His vices were not intellectual ones, at any rate.

"What sort of education did he have?" asked Lenox curiously. He stood up from his examination under the bed. "It must have been rather atypical. One of my friend Thomas McConnell's footmen is quite illiterate."

"I'm afraid I don't know. As I told you before, I didn't pay the lad much attention."

"I don't blame you if he was always on about Hegel," murmured Dallington, then laughed at his own joke.

There was really very little to see in the room. Lenox examined the entire bed and its frame for anything hidden—a note, a diary—but found nothing. The side table was similarly unrevealing. A small shelf in the corner had an assortment of meaningless trifles: a jar of ink, a picture postcard of Stratford with nothing on its reverse, a ball of black India rubber. The only thing that intrigued Lenox was a scrap of paper that read, *When's your birthday? C. said you would turn 20 soon. Did you have the day off last year?*

"Does this note mean anything to you?" asked Lenox.

"I was curious about it myself," said Ludo. "I asked Collingwood, and he said Elizabeth sent it, through him—we let the staff have their birthdays off, but she realized she didn't know Clarke's. She knew all the others."

"Wouldn't Collingwood have found that

out? I imagine days off are within his purview."

Ludo shrugged. "You know how solicitous my wife can be. She felt badly to think that we hadn't given him his birthday off."

"I see."

The closet was the last place in the room that hadn't been searched; in fact both Dallington and Lenox had run their eyes over everything else, shaken out the books, felt for lumps in the pillows. Lenox opened the closet, vaguely hoping to see something revelatory—something covered in blood, say—but he was disappointed. There were two tidy suits of livery, both black, such as a footman might wear, and four shirts.

"We provide them, of course," said Ludo.

There was also a very fine gray suit, his one personal suit, that looked expensively tailored. On a shelf behind these was a stack of shirts. Lenox shook out and refolded each, then did the same with two pairs of trousers, checking the pockets, three pairs of socks, and a night-shirt.

"Defeated," said Dallington.

"Probably," replied Lenox.

He knelt down and looked at the shiny black shoes on the floor of the closet. He groped inside the left and found nothing, and then he groped inside the right and found—something.

He pulled it out and saw that he was holding a gentleman's signet ring, made of heavy greenish-yellow gold. On its oval face was an intricately worked griffin with a small ruby as its eye.

"Good Lord," said Dallington. "It looks like an heirloom."

"I should think so. It's shined smooth from use on the outside."

"What is it?" asked Ludo, still in the hallway.

"You can come in," said Lenox.

"I'd rather not."

The detective flipped the ring. On the reverse of the griffin were two initials: *LS.* "I think perhaps you'd better," he called out to Ludo.

"What is it?"

Lenox went to the hallway, holding the ring up between his thumb and middle finger. "Does it look familiar?"

For a long time Ludo peered at the ring uncomprehendingly. "What is it?"

"I believe it's your ring. Unless there's another *LS* in the house."

Realization dawned on Ludo's face. "The thieving bastard! That's an old Starling family ring. I had it engraved when I was at university."

"You didn't give it to him?"

"Give it to him! Never in a century of Sundays!"

"Then I'm afraid he may have stolen it. I'm surprised, however. Would his duties as a footman have taken him near a jewelry case?"

"Anything's possible."

Lenox frowned. "Perhaps somebody else took it and put it here."

"It even could have happened after Clarke's death," said Dallington.

"Yes." Lenox examined the ring, holding it an inch from his eye. "Ah—or perhaps not," he said.

"Why not?" asked Ludo, still in the hall.

"There's another engraving, on the bottom inside of the ring, opposite your *LS. FC.*"

"Frederick Clarke," said Dallington.

Lenox nodded.

"The ruddy nerve," said Ludo.

"Did you wear it often?"

"That? No. That doesn't mean I intended it as a present for a footman."

Lenox peered around the room, the ring now in his clenched fist. He gave the bed a tentative prod and thought over what he had seen. From the kitchen a sound of heavy washing filled the room's new silence.

"It's strange," he said. "A strange room."

"Why?" asked Dallington. "Strikes me as in the normal run of things for a footman."

"Does it really? It's extremely spartan, for one thing. I doubt the other servants' rooms are as unadorned as this one. Could he possibly have been here four years and left so little a mark?"

"Perhaps he moved between rooms?"

"I doubt it. Ludo?"

"No, I don't think so."

79

"I think he's one of those people who lives a life of the mind. Did he often take books of this sort from your library?"

"Yes, quite regularly according to Collingwood."

"Yet contrast that with this ring." Lenox held it up again. "Why take such a personal bauble for himself? From everything this room has to show, he cared nothing at all for physical comfort or ornament, but this is what he chose to steal?"

"Worth a damn lot of money," said Ludo.

Lenox shook his head. "No. It's not about the money. He engraved his initials on it. That shows he valued it."

Dallington said, "Of course."

"Something odd was happening in this young man's life. Intelligence combined with menial labor . . . I wonder, is it possible he had found his way into crime?"

"Of course he had," said Ludo. "My ring."

"Not that, no. Think: a well-tailored suit, a signet ring . . . it looks to me as if he might have been playing the young aristocrat. Some scam or other, couldn't it be?"

"Perhaps that's why he reads," added Dallington excitedly. "To impress people—to seem like a varsity man!"

"I say, could I have that ring back?" said Ludo.

"Of course, here it is."

After handing Starling the ring, Lenox stood in the doorway of the room for a long time, thinking. Nobody spoke. The rhythmic sound of washing—what must have been the sound of Frederick Clarke's life—wore on like the blank, unvarying noise of an ocean.

"Something deep is happening here," said Lenox. "Deeper than I realized at first."

chapter ten

An interview with Jenny Rogers left Dallington perhaps half in love—she was extremely soft-spoken, with an endearing way of furrowing her forehead to show how intently she was listening —but yielded little helpful information. What was most interesting to Lenox was that she seemed genuinely sad to have lost her friend. It made Frederick Clarke more real, made his death seem graver, when she talked with a smile on her face about him.

She had been working at the Starling house for a year. "I'll never forget," she said, "at the end of my first week he took a piece of the cake they was having upstairs—Mr. Starling's cake," she added, remembering he was there, "and put a candle in it for me. 'Happy first week,' he said."

As far as she could recall, she had never seen him wear a gray suit or a gold ring, or indeed anything other than his footman's livery. He always had his nose in a book.

She had oberved occasionally in the past that he had scrapes on his hands.

"Occasionally," murmured Lenox after she had been dismissed down the opposite hallway (the staff were segregated in their sleeping quarters, men down one hall and women down another). "If it was an ongoing condition it means there's no significance in their directly preceding his death."

"They still might be related."

"Perhaps."

Betsy Mints was even less helpful than Jenny Rogers. A small, thick woman, she had a deeply stupid face that was red from the constant heat of cooking over fire. In conversation, however, she was witty enough, in a voluble northern way. Her experiences with Frederick Clarke were extremely limited. She thought he was quite handsome, very efficient, and rather rum—quiet, inward, that is to say—but that was the extent of her analysis of his character.

Lenox had higher hopes for Jack Collingwood, the young butler. For one thing he directly supervised Clarke. Lenox and Dallington sat at a table with him while Ludo hovered anxiously behind.

"I apologize for the lateness of our meeting," said Lenox.

"Not at all, sir."

"It's nearly ten o'clock. You must be off soon."

"Yes, sir."

"From what I understand, Frederick Clarke was a good footman?"

"Entirely blameless in the conduct of his professional duties, sir."

"Did you like him?"

"Like him, sir?"

"Were you friends?"

"No, sir."

"What was your impression of his character?"

"Mr. Clarke was quiet and studious. He preferred to be in his room, reading, if he had spare time. He spoke to me once or twice about going back to school. I dissuaded him from it, of course. He was excellent in his work and could have risen to be a butler in due time." This said as if there could be no higher conceivable ambition.

"Who do you think killed him?"

"I have no idea whatsoever, sir. A vagrant, I might venture."

"But to what end? Did he carry money?"

"No, sir. He and I both have our wages deposited in Mr. Starling's bank, and I never saw Mr. Clarke spend his on anything. As for household money, that is my province exclusively."

"What was his day off?"

"Thursday, sir."

"That's all?"

"The family eats a cold collation after church services, following which the servants have Sunday afternoon to themselves."

"Did he leave the house or stay in?"

"Left, sir, invariably. That's quite usual, however."

"Did you ever see him wear a gray suit?"

"No, sir."

"Or wearing a gold ring?"

"No, sir."

"Did you ever celebrate his birthday?"

"No, sir."

"And you saw cuts or scabs on his hands?"

"Yes, sir. I reprimanded him once—his only reprimand—for having unsuitable hands. Of course under his white gloves it didn't matter, but then it's the principle of the thing, I believe."

"Did you ask him where he got them?"

"No, sir."

Lenox sighed. "I take it you've spoken to Inspector Fowler?"

"He has," interjected Ludo.

"I can find out more from him, but what were you doing at the time of his murder?"

"I was here, sir, with Jenny and Betsy."

"So I understood. Why did he go out?"

"To fetch the bootblack."

"Did he speak of meeting anybody?"

"As I told Mr. Fowler, no."

"Is it normal for one of you to leave so soon before dinner?"

"Oh, yes, sir. There are always last-moment tasks."

"Well, thank you, Mr. Collingwood."

"Yes, sir."

When Collingwood had walked down Frederick Clarke's old hall, Ludo motioned Dallington and Lenox up the narrow staircase to the ground floor of the house.

"Mr. Starling, is your family about?" asked Dallington.

"Why do you ask?" said Ludo.

"It would be useful to speak to them."

"The boys are out. They generally are at night. Elizabeth will have been retired this hour or more."

"Perhaps tomorrow," said Lenox. "Would you mind if Dallington attended the funeral?"

"No," said Ludo, though looking as if he rather would. "You can't attend?"

"Meetings."

Ludo looked relieved. "Shall we just let the Yard handle it, after all?"

"With your permission, I would like to keep an eye on it," said Lenox. "Grayson Fowler is an excellent detective. Still. I can't quite identify what bothers me so much, but it's there."

"Well—all right." They were now in the entrance hall. "Good night."

Just as Lenox and Dallington said good night, however, a voice stopped them. "Who's there?" rang out from the drawing room in a cranky old tone.

"Only a couple of friends, Uncle Tiberius," said Ludo in an agitated way. "We're on our way out." He added in a confidential tone, "I'll come along and go to my club. I rather fancy a hand of whist."

"Wait!" cried the old man. He appeared in the doorway, holding a candle and dressed in a rumpled suit. "Is it the inspector again? I want to speak to the inspector!"

"No—only my friends," said Ludo. He looked irritated. "John Dallington, Charles Lenox, may I please introduce you to my father's uncle, Tiberius Starling."

"How do you do?" the two visitors asked.

"I remembered something to tell the inspector."

"It can wait until tomorrow."

"We're acting as inspectors, too," said Dallington mildly, earning for his troubles a look of pure vexation from Ludo, who was almost physically harrying them out. They paused by the door.

"Good, good," said the old man. "I remembered something about Clarke. The packets."

"What packets, blast them?" asked Ludo.

"Under the servants' door," said Tiberius. He looked at Dallington. "I sit down there, you see, because they have that cooks' fire. It warms up these old bones. One day I was alone down there —it was Sunday morning—and a packet came under the door. I hobbled over to fetch it for 'em, and it was unsigned. I opened it, and what do you think was inside?"

"What?" asked Dallington.

"A note! A white note, worth a pound! Not even a coin!"

Money. All notes issued by the Bank of England were printed in black on one side and blank on the reverse and were called white notes.

"Oh?" said Lenox.

"I thought it was empty—that's why I opened it—but down marched Frederick Clarke, who by rights should have been out on a Sunday, and he told me it was his, he was expecting it. I asked what was inside, to test him, you see, and he told me. Well, I had no choice but to give it to him then."

"You said *packets,* plural."

"It happened again two Sundays later, but he was there to scoop it up before I did."

"Why did you never tell me this, Uncle?" said Ludo.

"Forgot. But now he's dead—rich as he would please."

"How much did you pay him a year, may I ask, Ludo?" said Lenox.

"Twenty pounds."

Dallington was shocked. "My God, how dismal!"

"It's on the lower side, yes, but that includes room and board, of course," said Ludo, bristling.

"I'm sorry—quite sorry. I didn't mean to be rude. I haven't any idea what any servant earns."

Lenox ignored this all, deep in thought. At last he said, "Five percent of his yearly wage, slipped under the door so nonchalantly. What was that young man doing with his life, I wonder?"

chapter eleven

Lenox and Dallington walked very slowly through the pristine, vacant streets of Mayfair, moonlight and lamplight enough to make it rather bright. They discussed the case and arrived at one essential conclusion: Ludo Starling's behavior was odd. Neither of them knew whether it was significant, but they concurred upon that fact. As for the packet, or packets, that Frederick Clarke had received, Lenox was inclined to believe that Clarke had been the participant in some variety of fraud or chicanery.

They stood at the corner of Hampden Lane discussing it until they were neither content nor unhappy, then parted. It was past midnight. They agreed that Dallington would attend the funeral and then report in to Lenox.

When he went inside his house, Lenox was surprised to find a figure on the small chair in the hallway. It was Jane.

"Hullo," he said, cheerfully enough.

"Hello, Charles."

"You sound upset."

She stood. "I am."

"What's the matter?" Dread struck his heart. "Is it Toto?"

"No. It's you."

"What have I done?"

"Are you aware of the time?"

"Roughly." He pulled his pocket watch from his waistcoat. "Fourteen minutes past midnight," he said.

"I came home at nine o'clock, and Kirk hadn't the slightest idea where you were, except to say that John Dallington had dragged you off."

"I don't understand what's wrong, Jane."

"Why didn't you tell me where you would be? Or leave a note! The most threadbare consideration would have satisfied. Instead I have had to worry for three hours, needlessly."

"Three hours scarcely seems enough to go into

such a panic over," he said. "I'd have thought you understood the nature of my profession."

This raised her ire. "I understand it well enough. You are under the constant threat of getting shot or stabbed or who knows what, while I wait at home and—what, politely wait to hear news of your death?"

"You're being absurd," he said in what he instantly knew, and regretted, to be a haughty fashion.

"Absurd?" Suddenly her anger had turned into tears. "To worry about you—that's absurd? Is this what marriage is meant to be like?"

As she started to cry in earnest, his resentment washed away and was replaced with regret. "I'm terribly sorry, Jane. For so many years I could come and go as I pleased, and now—"

"I don't have any interest in that. We're married now. Do you understand that?"

He tried to take her hand, but she pulled it away. He sat down. "I hope I do."

"I don't know."

"Really, I am sorry," he said. Still she wouldn't look at him. He sighed. "We never argued once during our honeymoon, did we?"

"Our honeymoon was lovely, Charles, but it wasn't real life. This is real life. And it's not fair on either of us to have you gallivanting around London, putting yourself in danger, over some obscure murder."

"Obscure murder? If our friendship had taught you nothing else, I hoped it had taught you that there is no such thing."

"It's past midnight!"

"When I'm in the House I won't be home till much later than this on occasion."

"That's different."

"How?"

"It's your job."

"Being a detective is my job, Jane."

Lady Jane's voice rose. "Not any longer!"

"As long as I live!"

"You're in Parliament, Charles!"

"So that's worth staying out late for? Are you ashamed to be married to a detective?"

She looked as if he had slapped her: suddenly still, suddenly silent. Without a further word she swept out of the room and ran up the stairs.

"Damn," he said to the empty room.

He sat down, and as the anger burned out of him and he returned to his right mind he felt a deep anguish. Not only had they not fought on their honeymoon, they hadn't fought in twenty years, that he could remember. There had been cross words, but never a true battle.

He worried that he had ruined their friendship, the best thing in his life, by telling her he loved her. "My heart is ever at your service," Shakespeare had written, and it was the line Lenox always thought of when Jane came to mind. Might it be that he would have served her better by staying silent?

He went to bed disconsolate, and slept very little.

The next morning she was gone before he woke, though it was barely half past seven. He breakfasted alone, reading the papers as he munched on eggs and ham and gulped down two cups of coffee. The Emperor of Japan had married, according to the *Times*. A chap named Meiji, of all things, and his wife was called Shoken. She was three years older than her new husband, which had apparently been the greatest obstacle to their nuptials. Suddenly the problems of the house on Hampden Street seemed a little smaller. He smiled slightly as he finished the article. It would be all right.

Walking down to Whitehall before nine o'clock, he knew his mind ought to be on the meetings of the day, the blue books he had to read, lunch with his party leaders at Bellamy's.

Instead he was focused entirely on Frederick Clarke's anonymous money drop-offs.

What could they mean? He still favored the thought that there was some kind of fraudulence at play, but then why would he have anything delivered under the servants' door? Wasn't that a dead giveaway?

There was good news, however. The case might be perplexing, and domestic bliss elusive, but professional happiness was close at hand.

In his short time as Lenox's political secretary, Graham had already proved a marvel. It had only been a few days, but he had filled each of them with furious activity, rarely sleeping longer than a few hours, the commitment he had always shown as a servant transferred to this new work. Aside from organizing the new office to within an inch of its life, he had gone over Lenox's appointment book, deciphered which meetings were most important, and canceled the rest, something that would save the grateful Lenox several hours a day.

What was most impressive, though, was his quickly growing acquaintance. It took men years to know the various faces of Parliament, but Graham was a quick pupil. This was an unspoken but important fact of life in the House of Commons, and Lenox hadn't known anything about it. Now, however, they walked the halls and various men Lenox had never laid eyes on nodded at them both. "The Marquess of Aldington's secretary," Graham would say, or "Hector Prime's chief counselor." Graham's principal gift in detective work had always been infiltration—making friends in a pub or a kitchen—and he put that gift to use here now in these more exalted corridors.

The apotheosis of this talent in its political form came that morning. Graham was waiting at the Members' Entrance, as he did every day now, when Lenox arrived.

"Good morning, sir," he said. "In ten minutes you must sit down with the Board of Agriculture. After that—"

Here Graham broke off and nodded his head at an enormously tall, thin young man with a giant forehead. "How do you do?" he said.

"Excellently, Mr. Graham, I thank you."

After the man had walked on, Lenox said in a low voice, "My God, that was Percy Field."

"Yes, sir."

"How on earth do you know him?"

Percy Field was the Prime Minister's own assistant, a famously accomplished and imperious lad from Magdalene College, prodigiously intelligent, whom the PM himself had declared more important to Great Britain's welfare than all but ten or twenty people. Field had little patience for most Members, let alone their secretaries.

"He snubbed me, until I took the liberty of inviting him to one of your Tuesdays, sir. I spoke to Lady Lenox in advance of the offer, and she readily consented. Mr. Field's attitude was cold when I first approached him, but he quickly warmed."

This was disingenuous; they were Lady Jane's Tuesdays, as they had been for fifteen years, a gathering of London's elite—say twenty or so people—in her drawing room. Even for Field an invitation would be a great coup.

"Well done, Graham. Extremely well done."

They went inside, up to the cramped office, and began the day's work. For the rest of the morning Lenox dutifully attended his meetings and read his blue books. The entire time, though, his mind was on the murder. As such it wasn't quite a surprise when he heard himself saying to Graham, "Send my regrets to the one o'clock meeting, please. I'm going round to fetch Dallington. I have to go to Frederick Clarke's funeral."

chapter twelve

What was the proper form for a servant's funeral? In general one attended, but then in general the deceased was old and respectable. What if there was the strong prospect of a title, which only scandal could preclude?

The moment Lenox laid eyes on Ludo Starling it was clear the man had been mulling over these questions all morning. In the event Ludo and his wife were present, but Tiberius and the Starling boys weren't. Jack Collingwood, Jenny Rogers, and Betsy Mints sat in the second row.

Alone in the first row was a large, thin woman, perhaps fifty years old but still well-looking, horsey and countryish. She wore a straw mourning bonnet, black, with a deep black crepe ribbon, a soft black gown, and a dark veil. When she turned back Lenox saw that she was rather plain-faced, but somehow still attractive.

"That must be the boy's mother," he whispered to Dallington as they took their seats several rows back. "The place of honor."

"Don't you feel a bit dodgy here?" asked the young lord. "We didn't know him."

Lenox nodded gravely. "Even so, we owe him our best, and this is a singular opportunity to see who he knew and what he was like."

The funeral took place in a small, appealing Mayfair church, St. George's, which Lenox knew the Starling family had generously endowed over the years. It was a distinguished building with tall white columns in front, steep stairs to the front door, and a high bell tower overhead, part of the Fifty Churches Act that Parliament had passed in the early eighteenth century at the behest of Queen Anne, to keep up with London's expansion in population. A pious woman, Anne had wanted to ensure that all of her subjects were close to a church. In the end the project fell well short of its target—a dozen churches or so had gone up—but they had left their mark. The great architect Nicholas Hawksmoor had built many of them, and even the ones he didn't build (like this) were in his style. They were called Queen Anne's Churches now—all much of a piece, beautiful, high, very white, and somewhat severe. Given Ludo's newfound affinity for discretion, it was surprising to find the service held in a firmly aristocratic church.

The most striking occurrence at the funeral happened just before the service began. With the church already full, six footmen in identical livery marched somberly down the center aisle and took an empty pew. They made for an arresting picture.

"I'd like to speak to them," said Dallington.

"Perhaps they were his real friends. It wouldn't surprise me. He couldn't have been proper friends with either of the women in his house or Collingwood, his superior among the staff."

"True, and he lived along that row of houses. All the footmen would have been in the alley constantly."

"Precisely."

The service was a modest one, without music save for Bach's *St. Matthew Passion* at the recession. Funerals in London tended to be grandiose (at one last year, Lenox had seen a procession of mutes and jugglers before the coffin), but this was a plain old English service —rather touching in its simplicity.

One rather strange absence was that of Inspector

Grayson Fowler of Scotland Yard. Perhaps the feeling of propriety that had nettled Dallington kept him away, but Lenox doubted it. Fowler was a particular type—old, grizzled, disagreeable to most people, and extremely sharp-witted. He was well past fifty years of age, and in his many years on the force had been one of the few people at the Yard of whom Lenox had entirely approved. In turn he had always liked Lenox, who had talked over cases with him many a time, interpreting clues and prodding theories to find their soft spots. Lenox decided that he would visit Scotland Yard that night, despite the curt note he had received when he tried to contact Fowler before. Perhaps it had been a bad day.

As they stood on the steps of the church after the funeral, nobody seemed quite sure what to do. A reception would have been appropriate, but Ludo hadn't mentioned one, and the boy's mother was from out of town—and an old family servant! It was shabby of Ludo, actually, and thus it made Lenox doubly glad when one of the six footmen did something gallant. He was a red-haired, freckled, very young-looking man.

To the group he said, "Since we appear to be at loose ends, may my friends and I invite you all to the second floor of the Bricklayers' Arms? It's one street down, and Freddie often enjoyed a pint there. Mrs. Clarke, may I take your arm?"

"Oh—yes," stammered Ludo. "Here, I insist

upon buying a round." He fumbled through his pockets and came up with a note, which the footman had the good manners to accept.

"Freddie," murmured Lenox to Dallington.

"Maybe I'll buy a round as well. Come along?"

"Graham will murder me if I don't get back. Come see me tonight though, will you?"

"Yes, of course."

A ragged procession had already begun down the street, and Dallington ran up to join it. Lenox sidled up to Ludo Starling.

"Where is the boy's mother staying?" he asked. "With you, I assume?"

"No. We offered."

"You don't know where?"

"A hotel in Hammersmith."

"But that's miles and miles away."

Ludo shrugged. "We offered, as I say."

"Which hotel?"

"It's called the Tilton. That's all I know. Listen, Charles—I feel uneasy about you looking into this murder. It's nearly been a week already. Fowler says we can't expect to discover who did this horrible thing to Frederick, and I don't want to detain you for the purposes of a—a fruitless search."

"Yes," said Lenox placidly.

"After all, what's the point? The House sits again soon, and we both have work to do before then."

"True."

"Will you drop it?"

"My priorities are certainly at the House, but if you don't mind I'll have Dallington look around a little more."

"Oh?" said Ludo. His face was difficult to read. "If he has the time, by all means. I just want to be sure you don't waste any time that would be otherwise spent productively."

"Thank you," said Lenox.

As he walked away down Brook Street toward New Bond, Lenox pondered this exchange with Ludo. There was no possibility whatsoever that Grayson Fowler had said the Yard couldn't expect to solve the case. For one thing it was against policy, and for another Fowler was an irascible, tenacious man, not given to accepting failure gracefully. What could be happening between Ludo's ears? Why ask Lenox onto the case and then try to kick him off? The title?

He was walking in the direction of Grosvenor Square. He was already late to see Graham, but it had occurred to him during the service that he hadn't seen Thomas and Toto McConnell in nearly a week, and he decided to go visit them.

It was Toto herself, big as a house, who answered the door. Her funereal butler, Shreve, stood behind her with a dismayed downturn at the corners of his mouth.

"Oh, Charles, how wonderful! Look at the size

of me, will you? I'm not supposed to be on my feet, but I saw it was you through the window."

"Shreve could have gotten it."

The butler coughed a muted agreement.

"Oh, bother that, I wanted to stand up anyway. Thomas was reading one of his scientific papers to me, something or other about dolphins, I can't keep up and it's dreadfully boring. I do like his voice, though, don't you? It's very soothing."

McConnell was standing before the sofa, beaming—still tall, still exceedingly handsome with his shaggy hair.

"How are you?" he said.

"Excellent, thank you. Any day now?"

"Yes," he said. "I think it's a girl."

"I *do* want a girl," said Toto, heaving herself onto the couch with an unladylike grunt, "but of course a boy would be lovely, too."

"Anything happening about the murder?" asked McConnell.

"Don't talk about that nonsense," said Toto crossly, her pretty face flushed. "I want to hear happy chatter, not about murders and blood. Just this once. After the baby comes the five of us can have a symposium on the subject, but right now I want to talk about nice subjects. How is Jane's garden, Charles?"

chapter thirteen

That evening Lenox was sitting at his broad mahogany desk, reading a blue book on the subject of England's commitments to Ireland. It was early September all of the sudden, after the endless warm summer of his honeymoon, and chill on the streets. Lady Jane had been out all evening, and he had stayed home, hoping to speak with her when she returned. He owed her a better apology and in his mind he worked over the words he would say when she came in.

As it happened the sound of the front door opening brought not her but a breathless Dallington.

"Lord John Dallington, sir," said Kirk, coming in after the young man yet again. "The young gentleman didn't knock, sir," he added with opprobrium. Between him and Shreve, it was a bad day to be a fastidious butler in London.

"I was in a rush, wasn't I? Lenox, it's about the case."

"What?"

"I spent the last five hours at the Bricklayers' Arms. I think we have a suspect."

Lenox stood up. "Who?"

"Jack Collingwood."

Lenox whistled. Append another unhappy butler's name to the growing list. During their interview Collingwood had sounded so very neutral about Clarke, appropriately sad but not, seemingly, very affected.

"What makes you suspect him?"

"I'll tell you in a moment. Graham, could you scare up a glass of brandy for me? Oh, but of course you're not Graham—Kirk, is it? Thank you." He turned to Lenox. "I sipped one glass of porter all afternoon, trying to keep my head clear, even though I bought five rounds. I have a terrible thirst."

"Make it two, Kirk, and I'll take mine warm."

"Yes, sir."

"I've found out why he had scabbed knuckles. Freddie Clarke. Everyone calls him Freddie, by the way—his friends."

"Why?"

"It doesn't help us. He was an amateur boxer, bare knuckles. Apparently they make these footmen of pretty durable material—he fought every other Thursday and trained whenever he could, including early mornings, at a ring in South London."

Boxing had grown up over the course of Lenox's lifetime, replacing fencing and the quarterstaff as the city's most prevalent combat sport. There were both aristocratic sparring rings and back-of-the-pub arenas devoted to it.

"Who did he fight? Was it rough or clean?"

"Clean—a nice place, expensive enough to be a drain on his income. He was great friends with his sparring partners."

"It's too bad. I thought the hands might be a clue."

"I did, too."

"What about Collingwood?"

"May I tell it chronologically, while it's fresh in my mind?"

"Of course."

Kirk arrived with the drinks, and Dallington downed half of his in one gulp. He looked at Lenox. "Oh, don't put on that irritable face," he said. "I hardly drink at all anymore."

Lenox laughed. "I didn't know I had any particular look on my face."

Dallington still caroused three or four days a month, out with the lively young things of the West End, with loose women and plentiful champagne in the dim dens lying under unmarked doors, the ones that only true revelers could discover. As a result he saw opprobrium in Lenox's eyes perhaps more often than it was there.

"Let me think," said Dallington. "I should begin by saying that the footmen you saw at the funeral were Freddie's closest friends. They came from various houses along Curzon Street and went to the pub once or twice a week together, in addition to meeting in the alley where he was killed, to smoke and chat."

"It makes sense—he didn't have any close friends in the house."

"On the contrary, he absolutely loathed Jack Collingwood, his superior and apparently a very strict taskmaster. They nearly came to blows three weeks ago when Collingwood called Clarke an idiot. Collingwood withdrew the insult when Clarke challenged him to fight. According to Jenny Rogers, by way of Ginger—that's the red-haired chap who spoke on the church steps —Freddie said he didn't care a whit about the job and would quit just so that he could fight Collingwood."

"That's why you think Collingwood is a suspect?"

"Partly. There's a great deal of anecdotal evidence about how little the two men liked each other. Ginger told me several stories—so did his friends—about that. Once Clarke dropped a silver tray as he was coming down the stairs, and even though it was undamaged Collingwood reported the incident to Ludo Starling. Apparently Collingwood was outraged when Starling refused to reprimand him, much less sack him. Suffice to say there was a good deal of animosity between the two men."

"Go on."

"What's far more damning for Collingwood is something that happened about a fortnight ago, four days before Clarke died."

"What?"

"According to Ginger, Freddie found Collingwood pilfering money from Elizabeth Starling's desk."

Lenox turned, his eyes wide with surprise. "Really?"

"Yes. Apparently Collingwood went pale, and Clarke left immediately. Still, they both knew what he had seen."

"Congratulations, John. It may be the answer."

"It may be."

Inside, however, Lenox felt a twinge of disappointment. He told himself it was stupid, but he had found himself drawn further and further into the case as the days went on, and while he hadn't realized it until now this return to detection had been deeply satisfying. In turn it made him doubt, for a fleeting second, whether he truly belonged in Parliament. If his old career felt so natural, so true, was it right to turn away from it? Was it vanity that made him want a more respectable, prestigious occupation? Partly, perhaps. He had always loved politics, it was true, and he knew he would make a good Member. Nevertheless he felt troubled in his mind. It would be a grave personal loss to give up detection altogether. A grave loss.

"Did Ginger or any of Clarke's other friends go to Inspector Fowler?"

"No."

"Or Ludo Starling?"

"No. Clarke himself said he wouldn't be a tale-teller unless Collingwood tried to get him sacked. Which makes it all the sadder, really."

"That doesn't mean Ginger shouldn't say anything. It's not telling tales if it's murder. A few coins is obviously a different matter."

"Sorry, I wasn't clear. That was just an additional piece of information. The reason Ginger and his lads won't tell is that they're trying to establish where Collingwood was during the half hour when Freddie might have been killed."

"Why? Surely that's the work of the Yard."

"Perhaps, but they feel that the stronger their case is, the more likely they'll be heard."

"It may be so."

"At any rate, that's what I got out of my afternoon at the Bricklayers' Arms. That and a hundred stories about Freddie Clarke."

"Did you talk to the lad's mother, incidentally?"

Dallington swirled the last sip of his brandy and then drank it down. "No. She only stayed for one drink, and then one of Freddie's friends chaperoned her back to her hotel. When he came back to the pub he said she was dead tired and of course pretty beaten up. Ginger is going out to see her tomorrow."

"I may as well see her, too."

"Oh?"

"I don't think it can hurt," said Lenox, "and it may help us discover something new."

"What about Parliament?"

"I'm in too deep now to give it up. I'll still ask you to look at things, but I want to be a part of it, too. Besides, Graham has made my life much more efficient. And perhaps it will turn out to be simple, and Collingwood will be the murderer as you say."

"It seems pretty damning."

"Indeed. Even if he did murder Frederick Clarke, though, I wonder if there was anything more to it than the change he stole from Elizabeth Starling. A job as a butler and a few shillings—are they worth killing for?"

"Don't forget his father was the butler, too. It could be a matter of family pride."

"Yes, that's true."

chapter fourteen

Lady Jane returned rather late in the evening, not much before midnight. For a moment Lenox wanted to comment on this and ask how it was any different from his own late homecoming the night before. He decided against it when he saw her impassive face, set for an argument. She sat at her mirror and began to let down her hair.

"Hello," he said, standing near their bed.

"Hello."

"How was your evening out?"

"Well enough as these things go."

"Where was it?"

She gave him a frosty look and was just about to answer when there was a knock at the door downstairs. Lenox, puzzled, trotted down the stairs, with Jane close behind him. Kirk was still dressed and awake and answered the door as they all stood in the wide hallway.

It was McConnell.

"Why, Thomas, hello," said Lady Jane. "How are you?"

He was red and flustered.

"Quite well, quite well." He looked at them blankly for a moment, then seemed to remember his purpose. "I came because Toto is having the baby."

"Why, that's wonderful!" said Lady Jane. "Is everything all right?"

"Perfectly—perfectly," said Thomas in a rush.

There was an awkward silence. Toto's last pregnancy had ended with the loss of the child some few months in.

"Shall we come back with you?" asked Lenox softly.

"I couldn't ask you—I couldn't—"

"We're coming," said Lady Jane.

They went in McConnell's roomy carriage, after Lady Jane had gone to fetch a parcel of things she had laid aside for the day when the baby came. She clutched it on her lap, occasionally giving Lenox's hand a squeeze. All of the anger between the newlyweds was dissolved, and they exchanged joyful smiles. Sitting opposite them, McConnell prattled nervously on.

"The doctors said she was quite healthy, and of course we watched her nutritional intake most strictly—most strictly—fascinating paper I read from Germany about prebirth care, they translated it over here—we gave her good dairy and beef, not too many vegetables—hearty fare, you understand—and I fully expect everything to go well—I feel quite certain it will."

Lenox and Lady Jane nodded thoughtfully and said "Oh, yes!" and "Mm, mm" in all the right spots.

When the carriage arrived only a couple of minutes later at the massive Bond Street house, McConnell darted out and into the door, apparently quite forgetting about his guests.

"He's got the nerves of all first fathers," Lady Jane said quietly as they walked up the steps to the open door. "I'm glad we came."

Lenox nodded, but saw something different in his friend's mien than Jane did. He saw a man looking for redemption, both for not preventing the loss of Toto's first baby (even though every doctor had concurred that it was an act of God) and for something greater: his whole mess of a life, which had begun so promisingly when he was a young surgeon and made such a happy, spectacular marriage, but which had somehow gone awry. This was his chance to amend all that. It was a fresh start.

Jane rushed straight upstairs to the vast second bedroom, which had been arranged for Toto's comfort and where a small huddle of doctors and nurses, all hired at great expense from the best hospitals in England at McConnell's insistence, consulted with each other. As for the doctor and his friend, their fate was to wait hour upon hour in McConnell's study.

It was a wonderful room of two levels; first a comfortable sitting room with desk and arm-chairs, plus a comprehensive laboratory against the back wall, and then, up a winding marble staircase inlaid with cherubim, a library full of scientific texts. The ceiling, twenty-five feet above them, was a white Wedgwood design.

"Would you like a drink?" asked McConnell, heading for the table with the spirits on it.

"Not quite yet—Thomas," said Lenox hastily, "before all that will you show me what you've been working on?"

McConnell looked at him inscrutably. "Of

111

course," he said after a moment. "Although I shouldn't touch any chemicals—I've been staying away from them for the past few weeks, and before that scrubbed my hands and arms very thoroughly whenever I worked at my table. For Toto."

Against the back wall were three long wooden tables, very rudimentary things. Stacked above these were many small shelves, on which were lined hundreds, perhaps thousands, of bottles of chemical. On the tables themselves were chopping blocks, microscopes, scientific instruments, and formic-acid-filled jars, some otherwise empty, some containing samples. In all, a first-rate chemical laboratory.

For a diverting half hour McConnell explained his various endeavors. His face brightened, and soon he was lost in the world of his work. It wasn't the same as surgery to him—Lenox had known him then—but it had its own merits.

After that Lenox acceded to the inevitable drink, a gin with tonic water, and he and McConnell sat, sometimes talking easily, sometimes silent. At one thirty Lady Jane came in and told them, very hurriedly, that all was well. Perhaps fifteen minutes later one of the doctors strode in with a quick step, causing McConnell to gasp and rise to his feet, but the news was the same. At two o'clock they had a plate of cold chicken and a bottle of white wine sent up and ate. After that, time seemed to slow down. Each had a book, but neither read much.

At three Lenox nodded off. McConnell coughed softly, and Lenox startled awake. It had been an hour since they had seen anyone and half an hour since they had spoken to each other.

"What names have you thought of?" asked Lenox.

McConnell smiled privately. "Oh, that's Toto's bailiwick."

There was a pause. "Are you very anxious?"

It was a personal question, but the doctor merely shrugged. "My nerves have lived in a state of high tension for nine months now. Every morning when I wake up I'm afraid until I check that all's well, and every night I lie in bed worrying. At school, were you nervous during the examinations? I was always worse off the day before."

"From all Jane says, things have gone well. My one regret about the summer is that we couldn't be here with you and Toto."

"We saw very few people—it was nice, very nice." Unsaid was that they had grown more comfortable with each other, that the pregnancy had consecrated their rapprochement. "Her parents have been wonderful."

"Did you let them know?"

"This evening? Yes, I telegrammed them

straight away, same to my father and mother. Her parents are on their way, and my father sent back his felicitations. Really I desire it to be two days from now and all well. What a terrible thought, to wish time away when life has so little of it anyway . . ."

"Why don't I step out and find a doctor?"

Just as Lenox said this, though, there was a wail at a far corner of the enormous house. Both men rose to their feet by instinct, and McConnell took a few steps to the door, pain and worry fresh again in his eyes.

"I've no doubt all is well," said Lenox.

There was another wail, long and loud. "One day men will be in the birthing room," said McConnell.

Lenox was shocked but said only, "Mm."

"I've seen a birth."

"It's better to let the doctors and the women handle it."

"Don't be retrogade, Charles."

Don't be radical, Lenox wanted to say. "Perhaps I am," was all he uttered in the event.

There was a third wail, and then a fourth some seconds later. McConnell paced to and fro as Lenox sat down again.

"The noises are quite normal," the doctor said, "but I never cared when I heard them before. It's awful to say—these women were patients of mine—but it's true."

A fifth wail, and then an even more terrifying sound: footsteps in the stairwell.

McConnell rushed to the door and flung it open. In his mind Lenox said a short prayer.

Outside of McConnell's study was a wide, rarely used salon, covered with eighteenth-century paintings in the bold Continental style. The doctor striding across it seemed like a figure out of myth, his loud steps and white robe in the dark room somehow laden with meaning.

"I congratulate you!" he called when he was close enough to be heard. His voice echoed across the vast empty room. "It's a girl!"

chapter fifteen

By the time Lenox left at 6:00 a.m. several things had happened. McConnell had burst out of the room and gone to see his wife and child, and come back fifteen minutes later positively beaming ("An angel! Both of them, two angels!"). Lady Jane, eyes rimmed with red, had come down to see Lenox and tell him all about the child, and then the two had agreed, in a hushed embrace, never to fight again. At last Lenox himself had seen the baby, a rosy-skinned, warm-bodied dab of human life.

Most importantly, the child had a name: Grace Georgianna McConnell. Already they were all calling her George ("Though we must never let the child think it's because you wanted a boy," admonished Jane). Her father seemed ready to burst with pride, happiness, and, perhaps most powerfully, relief, while her mother was (apparently) a composed, albeit slightly shaken, picture of maternal bliss. Lenox himself was immensely happy.

He left early to try to get home so that he could sneak a few hours' sleep. There were important meetings to attend that morning. As he went, Lady Jane was curled up in the second bed in Toto's room, sleeping across from the new mother, the crib in between them. Toto's hand was draped into it. As for McConnell, he had let the women sleep and been full of action. He gave the servants the day off, handed each of them a double florin, and ordered a crate of Pol Roger for them from the shop down the street, then sent eight telegrams to his friends and family. After that he ordered his horses up (apparently forgetting the day off—but nobody minded) with the plan of calling on these friends and family before the telegram could. It was as this plan was hatching that Lenox left.

Behind his heavy curtains at Hampden Lane the detective slept for two or three untroubled hours. When he woke his first thought was of some obscure worry, and then he remembered the happy conclusion of the night and it vanished. All would be well now, he thought. He hoped.

Meanwhile the uncaring world marched on, taking extremely little notice of George McConnell's birth, and Lenox had to dress hastily to make a meeting at eleven with several frontbenchers who were concerned about the strength of the pound.

"Kirk," he called from his study just before he left, "have you settled with Chaffanbrass?"

The butler looked blank. "Sir?"

"The bookseller across the way."

"I'm familiar with the gentleman, sir, but I don't understand your question."

A wave of irritation passed through Lenox before he realized how stupidly reliant on servants—on Graham—he was. "I could probably take care of it. Graham didn't brief you on that?"

"Mr. Graham has been so busy in Whitehall, sir, that I see very little of him."

"I generally pop over there and pick up books, and Chaffanbrass puts me down for them in his ledger. Graham goes over to pay."

"With what funds, sir, might I inquire?"

"Do you not have any ready money?"

"Enough to pay the deliverymen, of course, sir."

"I'd forgotten Graham went to my bank and withdrew cash for himself."

Kirk looked shocked to his core. "Oh, sir?" was all he managed.

"We developed our own little ways, as you can tell." Lenox smiled. "There's money on my dresser—would you settle with Mr. Chaffanbrass today, and explain why it's late? He counts on Graham coming in."

"Of course, sir."

"I hope I don't ask too much of you. I've rather forgotten what's usual."

"Yes, sir."

"You heard about the baby?"

"Yes, sir."

"Well—excellent, excellent." They stood awkwardly for a moment.

"Yes, sir. Will that be all?"

"Of course, go."

Lenox went down to Whitehall and had his meeting, though after the long night he had trouble keeping his eyes open—and trouble, truth be told, caring much about the taxation concerns of the rich, blustery bankers who were speaking.

After it was over he intended to go straight to the McConnells' house. Instead he found himself walking, almost involuntarily, toward Scotland Yard.

It was only a few steps away. Whitehall, the imposing avenue between Trafalgar Square and the Houses of Parliament, contained all the most important buildings of government (and was indeed now a word in Lenox's mind that conjured not a street but an entire small world and its structure, rather like Wall Street in America), including Scotland Yard. The Yard stood originally in two rather modest houses along Whitehall Place, which were constantly stretched to include new property in all directions around them as the Metropolitan Police expanded in size. It was an untidy warren of rooms, with its own smell—dusty paper, old wood floors, wet coats that had never been aired out, dormant fireplaces.

Lenox knew the constables who manned the front desk and simply nodded at them on his way to the back offices. He passed what had once been Inspector William Exeter's office, which now stood empty and bore on its door a plaque in the murdered man's memory. Without saying hello he also passed the office of Inspector Jenkins, the sole man at the Yard with much sympathy for Lenox's methods or interference.

Fowler's office was empty, but just momentarily —a cup of tea steamed on the desk, and a lit cigarette smoldered in an ebony ashtray. As Lenox stood uncertainly in the doorway a voice spoke to him from down the hallway.

"What are you doing in my office?"

"Hallo, Fowler. I thought I might have a word with you."

"Did you?"

He was distinctly unfriendly. This wouldn't have surprised the vast majority of people who knew Grayson Fowler. He was an essentially disagreeable man, not particularly handsome, slightly snarling, always half-shaven, and poorly dressed. Nevertheless, with Lenox he had, in the past at any rate, been affable enough, because Fowler was sharp and valued the quality in others.

"It's about Frederick Clarke."

"I imagined it might be."

"Can I come in?"

They were standing rather awkwardly in the doorway, with too little space between them. "I'd just as soon you didn't," said Fowler.

"I don't want to tread on your turf. Ludo Starling is an old friend of mine, and asked me some time ago whether I might—"

"I believe since then he's advised you to let Scotland Yard handle the case?"

"Well—halfheartedly. If we could just speak—"

"I'm afraid not."

"But if—"

"No!" said Fowler loudly and turned into his office, shutting the door hard behind him.

Lenox felt himself turning red with embarrassment. He stood there for a moment, utterly nonplussed.

Eventually he turned and walked down the

empty hall out into daylight again, hailed a hansom cab, and directed it to McConnell's house.

Jane was fetched for him by a happily tipsy young servant girl.

"How is Toto?" he asked his wife.

"She's doing wonderfully well, tired but resilient."

"And happy?"

"Oh, marvelously happy."

He smiled. "Do you know, it was wonderful to witness McConnell's joy. I thought I had never seen a man so happy." He shifted from one foot to the other. "I wonder, Jane, would you think of having a child one day?"

There was a pause. "I don't know," she said at last.

"It might be nice."

"Aren't we rather too old?"

He smiled softly. "Not you."

She returned his affectionate look and grazed his hand with her fingertips. "It's a conversation for another day, perhaps."

Hastily—feeling slightly vulnerable, in fact slightly hurt—he said, "Oh, of course, of course. I'm only caught up in the happiness of the moment."

"I understand."

"Now—let's take a look at this child, George. I assume she's with a nurse somewhere hereabouts?"

"I'm afraid you can't see her. Toto still has

121

her. She won't let the nurse take her away—'just a few minutes longer,' she keeps saying. You can't imagine how she beams at the poor little child."

"Too bad," said Lenox. "I've wasted a trip."

chapter sixteen

Strangely, the Palace of Westminster, that remarkable and ancient-looking panorama of soft yellow stone situated on the banks of the Thames (and better known as Parliament), was now just, in its fully finished form, about four years old.

This was so strange because it already seemed somehow eternal, and of course some parts of it were older. There was the Jewel Tower, a three-story building that stood over a moat, which Edward the Third had built to house his treasures in 1365. And to be fair, construction of the Houses had begun some thirty years before, so *parts* of the new buildings were at least that old. Still, for most of Lenox's life it had been a work in progress. Only now did it stand on its own, unencumbered by builders or provisional outbuildings, so glorious it might have been there a thousand years.

The reason for the construction of the new Parliament was simple enough. A fire.

Until the middle of the 1820s, sheriffs collecting taxes for the crown had used an archaic method of recordkeeping, the tally stick. Beginning in medieval England, when of course vellum was far scarcer than paper now, the most efficient way to record the payment of taxes had been to make a series of different-sized notches in long sticks. For payment of a thousand pounds, the sheriff cut a notch as wide as his palm in the tally stick, while the payment of a single shilling would be marked with a single nick. The thumb was a hundred pounds, while the payment of one pound was marked, obscurely, with the width of a "swollen piece of barleycorn."

It was a system that in the eighteenth century was already antiquated, and by William the Fourth's reign embarrassingly so. Thus it was in 1826 that the Exchequer—that branch of government that manages the empire's funds—decided to change it. This left one problem, however: two massive cartloads of old tally sticks of which to dispose. The Clerk of Works (unfortunate soul) took it upon himself to burn them in two stoves in the basement that reached below the House of Lords. The next afternoon (October 16, 1834) visitors to the Lords complained of how hot the floor felt. Soon there was smoke.

Then came the fatal mistake. A caretaker of the place, Mrs. Wright, believed she had solved the problem when she turned off the furnaces. She left work. An hour later, the entire group of buildings was almost wholly in flames. The conflagration, even though citizens of London fought it valiantly, consumed almost all of the old Palace of Westminster.

The new Parliament was spectacular. It contained three miles of corridors, more than a thousand rooms, and more than a hundred staircases. As he walked into the Members' Entrance to go to work, all of this rich history crossed Lenox's mind. He was a part of it now, too. Slowly but surely a serious burden, an intimidating sort of expectation, had settled on his shoulders.

It made him wonder: What if this position for which he had so long yearned and which he had won at so high a cost was in fact wrong for him? A bad fit? It nearly broke his heart to think so. His brother and his father, both his grandfathers, had served long, distinguished years in the Houses of Parliament. It would be almost unbearable if he were the one to let them down.

Still, still—he couldn't stop thinking about Ludo Starling's strange behavior, about the notes slipped under the door for Frederick Clarke, and about whether he had already discovered a truer vocation than politics could ever be.

Graham was sitting at an upwardly sloped clerk's desk in their cramped office, but stood when Lenox entered.

"Good afternoon, sir."

"Hello, Graham."

"If I may be so bold as to ask, sir—"

"You know what, I don't think clerks here are quite so deferential as butlers," said Lenox, smiling. "You can speak less formally if you like."

"As you please, sir."

Lenox laughed. "That's a poor start. But what were you going to ask?"

"Has Dr. McConnell's child been born?"

"Oh, that! Yes, it's a girl, and you'll be pleased to hear she's quite healthy. They're calling her George."

Graham frowned. "Indeed, sir?"

"You find it eccentric? Her name is Grace, really—George is more of a nickname, if that improves it."

"It would hardly be my place, sir—"

"As I said, I think these young political chaps are extremely brusque with their employers. Get used to treating me like a sheep to herd from appointment to appointment. And on that subject, I believe we have to discuss your pay. Your current salary is . . . is it a hundred pounds a year?"

Graham tilted his chin forward very slightly in assent.

"We must bump you up. Let me ask my brother what he thinks would be a suitable wage."

"Thank you, sir, but as you will recall these weeks were intended to be the probationary period of our new arrangement, and it seems premature to—"

"I think it's working out wonderfully. Probation lifted."

Graham sighed the mournful sigh of a man afflicted with a frivolous interlocutor just when he most wants serious conversation. "Yes, sir."

"What's on today?"

"You have lunch with various Members from Durham, to discuss your regional interests."

"I'm going as the man from Stirrington, then?" This was Lenox's constituency, which was quite near the cathedral city of Durham. It was the rather unorthodox way of the English system that a man standing for Parliament did not need to have any prior affiliation with or residency in the place he hoped to represent.

"Precisely, sir."

"Who are the other fellows?"

"The only one whose name you will know is Mr. Fripp, sir, who has made a great deal of noise on the other side of the aisle on behalf of the navy. Otherwise they are a range of back-benchers with primarily parochial interests. Here is a dossier."

Lenox took the sheet of paper. "What am I supposed to get out of this luncheon?"

"Sir?"

"Do I have any aim, or is it merely an amicable gathering?"

"From what I gather from the other Members' secretaries, it has in years past been primarily a friendly occasion, always held just now, before the new session begins."

"Pointless," Lenox muttered. "What's after that?"

"You have several individual meetings with Members of the House of Lords, as you see on the dossier, and a meeting of the committee for the railway system."

Lenox sighed, moving to the window. He held the list of his day's events at his side. "I'm glad it's soon that the session begins. All of this feels unhelpful."

"The alliances and friendships you make now will serve you when you begin to ascend within the party, sir, or if there's some piece of law you would like to see passed."

Half-smiling, the detective answered, "You've taken to this much more readily than I have, I think. Friends with Percy Field, planning for me to be Prime Minister. All I can think about is old cases. I read the papers in the morning a bit too eagerly, I find, searching out the crimes that have confounded Scotland Yard. It's a melancholy feeling."

"It has been an abrupt transition."

Unusually close though they were, Lenox would never have given utterance to the thought that passed his mind then—that it had been an abrupt transition into marriage, too, and not always an easy one. Instead he said, "My hope is that when the ball is truly in play, when people are giving speeches and defending their words and *acting,* that then it will all fall into place for me."

"I dearly wish it, sir."

"There's nothing worse than going to work with that slight feeling of dread, is there, Graham?"

"If I may be so bold—"

Lenox smiled. "You must be quite to the point, remember, quite rude!"

"Very well. Then I would say that this feeling will pass, and soon you will remember that you came to Parliament not only for yourself but for others. You do, in fact, represent the people you met in Stirrington. Perhaps that knowledge will lift your spirits."

"You're right."

There was a pause. "And, sir, one last meeting, which isn't on the list."

"Oh?"

"It may ease the pressure, sir. Mrs. Elizabeth Starling sent a note, asking if you would care to take dinner there."

Lenox grinned. "Did she? Please, write back and tell her I would."

chapter seventeen

Ludo, standing in his drawing room, looked miserable as he greeted Dallington and Lenox that night. Collingwood had brought them in (they shared a swift, questioning glance as he turned to lead them down the front corridor) and announced them, all in a mood that was both scrupulously polite and somehow obliquely dismissive. Perhaps he didn't think of a detective as a suitable dinner guest at the house, or perhaps he had something to hide and regretted their presence so nearby. And there was one last possibility: that he was still jarred by the violent death of someone with whom he had worked in close proximity, and so not quite himself.

One thing was sure. It had been six days since the murder, and if they didn't make a breakthrough soon the trail might well run cold.

Starling, perhaps for that reason, looked alternately flushed and pale.

"Oh, ah, Lenox," he said. "Good of you to come, quite good of you. And Mr.—er, Mr. Dallington, I believe. How do you do? You both received my wife's invitations?"

"Call me John, please."

"John—certainly. Yes, Elizabeth thought the least we could do to thank you for your work was have you to supper. It will be a family affair, only the seven of us—my sons, whom of course you know, Lenox, and my great-uncle, Tiberius. I think you met him."

"Yes—it was he who told us that Frederick Clarke had been getting money slipped to him under the door of the servants' quarters."

This agitated Ludo. Pleadingly, he said, "Oh, *don't* let's talk about Clarke. I can tell you it's cast a tremendous pall over life here, and I think we would all be much more comfortable if we kept to other subjects."

"As you please, of course," said Lenox. Dallington smiled slightly.

"In fact, one of the reasons I asked you here was to request that you drop the case. I have full faith in Grayson Fowler, and believe—"

They all turned as a woman's voice came from the doorway behind them. "Having amateur detectives wandering around London and buying drinks for footmen can only serve to draw attention to this unfortunate circumstance. Hello again, Mr. Lenox." She laughed to show she wasn't too serious.

"How do you do, Mrs. Starling. I hope you know John Dallington?"

With a wide, warm smile, Elizabeth Starling said, "My pleasure. I'm sorry if I sound rude on the subject, gentlemen, but Inspector Fowler's discretion is far in excess of what we expected, and we feel we can count on him entirely. Consider Ludo's request withdrawn. It was importunate to begin with, I think."

She had a charm to her that softened Ludo's impoliteness, and Lenox found himself nodding slightly.

"Where are the boys, dear?" asked Ludo.

"Do you take my position, Mr. Lenox?"

"Yes, certainly."

"Wonderful. I think Ludo told you about the honor that may soon accrue to us. We mustn't put a foot wrong."

"Did you like the lad?" asked Dallington, whose tone came very close to impertinence. His next words spilled over into it altogether. "Not to turn the subject away from the honor that may accrue to you."

"I did," said Elizabeth, "and Ludo, to answer your question, I believe I hear their footsteps on the stair."

In the event, it was not the Starling boys but the old uncle, Tiberius. He was wearing a hunting jacket with holes in the elbows, trousers would have been more appropriate on a pig farmer than a gentleman, and shoes that, being orange and black, looked frankly peculiar. His ivory-white hair stood straight up in a stiff prow. Upon entering the room he took a large handkerchief from his pocket and loudly blew his nose into it.

"Uncle, I had Collingwood lay out your dinner jacket. Did you miss it?"

"Damn thing doesn't fit. How do you do, fellows?" he said to Lenox and Dallington. "Have you found out who killed our footman?"

"Not yet," said Dallington. His own dinner suit was quite fine—he was something of a dandy— but he was smiling widely at Tiberius. A kindred spirit. "I must say, I admire your shoes."

"Cheers for that. They get some strange looks, but they're quite comfortable. Fellow in India made them for me. Black as midnight." He belched loudly. "When's dinner?"

Elizabeth Starling, only temporarily nonplussed, said, "Please, sit—some wine, gentlemen?" Lenox nodded his assent to the proposal.

Two young men came clattering into the room, as if they had been racing downstairs. One was quite fat and tall and the other quite short and thin, with a sparse, queasy mustache that looked as if it had needed careful tending and cultivation in order to exist at all.

The fat, tall one came forward first. "How d'you do?" he said.

"This is Alfred," said Ludo. "My oldest son. Paul, come forward." The mustache approached. "These are two friends of mine, Mr. Lenox and Mr. Dallington."

"Cor, not *John* Dallington, is it?" said Paul, who appeared to be the more enterprising of the two. The older boy looked around hungrily, mouth open, and then, his eyes failing to alight on anything edible, turned hopefully toward the dining room.

"It is John Dallington, yes. Have we met?"

"No, but I know your name. You're a legend at the varsity. James Douglas-Titmore said you once drank five bottles of champagne in an hour."

"Well—perhaps. Wouldn't be to dwell on my accomplishments."

Elizabeth Starling looked anxious. "Paul, I certainly hope that *you* would never undertake something so frivolous and dangerous."

"I wouldn't," volunteered Alfred, his vowels heavy and jowly. "Shall we eat soon, Mother, do you know?"

Paul looked at his brother scornfully. " 'Course you wouldn't."

Tiberius belched.

"Oh, dear," said Ludo, pinkening.

Collingwood came in and rang a small bell. "Supper is served," he said.

"Lovely," Alfred said and pushed toward the front of the line to get to the dining room.

"What'd he say?" shouted Tiberius, as half-deaf men will.

"Dinner is served," said Elizabeth.

133

"Good for him!" answered Tiberius with a cheerful smile.

"No, dinner is served, Uncle!"

"Always said he would come to good. Excellent lad. Dinner being served shortly, I expect? No, Elizabeth, it's all right, you can't be expected to remember everything."

As they sat to eat, Lenox observed a fresh face among the servants ranged at the side of the room. Clarke had already been replaced, then. Collingwood began spooning soup from a large silver tureen into bowls on the sideboard, which the new footman began to distribute. Very distinctly Lenox heard Alfred's stomach grumble; they were sitting side by side.

"How do you find Cambridge?" asked the older man.

"S'all right."

"You're at Downing, I hear? It's a lovely college."

"S'all right."

"The soup looks nice."

"Oh, it's lovely soup here," said Alfred fervently, at last giving his dinner companion the benefit of his full attention. "They use real cream. At Cambridge the soup is too thin, if you ask me."

"What do you study?"

"Classics."

"Oh?"

"Father wanted me to."

Ludo said grace, and they began to eat. Lenox assayed a few more conversational gambits with Alfred but gave them up when they failed to earn a response. He turned to Ludo, on his left.

"Did you study history, too?"

"Look, Lenox," said Ludo in a low voice, "I apologize for my speech, before. It's a difficult time in the house, as you can imagine. Between this lad dying, Paul going up to university for the first time, and the prospect of this title . . . well, a difficult time, as I say."

"It's quite all right."

"*Will* you leave the case to Fowler?"

"You truly fear my indiscretion?"

"No! Not that at all, you must believe me. It's simply that the more people are involved, the more attention the situation will receive. I want the murderer found, but I want it done quietly."

"Isn't that why you came to me at first?"

Ludo again looked stirred, as if Lenox were misunderstanding him out of sheer obstinacy. "As I told you, Fowler has proved quite a good sort! Listen, will you leave it off, as a favor to me?"

"Paul!" Elizabeth Starling, breaking off her conversation with Dallington, called down the table to her younger son, concern etched in her face. "Is that a flask of liquor I just saw you sip?"

"Yes, Mother."

"Goodness!"

"Not at all the thing," said Alfred, his glabrous pink face screwed up in judgment. "You mustn't get a reputation at Downing, Paul."

"What do you know, anyway? Douglas-Titmore said you haven't any friends, and you hadn't any at Shrewsbury either."

The detective's heart went out to Alfred, whose face crumpled up as if he were going to cry. "I don't think I had a single friend my first term at Oxford," Lenox said. "That was years ago, but I expect it's the same way now."

"It only starts in the second term," agreed Dallington.

"Is that true?" asked Paul, who apparently looked upon the word of a man who could drink five bottles of champagne in an hour as gospel.

"Oh, very true."

"Hand over the flask," said Elizabeth Starling.

Tiberius belched. "Tiberius Jr! Tibby!" he called out in a high-pitched voice.

"Not the cat, Uncle," said Ludo despairingly.

In the cab back through Mayfair, after supper had reached its merciful conclusion, Lenox and Dallington laughed together over the night's events.

"That family is a mess," said the younger man.

"I don't envy them that great-uncle of Ludo's, rich as he may be."

"Amusing old git, if you have the right sense

of humor. Anyway, do you plan to heed their request?"

"That I leave the case alone?"

"Yes."

"No, I don't. Of course not. In fact I think we should go visit the dead boy's mother in the morning."

chapter eighteen

Hammersmith was a genteel, factory-scattered borough of London, some five miles west of Mayfair and situated on a turn in the Thames. As Dallington and Lenox rode out early the next morning, they continued their discussion of the evening at the Starlings'.

"Did you have a chance to spy on Collingwood?" asked Lenox.

"Unfortunately I was occupied with Paul, the younger son. He asked me a thousand different questions about pubs at Cambridge. I'd be surprised if his innards survive a month of King Street, with all the drinking he seems to have planned."

Reminded by the word "drinking" that he had tea, Lenox took out his silver flask (a present from McConnell—its cloth case was in his family's tartan) and took a long sip. "I wonder whether Collingwood is capable of violence. It seems so unlikely that he would kill Frederick Clarke over a few coins—a pound at the outside."

"Who knows how important his position might be to him, or indeed whether there was something else between the two of them besides the money Collingwood stole. I'm going to see Ginger, Clarke's friend, after we finish here. Perhaps he'll know something more by now."

They had pulled up to a low-slung sandstone building, which advertised itself on a small placard as the Tilton Hotel. This was where Mrs. Clarke had chosen to stay during her trip to London for the funeral. The entrance hall had a sort of shabby grandeur, with very nice furniture that was all worn at the edges, a floor of beautiful tiles that had gotten dingy, and attendants in fraying uniforms. Lenox registered the place in his head as a piece of evidence; it wasn't the sort of place one stayed if one had tailored suits, as Frederick Clarke had.

A few moments later they were sitting with her in the tearoom next door. Lenox went to the counter and bought cakes and coffee, as well as a scone and jam for Mrs. Clarke's breakfast.

She was a striking woman, nearly fifty but still slender and well dressed. Her hair was black and her face very alive, at once shrewd and playful—though now these characteristics were only half visible under an outer layer of grief. Her wide mouth was pinched with anxiety.

"Thank you," she said when Lenox returned with the food. Her accent was less distinct than the average housemaid's—perhaps through conscious effort. "Mr. Dallington has been telling me about your credentials as an investigator. Extremely impressive."

"He plays a decent hand of cards, too," said Dallington with a grin.

She smiled faintly. "I'm sure."

"Is your hotel comfortable?" asked Lenox.

"Thank you, yes."

"I'm sorry for your loss. By all accounts your son was a fine young man."

"A good boxer as well," said Dallington encouragingly.

"His letters were full of boxing, I do know that. Which makes it seem so unfair that he didn't get a chance to fight back." She brought her handkerchief to her mouth, her eyes suddenly stricken.

"Did he like his work, too?" asked Lenox.

"Yes, he seemed to."

"He must have mentioned the people he worked with—Miss Rogers, Mr. Collingwood?"

"Only Mr. Collingwood."

"In a negative light?"

"Not always. I sometimes thought they seemed quite friendly, though Freddie did mention that the butler could be strict with the staff. He wouldn't have liked that." She nibbled at her slice of lemon cake.

"What were his plans?"

"Excuse me?"

"Did he hope to continue on as a footman?"

"He spoke of university, in fact. The new place, not Oxford or Cambridge."

For many centuries these had been the only two universities in England, but now others were springing up. "University College, do you mean? Here in London?"

"Yes, exactly. He said they offered a good education without all the snobbery. But just for the moment he was earning a decent wage and saving his money, I think. We never spoke about his plans, to be quite honest. I was always pleased for him to do whatever he liked. I only know he thought about university because we live in Cambridge, and when he visited me he said that he could never go anywhere like that —pointing at the university, you understand."

"I didn't realize you lived in Cambridge."

"Yes, these several years, and before I worked in London as well. It's where I grew up. My father was a gardener at Peterhouse."

"Did you come to work for the Starlings because you met them in Cambridge, then?" asked Lenox.

She looked at him curiously. "Why would you

think that? I came to work for the Starlings because they needed a housemaid and the hiring agency sent me there—you see, I had come to London because I wanted to see a bit of the world. I left when I inherited money from my uncle George and opened my pub. The Dove."

"Did Frederick like the Starlings?"

"He never mentioned it. I imagine he did since he stayed so long."

"Did you like working there?"

She shrugged. "I liked the girls on the alley —oh, yes, the one where Freddie died," she said in response to Lenox's surprised look. "We lived our whole life in that alley, the ten or fifteen of us. There was a great deal of gossip and chat. It pleased me to think of him there, running out for small errands and meeting people."

"A community," Lenox murmured.

"Yes, precisely."

Lenox made a mental note to interview other people "on the alley"—not just the footmen who had been friends with the dead lad.

"Did he ever wear a ring, that you recall?" asked Dallington.

"No," said his mother. "What sort of ring?"

"A signet ring? With a picture on the front, gold?"

"No." She shook her head firmly. "Certainly not."

"In your experience did he often have much

money? When he came to visit you on his holidays, for instance?"

"Oh, dear, no—he saved his money, I think."

"Did he dress differently after he moved to London? In a nicer suit, for instance?"

"Not at all. He had his old suits mended and wore them until they were threadbare. He always offered me money, though. Not that I needed it—the Dove does quite well—but still, the offer." She took a sip of tea, and a slight smile came over her face. "You can't imagine how wonderful he was to me. Mr. Clarke is dead, you see, and when Freddie came to visit he was so thoughtful—so considerate. What a nice boy he was."

"There, there," said Lenox. She had tears in her eyes.

"He did all the chores a man usually does in the pub, when he was home. Fixed squeaky doors and creaking chairs, carried the kegs, rousted the patrons who had too much drink and were acting loud. It was a treat for me, not to be on my own." Now she was really crying. "And he's gone forever."

Because of his work Lenox had seen so many grieving people in the last two decades that he was, to his shame, in some degree immune to their suffering. It was no different with Mrs. Clarke; he sympathized with her, but the rawness of her emotions—he could now feel detached from it. Inwardly he vowed to discover who had killed Freddie, if only to make amends for this own private callousness.

"Are you leaving town, Mrs. Clarke?"

She shook her head decisively. "Certainly not. Mr. Rathbone, who sold the Pig and Whistle some years ago, has come out of retirement to run the Dove while I'm away. I mean to stay here until I find out the truth."

"Can I ask—who do you think killed your son?"

Her tears started afresh. "I don't know!" she said. "I wish I did."

"Do you recall anything else he said about life at the Starlings', anything unusual? Anything about Mr. Collingwood?"

She thought for a moment, one delicate hand touching her pale chin. "He said that Collingwood was secretive, I remember. Freddie said, 'I don't have any friends in the house, only on the alley. Collingwood is far too secretive.' "

Freddie had his own secrets, thought Lenox, his mind on the money. "Did you ever send him money, by any chance?" It was a long shot.

She frowned. "No, not after his first month or so there, when I made sure he had enough. I didn't want him to go, you see."

"Oh?"

"He could have taken over the pub for me. Even if he had only wanted to live in London, he needn't have been a footman. He could have

143

taken lodgings and applied to be a tutor—he was excellent in books, you know—or any number of things. But he insisted on London, and on being a footman—and in fact on being a footman for the Starlings."

"Why the Starlings?"

She shook her head. "He heard me talk about my days there, I suppose. He said he wanted a few years in London, and then he would decide what he should really do with his life. Do you have children, Mr. Lenox?"

"I don't."

"They're mysterious creatures. You do your best with them, but in the end it's not up to you how they live."

Lenox took a sip of coffee, wondering to himself what could have made Freddie so adamantly desire to be a footman, a difficult job, and more specifically a footman at the Starlings', when other options were available to him . . . and how did his job in Mayfair connect with the large sums of money he had been receiving under the door of the servants' quarters?

chapter nineteen

Lenox had eaten little as he spoke with Mrs. Clarke, absorbed by her answers, and so at twelve thirty that afternoon he fell ravenously upon the lunch Kirk brought to his desk in the house on Hampden Lane. There was a roasted chicken, a fluffy hillock of mashed potatoes, and a beautifully charred tomato cut in quarters, along with half a bottle of dreadful claret that he nevertheless managed to get through most of. As he ate he let both Parliament and Frederick Clarke fall away from his mind and read a novel by Miss Gaskell about a small town somewhere in the Home Counties. When he was finished eating he moved to his armchair, reading on and smoking quite contentedly.

Only at two o'clock or so did he turn his attention to the tottering stack of blue books that Graham had put on his desk the night before. Their name was wonderfully evocative to Lenox (its origin was the rich blue velvet medieval parliamentary records were bound in), reminding him of harried politicians, deep matters of state, and hushed late-night discussions of strategy. As it happened, one in ten of the books—reports on every imaginable topic that affected Great Britain—was as interesting and urgent as he had imagined. The other nine would be dreadfully dull, reports from distant nations of the empire, coal statistics, a study of the increasingly serious accumulation of horse manure in Manchester.

Still, he was duty bound to read them all, or at any rate to skim them. He picked one up, spent half an hour in study, and then tossed it aside. Another. Another. Soon it was four o'clock and he knew far more than he had ever cared to about the state of Newcastle's police force and the shortage of English beef after the previous year's serious outbreak of a new illness called— and he had to double-check the name—"hoof and mouth" disease.

With four books absorbed, in their outlines if not in their details, he turned to a fifth. It drew him in almost like a novel—with the best novels he was at first still extremely aware that he was reading, but gradually the act of reading itself disappeared, and even turning the pages didn't remind him that there were two worlds, inside and outside of the book's covers. This blue book, though much more dense than a good novel, had for him that same imperative feeling.

He finished it in an hour flat, and when he was done he clutched it in one hand and, without a word to anyone in the house, made for the door and hailed a taxi.

He was after James Hilary. Although Hilary was nearly a decade younger than Lenox, he was one of the most influential men in Parliament, an urbane, learned, and fluent gentleman with a private fortune and a secure seat in Liverpool. He was irreplaceable within the party, connecting as he did the back bench and the front bench, the various offices of government to one another. If anyone would understand, it was Hilary.

As Lenox had expected he found the man—a charming, well-dressed, slightly sharp-faced sort of person—in his favored club, the Athenaeum. He was reading by a window in the great hall.

"There you are—may we speak?"

"Lenox, my dear chap, you look beside yourself. Is everything all right? Jane? I've scarcely said ten words to you since your wedding all those months ago."

"Oh, quite well, quite well. It's this." He thrust the blue book he had been reading into the air.

Hilary narrowed his eyes, trying to catch the title of the report on the side of the book. "What is it?"

"Can we find a private room?"

"By all means." He folded his paper. "I'm so pleased that you've hit the ground running. Your man, Graham, has been all over the House, too. Excellent."

They retired to a small chamber nearby and sat at a six-sided card table, where in a few hours four or five debauched gentleman would sit until dawn, playing whist for stakes rather higher than they could afford and drinking great drafts of champagne. Lenox hated the scene: the jollity, sometimes real but often forced; the insincere banter as each man privately, worriedly totted up what he had won or lost; the casual IOUs passed from rather poor men to very rich ones, both knowing that payment would be difficult but pretending it was all the same. The room set his teeth on edge. Still, he knew what he wanted to say.

"It's cholera," said Lenox.

"Oh, that? Is that what you're so worked up about, Charles? My dear chap, Bazalgette has solved—"

"He hasn't!"

Perhaps taken aback by the fierceness of Lenox's tone, Hilary began to look more serious. "What do you mean?"

"It's about the poor. They're still in danger— as anyone who read this report could tell you."

Cholera had been for much of Victoria's reign the chief social anxiety of London, England, and indeed the world. In England there had been epidemics in 1831, 1848, 1854, and just last year, in 1866. In the previous decade alone more than ten thousand people had died of the disease.

It had only recently become widely acknowledged that it was a waterborne plague, and the so-called Great Stink of several years ago had galvanized into action the politicians and municipal leaders of London. Joseph Bazalgette, a well-respected engineer working with the Metropolitan Commission for Sewers and its successor, the Board of Works, had designed a new sewage system for London that would make the water of the Thames safe to drink again, and after his plan had been published and executed a couple of years before, towns and cities across the country had begun to copy it. The reformers had won.

But there was a problem. Most of London was connected to the new sewage system, but the part of the city that had suffered the most deaths, East London, where the poorest people lived—it had not. This fact, with its implications, was what had so shocked Lenox. He had assumed before then, not paying very great attention to the matter, that all was solved. It wasn't. In fact a fresh epidemic was just beginning to show signs of emerging in East London. One of the primary causes of cholera—overfull cemeteries—was still prevalent there, and the water supply was horribly compromised.

Lenox explained all this to Hilary. "It's all right for the nibs, living around here, and for the middle class, but these people, James! You wouldn't believe the statistics! Italy has lost a hundred thousand people this year, maybe more. Russia the same. Everywhere in Europe. People couldn't abide the smell—the *smell!*—and so we have a new sewage system, but there's no interest in the death of people in our own city! It's the most shocking thing I've heard since I was elected!"

Hilary shifted uncomfortably in his high-backed wooden chair. "It's grave indeed, Charles, but I'm afraid we have more pressing concerns at the moment. This reform bill, for one, and of course the colonies—"

Lenox interrupted him. "Surely we have time to handle all of these things at once. As a start we should buy some of these private water companies, which care for nothing but profit, and turn them into municipal concerns."

"That would require a great deal of money."

"These are precisely the people we're supposed to represent. What if this were happening in a small town? Would we help them?" He threw up his hands in disgust. "Any evil can go hiding in London. It's always been the way, hasn't it?"

"Charles, you're new to Parliament. You must understand that we hold human life in the balance every day, and make judgments about how to help people based on our best sense. It's not pleasant, but it's our work. When you've been in Parliament a year you'll comprehend—"

"I'll deliver a speech. I don't care who listens to it—I don't especially care who wants to help me, Conservative or our side."

"A speech!" said Hilary with amused incredulity. "I should think it would be some months before you deliver a speech."

Lenox realized that he was in the reverse of his usual position: He was the petitioner, like so many grieving people who had come to solicit his services with varying success. It was a helpless, unpleasant feeling.

He decided to try a different tack. "I know I must seem callow to you, Hilary, but you've known me for many years. I'm not a hasty-minded person. I've read dozens of blue books, and of them all this was the one that affected me. Will you read it? Will you speak to people?"

Lenox was holding the book halfway out, and Hilary took it gingerly. "I'll read it."

Lenox stood up. "Thank you. Meanwhile I'll speak to a few of the Members I know. This is a worthy cause, you'll see."

"Well—I'm quite sure. But Charles, don't speak to too many people—let this move slowly."

The detective nodded, though he had no intention of adhering to the advice. He ran out of the Athenaeum with a dozen ideas swirling through his mind—to talk to this person, to write that one, to ask that gentleman to dinner and another gentleman's wife who could speak to Jane.

Underlying these plans was the thrilling notion, barely formed in all the hustle of the last hour, that he had found the purpose and motivation in his new career that had seemed so elusive only the day before.

chapter twenty

Though he now had a dozen things to do, he decided it was important to stop in for a visit at the McConnells'.

Jane was still spending nearly all of her time there. He didn't wonder at her devotion—he knew better perhaps than anyone else in the world the strength of her friendship—but did ask himself whether it took a toll on her. She would be happy for Toto, that was a given. But would she be sorry for herself?

She had been a very young widow. It was the one subject they never discussed, the sudden death of her first husband just a year into their marriage. Lenox tried to think back to Jane as she was then, at a time when he could be friendly but dispassionate in his analysis of her character. He remembered that she had been a very happy bride, and a very brave widow. What had she planned for herself, in the idle moments during the weeks before that first wedding? How many children? What names had she bestowed upon them?

It made his chest feel hollow, his lower stomach roiled. It was awful.

Still, he managed to put on a cheerful face for Thomas and spent half an hour closeted with him, drinking a dram of whisky with the new father, who paced back and forth, an unshakable grin upon his face. It was the happiest, quite literally the happiest, that Lenox had ever seen him.

Jane came downstairs, brushed a kiss on his cheek, said a few quick words—amiable enough, loving enough—and went back to be with Toto, who was apparently still rather weak.

"Another sip of Scotch?" asked McConnell when she had gone.

"Thanks, yes."

McConnell poured two from his sideboard and handed one to Lenox. "To George!"

"With all my heart."

They drank. "I think all my toasts from now on will be to her," said McConnell thoughtfully, looking out of his window at the soft pink and white fall of evening, buildings half lit, home-ward-headed people scattered over the cool streets. "Whether we toast the Queen or a newly married couple, in my own mind I'll know who my toast is really for. Little George McConnell."

Lenox smiled. "What's it like?" he asked quietly.

"What is it like? It's . . . it's like being given your own life to start over. I don't think I've ever thought for a moment about what I ate or what I drank or whether I hit my head. I don't think I ever thought for a moment about my education, not really."

"Oh?" Lenox felt slightly crestfallen—not envious, but sad that the brilliant, shimmering happiness of McConnell's face would never show on his own.

"Other parents said I would care more about her than myself, and I see now that's what they meant. All of the choices that are quick and painless for my own old bones seem so important when they're for her. Where will she go to school, I wonder?" In a private reverie he fingered a book on the shelf next to him. "What will she learn there?" He looked at Lenox. "It's the most wonderful thing you can imagine."

"Is Toto holding up well?" asked Lenox after a silent moment.

"Oh, she's making jokes again. And between us all is well." This was an unusually intimate thing for the doctor to say, and perhaps he realized it, but, caught up in his own exhilaration, he went on. "When one is unhappy and trying to hide it—when one has a secret trouble—there's an antic cast to everything in life. Now things are serene again."

"It's very finely put," murmured Lenox.

Then a thought occurred to him. It was that turn of phrase: "an antic cast." It put him in mind of someone.

Ludo Starling.

If one has a secret trouble . . . and now it occurred to Lenox in a fell stroke what should have occurred to him all along. That Ludo himself was certainly a suspect in the murder of Frederick Clarke.

Everything about his behavior had been odd, but more than that, there was some indefinable disturbance in his mind that was obvious if you spent three minutes in his presence.

Of course it was a problematic idea. For one thing, Ludo had an alibi (but hadn't he been quick to deliver it?). Dallington would have to check whether he had in fact been playing cards at the hour when Clarke was killed. For another thing, he had approached Lenox. Why would he have done that, had he been the murderer?

And yet the detective's intuition was pulsing with the certainty that Ludo was concealing something.

"What is it?" asked McConnell. "You look peculiar."

"Nothing—nothing. I must be going."

"Is it about your case? Shall I lend you a hand?"

Lenox smiled at him. "Your place is here. Tell Jane I'll see her this evening at home."

"As you wish, of course."

On the way to Ludo's house Lenox pondered their encounters over the past few days. There were Ludo's constant pleas that Lenox drop the case. There was the invitation to dinner, ostensibly in the spirit of friendship but in fact as an excuse for Elizabeth Starling to make the same request.

It was all exceedingly strange.

Ludo's house was brightly lit; it was nearly night by now, with only thin purple bands of light visible below the black of the horizon. Lenox knocked on the door, and Collingwood—whose complicity suddenly seemed like a possibility—answered.

"Is he in?" asked Lenox, barging past.

"Yes, sir. Please—" Collingwood had been going to invite him to sit and wait, but Lenox had already taken a place on the sofa in the drawing room. "Just a moment, please."

Ludo appeared. "Oh, Charles," he said. "How are you?"

"Do you know why I'm here?"

"To thank us for supper? It was our pleasure, I promise you."

"I do thank you, but no. I have some questions about—about Frederick Clarke. And you."

"And me?"

"Yes."

"Very well. I was just on my way to supper and a hand of cards. Will you walk with me?"

"As you please."

"Just wait here a moment, if you don't mind. You'll find something to read in the bookshelf if you like."

Ludo left. Lenox felt suddenly nonplussed: What was he going to say? Perhaps coming here had been a mistake. It was the fervor of his meeting with Hilary that had made his blood race. He was behaving impulsively. Now he resolved that he would ask Ludo only the most innocuous question, and leave it till the next day to collect more facts.

Then something rather strange happened. Having expected Ludo to be gone a moment, Lenox waited nearly twenty minutes before the man appeared again. At first he was annoyed, then puzzled, and finally truly perplexed.

"Sorry for the delay. I had to get my papers in order before I went out for the evening. It took longer than I expected, but my secretary is coming by to pick them up in a little while, so it was quite necessary. Parliament sits within the week, as of course you know."

"It's quite all right."

"Are you nervous? I was, my first time. Here, this way. If you don't mind terribly, we'll go down the alley. A bit ghostly, but it's the fastest way out."

"Not at all."

They went through a back garden into the brick

alleyway. Ludo was chatting amiably on, much more self-assured now, when Lenox heard rapid footsteps behind them.

He turned to see and with one shocking glance realized it was a masked man, bearing down on them.

"Ludo!" cried Lenox.

"Wha— oh!"

The man in the mask had barreled into them, and in the confusion of the next moment Lenox saw a glint of silver. A knife. He lunged at the man in the mask—a black cloth wrap, he noticed, though it was now very dark—but was too late.

The knife plunged into Ludo—Lenox couldn't see where—and the masked man, silent all the time, withdrew it and sprinted down the alley, toward the busy thoroughfare at the end of it. Lenox caught sight of something green, trousers or a shirt perhaps, in the quick glare of street-light that bathed the man before he turned right.

"There's blood!" said Ludo, raising his hands.

"Where is it, Ludo?"

"Get my wife!"

"I'm going to get help. Where—"

"She's in Cambridge with Paul—get her! Get the police!"

"Let me look at the wound first."

This he did. There was blood everywhere and

a deep cut, he could see. Soon he ran down the alley, his mind fluttering with the implications of a second attack in the exact spot where Frederick Clarke had been murdered.

chapter twenty-one

"It could be—and I don't say it is, mind—it could be a madman. Someone who lives or works quite near here."

This was Inspector Fowler speaking. It was an hour later. Ludo, pale but well, sat in his own drawing room, a roll of bandage around the thick part of the thigh where he had been stabbed. He had insisted Lenox stay when Grayson Fowler arrived. There was also a young constable in the room, the one Lenox had fetched. Ludo had rejected his initial instinct and said he felt well enough to let his wife and son stay in Cambridge overnight. He told Lenox this privately, perhaps ashamed of his neediness in the alley. Lenox could hardly blame him, however; his own thoughts had flown to Jane when the masked man was barreling toward them.

"I very much doubt it," he said in reply to Fowler's proposition.

The inspector gave him a poisonous look. It was already a matter of some discomfort to Lenox that Fowler had been so rude at Scotland Yard, and apparently his anger hadn't abated. "Oh?"

"Ten houses' worth of people use that alley, but the two men who have been attacked both live here. It could be a coincidence, I suppose."

Fowler sighed and took his notepad out again. "Tell me one more time what you saw, both of you."

Ludo said, "Almost nothing. A black mask made of wool or perhaps some other kind of cloth. It was a man, I feel sure of that."

"Do you recall any particular odor?" asked Lenox, earning another dirty look from Fowler, though it was the right question. "I don't, but you were closer to him."

"None. He was about my height, a few inches under six foot. Strong."

"Mr. Lenox?"

He furrowed his brow. "All I can remember in addition to that is the color green, either his trousers or his shirt. I'm trying to remember—I think he must have worn boots, because his footfall was very heavy, and they didn't make that click of dress shoes. More of a thud."

"I'm skeptical of that sort of analysis, taken in the heat of the moment, but I thank you. Mr. Starling, I'll stop by again in the morning, and we'll post our man in the alleyway again. We took him from his place too early. Constable, you may resume your beat."

"Nobody could have known this would happen," said Ludo bravely.

"I must be going, too," said Lenox.

"Oh—but really?"

"Unless you're unwell?"

"Oh no, quite well, thank you."

"Is Alfred in this evening?"

"He should be, yes." Ludo tried a weak smile. Even apart from the exonerating circumstances of the attack an hour before, Lenox when he saw this smile had trouble believing that the man on the sofa, a ginger hand on his leg, was any kind of murderer. "We never did speak."

"I only had some elementary questions, nothing you need to be worried with just now. Do you feel safe?"

"Of course—Collingwood is here, and two or three others. I shall be quite safe if I stick to the house and the larger streets. It will be a relief to have a constable stationed in the alley again."

"Indeed. Good-bye, then. I'll be by to check on your health tomorrow, if I may."

"Thank you," said Ludo, and looked genuinely grateful.

On the walk home, Lenox wondered if he himself felt as secure. It had been a jarring, horrifying moment, and the sight of that silver blade had raised every animal instinct in him to flee.

The house on Hampden Lane was empty, and seemed twice as empty because it was twice as large now. Lenox sat in his study, reading *Cranford* again, struggling to focus after the evening's intensity. Gradually the story absorbed him, however, and he relaxed.

When *Household Words* had published *Cranford* he would have been . . . what, twenty-three or twenty-four? He hadn't read it as it was serialized, and in a way he was glad. He often envied people who hadn't read his favorite books. They had such happiness before them.

The front door opened, and he went out into the hallway prepared to see Jane. In fact it was Graham, home late from Parliament.

He looked sheepish. "I scarcely like to take the liberty of using the front door, sir, but I hoped to visit you in your study."

Lenox waved a dismissive hand. "You should use it as if it were your own."

"No, sir, I continue to live in the same quarters, and I will continue to use the servants' door."

The detective frowned. "That hadn't occurred to me. These secretaries have their own rooms, don't they? What do you have—two rooms to yourself?" It was a fact that no matter how close Graham and Lenox had been as butler and master, there was some final estrangement; it would have been deeply embarrassing for Lenox to see Graham's rooms.

"Yes, sir."

"You should have your own rooms, I fear, in some building down Whitehall."

"Oh, no, sir—"

"For that matter, we still need to settle your wages. What do these bold young secretaries make?"

Rather miserably, Graham said, "Rather less than an experienced butler, sir. Many of these gentleman are highborn, with private fortunes."

The briefest look of fleeting pain crossed Graham's face, and Lenox knew in an instant that he had failed to recognize his friend's position; Graham was a former servant, forced to deal on equal terms with those he might have served in other circumstances. Had someone mentioned something?

Lenox couldn't say any of this, or even inquire after Graham's happiness in his new position, so he said, "Damn 'em all, you're twice as useful. We'll put you on an extra ten pounds a year. And," he went on awkwardly, "you must come to our next party."

"I couldn't, sir—"

"You must. It will be wonderful. Did I tell you how delighted McConnell was about your rise in the world?" Lenox laughed. "He said you'd be Prime Minister one day, which really I wouldn't put past you. Has anything gone on today?"

Grateful to fall back on work, Graham said, "Oh, a great—"

Lenox interrupted him. "But I've forgotten!"

"Sir?"

"Cholera!"

"I—"

"You look puzzled. I don't have cholera, you needn't worry about that. But the blue book on the subject, my God!"

Lenox spent the next five minutes telling Graham about the failings of the current sewage system, then recounted the conversation with Hilary.

"That was profoundly inadvisable, sir."

"Why?"

"I've studied the other clerks and secretaries, and in general it seems the safest policy is to gather several backbenchers before approaching a frontbencher."

"James Hilary and I are friends. I sponsored him for the SPQR club, as you know."

"That's precisely the problem, sir. He would have been confused as to whether you were approaching him as a friend or colleague. To cloud the issue in that way risks making you seem unserious."

"What do you think I should do?"

"Percy Field is the person I've been watching

most closely, sir, the Prime Minister's secretary. If there's an issue he supports, he links several Members who might be interested in it and schedules them an appointment. It gives him tremendous power, and it helps the Prime Minister to no end by giving him a sense of the feeling within the party."

"You want to speak to other MPs, then?"

"No, sir! I mean that you must behave as he does, using Mr. Hilary or Mr. Brick as your Prime Minister. You must convoke a group who agree with you on the subject and approach someone with greater power as a forceful unit."

Smiling, Lenox said, "You're far wiser than I am. Let's do it your way."

The front door opened, and Lenox stood. Since he had returned from Ludo's he had felt an indefinable tug of uncertainty, even unhappiness, and now he remembered why: Lady Jane. They had seen so little of each other over the past few days, and what conversation they'd had had been disconcerting.

Graham stood up, nodded to Lenox, and left. Lady Jane spoke a word to the butler—former butler—in the hallway and then breezed into the room, pink from the chill, smiling, and lovely.

chapter twenty-two

They said hello to each other. Lady Jane was still smiling but seemed slightly detached. He knew that when she was out of countenance she covered it up by talking, and that was what she did now, very gaily.

"The baby is wonderful, not a sound out of the poor dear. Toto makes much more noise, grumbling and disagreeable but I think secretly she's happier than she can quite grasp. It is hard to have a boy's name, though, isn't it? I hope they'll call her Gracie by the time she has little playfellows, or I fear she'll be teased for it. The Longwalls have just had a child, a boy, and Toto thinks he might make a suitable husband. Can you imagine? And you'll never guess what he's called."

"George?

She laughed and took off her long gloves, finger by finger. He recalled fleetingly how intimate he had once found that gesture. There wasn't precisely fear in his heart, but a kind of melancholy ambiguity, an insecurity.

"Not George, no. Charles! Charles Longwall. I thought it quite funny to imagine you having an infant namesake out there in London some-where."

This brought them awkwardly close to the subject of their conversation earlier that day, and Lenox said hastily, "Longwall—a very English name."

It didn't mean much of anything, but she took the cue from him. "I always thought the same thing about Reggie Blackfield."

"And do you remember Henry Bathurst, who was foreign secretary?"

Finally shorn of her gloves, hat, and earrings, which she dropped into a silver tumbler on Lenox's desk, she came and whispered his cheek with a kiss. "I'm going to ring for some food." She picked up a glass bell and gave it a brisk shake. "Have you had a long day?"

"Now that you mention it—"

Kirk came in. "You rang?"

"I'd like some supper, if Ellie is still awake," said Lady Jane. "Whatever there is."

"Bring up a bottle of wine as well," added Lenox.

"Yes, sir."

When he had gone, she said, "What were you saying?"

"I did have rather a long day. I was attacked." He laughed to defray the concern that immediately showed on her face. "I'm quite well, I promise. Starling didn't have such a happy run of it, however."

"What happened?"

"He was stabbed in the leg."

Lenox told the story. She made all the right noises, but he couldn't help but notice that she wasn't sitting beside him on the sofa, as she usually did, but across from him on a chair; couldn't help but notice that after she had made sure he was unharmed her eyes flew more than once to the door, as if she were more interested in her food than in his story. Was he imagining her indifference?

For so long she had been his best listener, and in turn he had tried to be hers. During their honeymoon, marriage had seemed to twine together the best elements of their friendship and their love. Now, however, he felt robbed of both.

At last her food came, and his wine. She ate happily—there was a cottage pie and some turnips.

"Made of real cottages," he said, repeating an old joke she loved.

She rewarded him with a laugh and then, perhaps observing something in his face, put down her fork and came over to the sofa. "Are you all right, Charles?" she said, taking his hand in hers.

"Oh, quite all right. A bit tired perhaps."

"It's been difficult, I know—I've spent so much time at Toto's, and you've got both Parliament and this poor boy's death."

She had missed the point. "It's nice to sit here with you," he answered her.

Or perhaps she hadn't. "I don't know if I'd like to have children," she said softly.

"Oh—that, put it out of your mind."

She gazed at him unhappily. "I will, then," she said at last.

Soon they went to bed, neither of them quite tranquil in their heart.

The next day was exceptionally busy for Lenox. After her long hours at Toto's side, Lady Jane slept late, but he was awake and reading a blue book over eggs by six in the morning. There was a succession of meetings to attend; Graham had laid out what he needed to read before each of them, and as Lenox finished the last of his tea they spoke about each in turn.

It was difficult to be patient about cholera, but Graham would begin to canvass for support among the secretaries of other backbenchers. Listening to Graham's strategies was an education for Lenox, who had believed—naively, and against all the evidence—that a good idea would always win out in politics. The murky world of favors, exchanges, and alliances was new to him, but Graham was already emerging as a master of it.

"How many days before I can take this to Hilary again, or Brick, or the Prime Minister?" asked Lenox as he was putting on his overcoat, ready to go to Whitehall.

"Parliament opens very shortly, sir. There will be a great deal of official business to accomplish, and people are often bursting with ideas in the first days, from everything I understand."

Lenox nodded. "So I've heard. I don't want to get lost in the shuffle of things."

"No, sir, certainly not. I think we must wait a week or two. When we have support and the House has quieted down, and the less committed Members have returned to their clubs after their bursts of initial enthusiasm have subsided—then we may strike. I recall from your account of the conversation that Mr. Hilary laughed at the idea of you giving a speech in your first weeks."

"He did."

"Without support—as simply a wild gesture, sir—his incredulity at the thought of a speech might be correct. With the proper support, however, it could be powerful."

Lenox nodded thoughtfully. "Perhaps I'll begin to write something out."

"That would be wise, sir. As I understand it the best speeches are heavily revised and compressed, never off the cuff—very brief, full of conviction, even inspirational, but always with a practical bent."

The detective laughed. "Yes. Although I've heard enough tales of new Members who write a perfect speech and forget every word of it the moment they stand up. Still, we must try."

"Indeed, sir."

After a long day of meetings—the most tedious was with a gentleman from Durham who represented northern farming concerns—at five o'clock Lenox was in his office. He was running through potential clerks, Graham at his side. They were all young, bright boys from middling backgrounds, the sons of merchants, schoolteachers, doctors, small landholders. A job as a clerk was moderately paid and, better still, might lead to a job as a personal secretary. Even if that route failed, a Member with influence could be a wonderful ally for a young gentleman hoping to make his career. There were jobs in the City, jobs in the colonies, government sinecures in Ireland and Scotland.

He had interviewed four boys and now was sitting across a desk from the fifth. This was by far his favorite. The lad, one Gordon Frabbs, was very young-looking, with pale blond hair and a dense of freckles on his cheeks. He had an earnest air about him and was cleverer by half than any of the other boys. He had Latin and some Greek, was excellent at sums, and could even draw skillfully. What weighed against him was his age—he was only fifteen, on the callow side for this sort of job—but otherwise Lenox approved. He wondered as they spoke whether Graham would agree.

"You can write a good hand?"

"Yes, sir."

"Can you read quickly?"

"Yes, sir."

"With comprehension?"

"Yes, sir."

He pushed *Cranford* across the table. "There, read the first chapter of that as quickly as you can, and I'll ask you a few questions about it."

Frabbs grabbed the book as quickly as if it were a life preserver and he was drowning, and began to scan the lines, biting his lip and with a look of immense concentration on his small face.

There was a knock at the door. Expecting it to be the next candidate—they were running behind —Graham went to the door.

Instead of another seventeen-year-old lad, though, Dallington came rushing in. "There you are," he said.

"What is it? I'm in the middle of seeing clerks."

"Never mind that—Ginger came to the Beargarden and told me that they've arrested Collingwood."

"What? Why?"

"It was he who killed Frederick Clarke and attacked Ludo Starling."

Lenox stood up immediately. "Mr. Frabbs, you're hired. Graham, give him his desk."

"Am I really, Mr. Graham, really really?" Lenox heard Frabbs say as he left, the boy's voice squeaking with delight.

chapter twenty-three

"How do you know?"

That was what the detective asked his apprentice as they rolled through Whitehall in a hired brougham.

"Fowler caught him last night after you left."

"Fowler?"

"He pretended to leave—this was Starling's plan—and fetched back quickly to the alley door to take everyone by surprise. He was convinced it might be Collingwood, apparently."

"Perhaps he's spoken to Ginger, too. Did you ask him?"

"Damn, I didn't. That's true. I thought we had an advantage."

"It's not a competition," said Lenox. "I would be just as pleased if Fowler caught the murderer as if we did." This wasn't true at all, but he felt he needed to say it.

"In any event, Ludo ordered the entire staff to wait in the living room, and Fowler went through all of the rooms."

"What did he find in Collingwood's?"

"It wasn't in Collingwood's room. That was what Fowler hoped, and he searched it high and low, but no such luck."

"Well?"

"Among the staff only Collingwood has a key to the larder. It was in there. A bloody knife, a black wool mask, and a green butcher's apron. It was you who saw the flash of green, wasn't it?"

"It was I, yes."

"He arrested Collingwood straightaway, for assaulting Starling. The house was in a stir about it, of course." Suddenly there was a silence, and Dallington stared moodily at the carnation in his buttonhole, fiddling with its stem. "Charles, I've told you a lie."

"What?" said Lenox, shocked. "It wasn't Collingwood?"

"No, no—not that. About Ginger. It wasn't he who came to me at the club."

"Then who—" Suddenly Lenox remembered with perfect clarity the light banter, the looks of curiosity, that had passed between Dallington and the young housemaid. "Jenny Rogers, was it?"

The younger man nodded guiltily. "Yes."

"It's bad—very bad. Not so much that you lied, though you ought to deplore any action of the sort, but that you have a—a friendship with a suspect."

"A suspect!" cried Dallington. "Surely not!"

"Not a very likely one, of course—but certainly she had the opportunity, and she knew the alley well enough to find that loose brick. The weapon."

"But—but motive!"

Dallington looked pale, and Lenox decided he had been hard enough on the lad. "It's unlikely, as I say. Almost impossible. Still, it was unprofessional of you."

"I don't get paid," said Dallington miserably. "I'm not a professional."

"It's not so bad. Look—we're here. Wait, before we go on we must think for a moment. Hold here a second, sir, and it's a shilling for you," he called out to the cabman.

"What is it?" asked Dallington.

"Well, only this—do we believe Collingwood murdered Frederick Clarke? Or that he attacked Ludo Starling?"

"It certainly seems likelier now."

"Let's take this as part of your education, John. *Think!* Why would Collingwood have attacked Ludo Starling? How could it have benefited him?"

Dallington frowned. "Perhaps Starling knew Collingwood had killed Clarke?"

"Then why on earth wouldn't Ludo have told us? All he wants is for this scandal to end!"

"Still, you must admit Starling is acting peculiarly."

"There! That's certainly true. We have to think about his motivations in all this. But then, listen —is there anything strange about what Collingwood hid?"

"What?"

"Even granting that he may have had a green butcher's apron—which I feel far from sure of—why would he have worn it?"

"To keep the blood off?"

"Fair point. Still, I find it a singular piece of evidence. Then, last of all, the larder."

"Well?"

Lenox shrugged. "Why choose a place in the house so closely associated with himself? Besides which certainly Collingwood isn't the only person with a key."

"Ludo!"

"That's one. Or, for that matter, another member of the family whom we've both observed at the trough."

"Alfred—but why on earth would he attack his father?"

"I don't say he did, just that he may have had a key, somehow, and if so he may have lost it—misplaced it—given it away. Anything."

"It's true."

Lenox stepped out and paid the driver. "Bear that in mind as we interview Collingwood. If we have a chance to, that is."

"I doubt he'll still be here."

Dallington was right. They saw Ludo, who looked heartily sick of them, and he recapitulated briefly what they already knew.

"Do you believe Collingwood was capable of

murdering Frederick Clarke?" Lenox asked.

"I don't know, to be honest. Look, I'm late for a game of whist."

"The Turf?"

"No, we're playing at the house of a chap I know. I must be off."

"How's your leg?"

"My leg? Ah, that—it's painful but healing, thanks."

When they had walked a block away, Dallington said to Lenox, "Maybe we should go to the Turf."

"His club?"

"We agree that his behavior is strange. Shall we see whether he was playing cards during the time Frederick Clarke was killed?"

The Turf was a very new club—it had been founded in 1861—but already a very exclusive one among the younger generations. The game that had taken London by storm in the past several years, whist, had actually been invented there and then certified by the much older Portland Club, a more staid place where the game of choice was generally contract bridge. The Turf had a comfortable house in Bennett Street in Picadilly, with many small rooms for cardplaying, a fine cellar full of wines, and a notably discreet staff. Many of the surfaces in the building, the doors, chairs, and tables included, were embossed with the club's emblem, a centaur.

Dallington, who was a member, asked the porter if he could look through the sign-in book, passing him a coin; everyone who entered the Turf, member or guest, had to sign the book. After they had signed it themselves he and Lenox looked back to the date when Ludo had been playing cards. "For ten hours or more," Lenox recalled him saying, or something like that. It wasn't at all uncommon for these games of cards to go on for days, with players dropping in and out to eat or sleep for a few hours, and then returning to see a mix of old and new faces at the table.

Ludo's name wasn't in the book.

They checked the date twice, and for good measure each day on either side. "There, Frank Derbyshire," said Lenox. "That was the group he said he was with."

"He was lying!"

"He might have been. Or he might simply have walked in with a crowd and not bothered to wait around for his turn to sign the book. Still, it is suspicious, I'll grant you that."

"This is it!" said Dallington excitedly. "Ludo is involved, even if we don't know how!"

"Patience. Let's go see Frank Derbyshire."

Dallington flipped to the front of the club book and studied the names on the most recent page. "We may not need to leave the building," he said after a moment. "Derbyshire signed in an hour ago."

chapter twenty-four

There were servants stationed at the door of every card room that was in use, in case the players needed a fresh cigar, or a cutlet to eat during play. Dallington, who knew many of the servants by name quietly asked each whether Frank Derbyshire was there. The third one said yes.

Derbyshire, an ugly, carrot-haired, very rich young man, was annoyed at the disruption. "What in damnation is it, Dallington?" he said. "I don't owe you a cent, and there are no places at the table. Monty Kibble is ahead thirty pounds, and I'll be damned to hell if he isn't cheating. I need to get back in there and catch him." A moody puff on his cigar.

"It's not about cards."

"Well, what else is there?"

Lenox smiled, then realized it wasn't a joke.

"Ludovic Starling," said Dallington, whom they had agreed would be the one to speak to Derbyshire.

"Who's that?"

"Ludo—"

"No, this gentleman."

"Ah. This is my friend Charles Lenox. Lenox, Frank Derbyshire."

"Lenox the detective? That's right, you are, too, Dalls," said Derbyshire, giving them a nasty grin. "Playing about at bobby?"

Something happened then that shocked Lenox: For a single moment Dallington's face showed a mix of shame and hurt that was piercing. He covered it with a sardonic laugh. Suddenly Lenox understood the cost to his pupil of this occupation: dismissed for so long because he didn't work, because he drank and played, and now dismissed because he *did* work.

Dallington went on, "Did you play cards with Starling recently?"

"Yes, strangely enough. He usually plays with an older set, doesn't like the university crowd down here on the second floor. But he wanted a game and got one, by God. I took him for eight pounds and a halfpenny."

The impeccable memory of the gambler, thought Lenox. "How long did you play for?" he asked. "Ten hours, was it?"

Derbyshire snorted, and then something from the snort caught in his throat and he coughed horribly on his cigar smoke, hacking for what seemed like an entire minute. At last, eyes watery, he gasped out, "Never!"

"How long, then?"

He was still hoarse. "Couldn't have been more than four hours."

"What day?"

"Would have been about a week ago. It was eight days, in fact, I remember."

The day of the murder.

"What happened?"

Derbyshire looked at Lenox strangely. "What happened? Nothing unusual. I took the eight pounds and bought as much wine as I could carry to take over to the old Rugbeian match. We drank 'em all. I still have the halfpenny." He grinned.

"You're sure about the day?"

"Yes!"

"What time of day was it? This is important. Late? Afternoon?"

"Early evening."

"You're sure?"

"You can stop asking me that. I'm certain."

They let Derbyshire go, amid a variety of hacks, coughs, and eructations, back into his card room. As he turned he invited Dallington to play that night and shrugged at his decline.

"Inconclusive," said the younger man to Lenox, hands in pockets, a disappointed look on his face. "He was probably there."

"You're sharper than that, surely. Think— we've just caught Ludo in his first lie, and if he would lie about six hours, wouldn't he lie about matters of greater moment?"

"Anyway, why wouldn't he have signed the book if he simply wanted an alibi? It might have been an exaggeration."

"He was too specific for that, as I remember it. This is incriminating, somehow or other."

"So Collingwood is innocent."

"I don't stipulate that point," said Lenox. "There have been half a dozen cases during my years in London when a man who had been arrested seemed innocent, another suspect having emerged, only for the first man arrested to be proven guilty. In one instance, Smethurst back in '52, the second man was covering up for an entirely different crime. Embezzlement."

They were out on the street now, the light low. They passed a fruit and vegetable cart, and Dallington swiped an apple from it and flicked a coin at the cart's owner, who caught it and touched his cap in one quick motion. Dallington crunched into his fruit as they walked down toward Green Park.

"Tell me, what shall we do next? Or what shall I do next, as you must be in Parliament tomorrow?"

"I think we must go see Collingwood himself, and I would like to go to the boxing club. It still bothers me that Clarke had money slipped to him under the servants' door. I reckon Collingwood wouldn't have tolerated secret doings among the servants, strange business that touched the house. And then Clarke's peculiar room . . ." Lenox shook his head. "I feel quite sure we're missing something."

"Must you go back to work?"

"No. I don't have any particular role in the state opening of the House, beyond observation." He looked at his watch. "It's only six o'clock. We should be able to find our way to Collingwood if we get there before eight. We'll pass by the Starling house along the way, to wish Ludo a swift recovery."

As a shortcut they took the fateful back alley, now gloomed with shadows. Fetching up at the back stoop of Ludo's house on Curzon Street, Lenox said, "Out of curiosity, which house belongs to Ginger's employer?"

"It's three down," Dallington was saying, when they heard the short, urgent rap of knuckles on a window. They looked up. It was coming from behind a curtain on the second floor.

The curtain pulled aside, and they were both surprised to see Paul, Ludo's younger son. He held up a finger: Wait.

He had raced down the stairs, evidently, because when he reached them he was breathless. "Dallington!"

"What is it? Didn't you like Cambridge during your visit?"

"Oh, bother Cambridge. It's Collie!"

"A dog?"

"Collingwood, you ass!"

Dallington raised his eyebrows. "I see."

Paul looked appalled at what he had said to

his drinking hero. "I'm sorry. I'm too used to speaking with Alfred. Anyway, no, it's about Collingwood. They've arrested him!"

"So we heard."

"But don't you understand, it's impossible!"

"Why?" asked Lenox.

Paul threw up his arms with the despair of someone who feels that he should be understood but isn't. "Ask Alfred. Collie was our friend— our best friend. When we were children and he was a footman, he let us jump on him over and over, and just laughed. When he should have given us a lashing for stealing from the pantry, he smiled and looked the other way."

"There's every chance—"

"No!" Paul looked as if he were going to cry. Suddenly he reminded Lenox of Frabbs, his new clerk at Parliament: youth dressed up in the maturity it didn't possess. "He couldn't even bear to watch the foxes die at the hunt!"

"Paul!" From the back step Elizabeth Starling, red with emotion, almost shouted her son's name.

"Damn," said Paul under his breath, his face suddenly fearful. He ran up the steps and past her.

She ignored Lenox and Dallington and closed the door.

"Do you give that any credit?" asked the young lord.

"It was in Collingwood's professional interests to befriend these lads."

"I don't know, Lenox. Their father is at the Turf constantly, and their mother is a bit too protective. You saw. He seemed genuinely upset."

"He did. Unfortunately this is a field in which sentiment is of little practical value."

chapter twenty-five

Walking down Curzon Street, they saw Ginger leaning against the wall of a small alcove in front of the house he worked in. He had a pouch of tobacco in his hand and was loading a pipe with it.

"John!" he called out in a theatrical whisper.

"Hiding?" Dallington asked when they were close.

"The butler's strict."

"Have you heard about Collingwood?"

Puffing away now, he said, "Everyone in China's heard of it, much less Curzon Street. I can't believe he attacked Starling!"

"Mm."

"We've all wanted to do it, mind, to our masters," added Ginger with a dark grin, "but it's sheer madness."

"You still think he did it, then?" asked Lenox.

"Collingwood? Of course. They found the apron and the knife in his larder."

"Does nobody but the butler go into the pantry?"

The lad shook his head. "They're afraid of theft, these rich families."

"Doesn't it puzzle you that he attacked Ludo? What would his motivation have been, for heaven's sake?"

"I'll tell you what it is. He knew he was going to get pinched, and he wanted to turn attention away from himself."

"By hiding the evidence in a place that could only be attached to him? I don't think so."

Ginger shrugged. "Well, he was the only person with any reason in the world to kill poor Freddie."

Unless the lad had a secret life, thought Lenox. They had to get to that boxing club.

First, though, they went to Newgate Prison. A quick, silver-laden handshake with a jailer Lenox had known for a decade and they were through to a bare room with two battered tables and four battered chairs in it.

When an unseen hand shoved Collingwood through the door, it was apparent instantly that the last hours had robbed him of the dignity of office and person he had borne during their previous encounters. He would have been searched for weapons, had his money taken from him and—possibly—been entered in a logbook, had his hair shorn off, and been bathed in cold, filthy water. As a remand prisoner he had been permitted his old clothes, but they looked rumpled and now absurdly formal after the travesties of the day.

Collingwood's face fell when he saw Lenox and Dallington. "Hello," he said, the "sirs" dropped from his speech.

"How do you do, Collingwood?"

"I had hoped it might be Mr. Starling, or perhaps my brother."

"No, I'm afraid not." Lenox didn't have the heart to tell him that prisoners could only receive two or three visits a year, and that unless his friends had ready money only his lawyer would visit. "We came to ask you whether you murdered Freddie Clarke."

For a tense moment, everything hung in the balance. Then the man spoke. "No, of course not. The idea is outlandish."

"Did you attack Ludo Starling?"

"Mr. Lenox, my father was butler to Mr. Starling for twenty-five years. I myself ascended to that position upon his death and considered it the fulfillment of my only professional ambition. Both my father and I, and my brother, who is a butler in Sussex for the de Spencer family, take tremendous pride in our work. The answer, you'll have deduced, is no. I did not stab the man who has employed me these dozen years."

The words were civil but the tone of derision in them acidic. It was convincing. "Who besides you has the key to the larder?"

Collingwood's self-belief seemed to flicker for a moment. "I—nobody else."

"None of the other servants, you mean. Perhaps Mr. Starling has it? Mrs. Starling?"

With transparent relief, he said, "Oh, of course."

"Master Alfred?" Lenox said in a speculative tone.

Collingwood reddened. "I've had a soft spot for Mr. Starling's sons for many years now. I'm not sure who told you—"

"No, no, only a guess."

"Did Paul have a key, too?" said Dallington.

"No."

"You're sure?"

"No! Paul wasn't involved, I tell you."

Lenox thought for a moment. "Very well. As for Alfred . . . I hardly think it was a serious dereliction of your responsibilities to give him the key. And since any one of them might have lost theirs . . ."

"Yes! Precisely what I thought—precisely. I'm being plotted against. This was all prearranged."

"Do you own a green apron?"

"Absolutely not. Am I a woman?" he asked bitterly. "A butcher?"

"A knife?"

"There are knives in the kitchen, of course, but I've never had need to use them."

"We'll have to check whether any are missing from the cook's set," Lenox murmured to Dallington.

"Yes!" said Collingwood. "Do that! Please, check!"

Lenox decided to shift tacks. "What did you think of Freddie Clarke?"

"Think of him?"

"Were you friends? Did you clash?"

"We didn't clash. He kept to himself, very diligent in his duties. Can't say we were friends, though."

"Did he have much money?"

Collingwood laughed and rubbed his tired eyes, taking some genuine pleasure in their company for the first time. "That depends how many envelopes came under the door, doesn't it?"

"You know about that?" Dallington asked incredulously.

"The older Mr. Starling—Tiberius—he told me about it the moment it happened. He often came to me for a measure of brandy, and we had many conversations."

The man had been bosom friends with everyone in the house, Lenox thought. Why would the Starlings ever have believed Frederick Clarke's word against the butler's? And therefore why would Collingwood have felt the need to take such drastic action in order to protect his job? It didn't add up.

"Where do you think the money came from?" asked Dallington.

Collingwood shrugged. "I don't know."

Delicately, Lenox put the crucial question to the butler. "Mr. Collingwood, if I might ask: Did you ever take anything, small change, trinkets, from your employers?"

"Never! And whoever told you that can go straight to hell!"

"If you're worried we'll tell, you—"

"Never!" he bellowed, standing up and slamming his fists on the table. "Who told you that?"

"Frederick Clarke saw you taking coins from Mrs. Starling's dresser. Admit it." Dallington, shrewdly, had taken on the role of the villain. He caught Lenox's eye and nodded.

Quickly the older detective played along. "No, no, John, we don't know if it's the truth—"

"How much did you steal?"

Collingwood, now more aggrieved than enraged, said, "Nothing. It's a damnable lie."

"Well, tell us about the incident anyway," said Lenox encouragingly.

"It was nothing. I organize the desk in that particular chamber every morning, and Clarke came in to refill the coal scuttle just as I was placing Mrs. Starling's spare coins in the small wooden box where she keeps them. Clarke must have had the impression that I was taking them, as he turned and left right away. The idea that I would kill him for that—it's preposterous. Beyond preposterous."

"Then what did you kill him for?" asked Dallington.

"I didn't!"

To forestall another tirade, Lenox quickly interjected, "We mustn't be hasty. There may be another answer."

"There is! Find it!"

After this burst of energy Collingwood seemed to crumple, and there was very little further conversation. As they left the prison, Dallington asked what Lenox thought.

"I'm not sure."

"He seems innocent, doesn't he?"

"Certainly I don't think he killed Frederick Clarke over that incident, as Ginger believes."

"Of course not."

"Still, we can't know why Fowler arrested him. If only he would speak with me."

"Fowler? Of course he arrested Collingwood for the apron and the knife in the larder, which we've proven to ourselves are inconclusive."

"I wouldn't venture to guess at Inspector Fowler's motives. He's making himself a mystery. One thing, however, that I noticed: Collingwood has a temper."

"Wouldn't you, in jail for a crime—for two crimes—that you didn't commit?"

"Perhaps. Still—someone killed Frederick Clarke, and someone attacked Ludo with a knife. The strongest pieces of circumstantial evidence both point to this butler. We may be too clever for our own good."

They arrived at a line of cabs. "Care for a drink?" Dallington asked. He grinned. "There's a lad at the Jumpers who's going to try to eat four hard rolls in a minute. I have a shilling on the other side."

"Diverting as that sounds, I must go home," said Lenox. "As you know, the Queen's opening Parliament in the morning."

"Well, if you prefer the Queen to an eating contest, I can't say I admire your priorities." Dallington laughed. "Here, take the first cab. I say, good luck tomorrow, Lenox. Pass a law making Fowler tell you everything if you find a moment."

chapter twenty-six

On the next morning he opened his eyes with the feeling that at last he would truly belong in Parliament, truly be one of them, for the first time. If the issue of cholera had given Lenox the realization of his responsibility, a purpose, the chamber's opening reminded him of the gravity of his new work. After so much prelude he was ready for the real thing.

Jane was at home, thank God, and for the first time in what felt like years they spoke in their old, familiar way, as they had when they were friends (and she certainly would have been the one to straighten his necktie and brush off his jacket, as she did now). What a relief it was.

"Well—try not to fall in love with the Queen and leave me," she said with a laugh as she inspected him. He was dressed and breakfasted. It was almost time to leave. "No matter how good her speech is."

He smiled. "I'll send a note if it happens. From my new home at the palace."

"It's the least you could do, really."

"Are you going to see Toto?"

"I think I'll take a day to myself, at last. I love

her—as well you know—but she's run me ragged."

"Anyway, they're quite safe now."

"Exactly. I need the morning to catch up with my correspondence, and I'm having lunch with Duch." This was the Duchess of Marchmain, Dallington's mother and one of Lady Jane's closest friends. "Then we're going to call on Emily Pendle, the bishop's wife—in Berkeley Square?" In exasperation at Lenox's blank face, she said, "Surely you know her."

"I misplaced my master list of all the bishops' wives, I'm afraid."

"He'll be there with you, of course." All the bishops of the Church of England had, *ex officio*, seats in the House of Lords. "She's going through a terrible time, poor dear, with her father. He's been ever so ill. We thought we'd try to cheer her up."

"Are these shoes fine?"

"Oh, I daresay they'll pass." She smiled. "Yes, quite shiny, of course. I think Graham had the boots around to shine them five times yesterday."

"Graham! I haven't even thought of him today!"

"You're lucky to have me, then. I congratulated him and gave him the morning off, then told him to come back at three so we could greet you together and hear all about it."

Lenox frowned. "You can't give my political secretary the day off."

"I'll give him the week off if I like."

Now he smiled. "You know, I am lucky to have you."

It was the first awkward note. She handled it by going to the hook where he kept his cloak and taking it down. "You are, of course," she said lightly.

"Emily Pendle will be cheered by three, then?" he asked, trying to restore the tone the conversation had had.

"It won't be for lack of trying if she's not."

There was a moment's silence, and then they were saved from truly talking by the doorbell. Kirk's footsteps echoed down the front hallways, and both of them peered curiously at the door.

Was it a message about Clarke, Lenox wondered wildly? Who was guilty? What had happened?

But no—it was his brother's reddish, cheerful face that popped through the door. "Hallo, Member for Stirrington," he said brightly. "You, too, Charles." At his own joke he laughed loudly. "Imagine, Jane giving her speech in Parliament."

"I think I'd do a fair job," said Lady Jane with mock hurt. "Better than some of the gentlemen I've heard from the galleries."

"You would! I don't doubt it! Only—the figure

of a woman—the benches—a dress!" Edmund dissolved into laughter. "It's exceedingly comical, you must admit."

"Not so comical as all that, Edmund you great oaf," said Lady Jane, frowning. "After all, the Queen is speaking there today."

"It's true, you're quite right." Edmund looked at his watch. "Lord, Charles, we must be on our way. The crush of carriages around Whitehall, you wouldn't believe it. The Queen's only an hour away; we should already be seated!"

Lady Jane bestowed a kiss on Charles—still such a thrill, after all this time!—and the two brothers hurried out of the door.

When they were sitting in the carriage together, Edmund asked about Ludo Starling. "They've arrested somebody?" He had always taken a deep interest in his brother's work and liked to solve the crimes of his small village—a missing silver plate, for example, or a stolen horse—using only the evidence in the newspaper. He would bring his deductions to Charles with frankly unbecoming pride and boastfulness.

"The butler."

"I've never liked Ludo Starling, not that it's here nor there."

They were in Whitehall now, and it was indeed crowded. The mall from Buckingham Palace was entirely cut off for the Queen. "Oh, bother murders. What are we to do today, Edmund?"

The question was more complicated than it seemed. This was one of those many days in England when a host of old traditions come back to life, and ceremonies with obscure and absurd origins are carried out with the utmost seriousness.

"You and I will start by going to the House—the House of Commons."

"Won't it be jammed?"

"Here, let's go out on foot. It's crowded. No, it won't be too jammed. Do you really not know this ceremony? Right at the moment, the Yeomen of the Guard—that's what we call the Beefeaters when we like to be formal—anyway, those chaps in red uniforms, who get a ration of beef every day—they're poking around the cellars in case somebody wants to emulate Guy Fawkes and blow us all up."

"What a relief," murmured Lenox with a grin.

They were halfway down toward Parliament now, and the crowds were growing denser. "At just this moment an MP—this year it's Peter Frogg, the lucky blighter—is being taken prisoner."

Lenox laughed. "What can you mean?"

"In case we try to kidnap Queen Victoria, of course. He sits in the palace and gorges himself on wine and food and makes pleasant conversation with the royal family, generally. Plum job. Then the Queen comes down here in her coach —she'll be on her way now."

The Members' Entrance was crowded with politicians, and a roar of noise was audible even from fifty feet away. The porter, waving away their identification, said, "You oughter have come earlier, for shame, sirs," and pushed them into the throng of people.

"This way!" shouted Edmund. "Let's slide through! I made sure we could both be in the Commons! That way we'll get to see the Queen!"

"Why will we get to see the Queen?" asked Lenox when they were through to a quieter corridor. "And why on earth won't it be jammed?"

"Most people are in the House of Lords—where they give the speech, you know—or in the Queen's Gallery"—the hall that connected the Lords and the Commons. "Only a few dozen of us will be straggling around the Commons. Look, here it is."

They took their place on a green baize bench. Lenox was, to his surprise, rather fluttery in his stomach. "Edmund, how will we see her speech, if it's in the House of Lords?"

"Let's talk of other things for a moment—I want to hear about Ludo Starling."

"But—"

Edmund smiled fondly. "Let it be a surprise, Charles."

So they talked of Ludo Starling, Freddie Clarke, and Jack Collingwood for some while, pausing occasionally to greet a Member they both knew, or more often one that Lenox knew by reputation and with whom Edmund exchanged a few cryptic words about various bills in the offing for the new session. Strangely enough the room was indeed empty but for a dozen or so men.

Edmund was asking questions about the case when there was a hush. A man in tremendously ornate garb appeared at the door of the chamber, and to Lenox's shock a gentleman at the far end got up and slammed the door in his face.

"My G—"

"Shh!" whispered Edmund urgently.

Then there was a very loud rap at the closed door of the chamber. Lenox jumped a foot in the air. Edmund laughed into his sleeve.

"That's the Lord Great Chamberlain," he whispered. "It means the Queen has entered the building—through the Sovereign's Entrance, of course, on the other side from ours—and taken on the Robes of State. We slam the door in his face to show we're independent—that we don't have to listen to a monarch."

Another loud rap. "What do we do?"

"Now we'll go. Wait—the Speaker leads us."

So they processed down the silent Queen's Gallery, and through to the *red*-benched House of Lords.

Suddenly there she was, in her person; Lenox, no great admirer of power, was so enchanted he could barely stand when he saw her on her glorious golden throne: the Queen.

"Bow at the bar!" said Edmund urgently. "We must bow!"

They bowed.

chapter twenty-seven

She was a roundish, placid, unbeautiful woman; in her youth she had been not pretty but slim and eye-catching. Now she contained all the majesty of England in her rather waddling gait and intelligent, indifferent face. She had survived half a dozen assassination attempts, given birth to children, and seen empires fall. Whether because of her position or her person, she was captivating to behold.

The speech addressed a number of issues for the Houses to take up. To Lenox's annoyance Edmund kept whispering questions about the case. These received at best a nod by way of reply, but still Lenox found himself missing chunks of the speech. It was nearly the end when he could concentrate.

"My Lords and Members of the House of Commons, I pray that the blessing of Almighty God may rest upon your counsels."

With that the speech ended, in the same words it did every year. For the rest of the day there were a thousand things they did, each of which half confused and half delighted Charles. They elected the Speaker (a reelection, and a matter of no drama) and then, per tradition, several Members "dragged him unwillingly" to the Speaker's bench.

"Ages ago it was dangerous to be Speaker—you could be killed if you said something to displease the monarch—and that's why we do it. Daft, of course, but good fun when the Speaker is such a magisterial figure for the rest of the session."

They debated the speech and passed a bill—again per tradition—declaring their autonomy from the Queen's rule. Several people stopped and clapped Lenox on the back forcefully, saying welcome, Members from both sides of the aisle. He found it tremendously collegial of them.

On it went for hours and hours, all of it fascinating. What it reminded him most of was being new at school, when he was twelve. There was the same overwhelmed, excitable feeling, as if a new adventure had been embarked upon and now there was nothing to do but figure out its multitude of small necessities, rules, traditions. At Harrow—his school—there had been the same sort of insular world, with its own terminology: Teachers were beaks; a bath was called a tosh. It had taken weeks before he felt at home with all the slang.

Finally, a little after three that afternoon, Edmund led him out through the Members' Entrance again.

"Well?" he said when they were a few streets clear of the din of Parliament.

Lenox simply grinned and told him what he had been thinking about Harrrow, where Edmund had been, too.

"It makes a strange impression, doesn't it? Don't worry. You'll soon feel at home there. Look —a pub. Let's duck in for a celebratory drink."

They spent an hour then drinking to each other's health, the Queen's health, and the House. It was a pub called the Westminster Arms, with honey-colored walls and low raftered ceilings and the gleam of brass and glass everywhere.

"What's all this about cholera?" Edmund asked finally, after they had sat down with their drinks.

"What did you hear?"

"Hilary spoke a word to me in Bellamy's. Said he was rather taken aback by your insistence that it be addressed."

"Insistence? Of course I was insistent."

"Things move slowly in politics, Charles."

"They ought to move a sight faster."

Edmund smiled indulgently. "No doubt you'll change it all?"

"You think me foolish?"

"No! The farthest thing from it—I'm full of admiration for you—but this is a matter I know about. Perhaps you may be a bit innocent. It will be difficult."

"Graham has a plan."

"Does he? Then things will be well. I was surprised about that, by the way. Not that you deemed him worthy for the position, but that you considered it wise. There was a rumble among the secretaries. They fell in line after Percy Field, however."

"I wondered if it were taking a toll on Graham."

"Be careful. You compared the House to Harrow—well, it's just as rigid and orderly. They don't like people jumping the queue."

"Graham's thought was to find a group of Members who felt the same way about the issue of cholera. With strength in numbers we could approach a frontbencher—Brick, Hilary, you."

"I'm not a frontbencher."

"In all but name, Edmund."

"At any rate, you needn't gather a group to speak to me."

"What did Hilary tell you?"

"Pretend he told me nothing."

Lenox recounted the same story he had for Hilary, dwelling on the potential risk to the people in East London of a cholera outbreak.

"It's unquestionably a valid concern," Edmund finally answered, sipping at his pint of mild ale. "You must keep me apprised. Wait, though— about Ludo—isn't—"

"Just a moment, before you go and change the subject please."

"Me?" said the baronet innocently.

"I know you too well for that, Ed. What's wrong with it? I hate you being tactful. It irritates me."

Edmund sighed heavily. "I'm sorry, Charles. It's only that there's so much against it. A major public works has just finished, at tremendous expense and after tremendous difficulty. No public body backtracks this quickly. 'We just finished with all that bother' will be what people say. I promise you."

"They won't! Did you hear a word I said? The imminent danger of it all?"

"I know, I know. It's only a feeling. I hope I'm wrong."

At home Lady Jane was full of a dozen questions, and Graham—whom Lenox studied closely for signs of anxiety—was full of good cheer and shook his hand solemnly, before going straight back to work into the night with Frabbs. There was an ominous pile of blue books on Lenox's desk.

"Now, how *was* it?" asked Lady Jane when at last they had settled on the sofa, her hands clasping his.

They spent an hour in close conversation, absorbed in each other as they had been that morning but so rarely in the past week. He fell ravenously upon a shoulder of lamb and fresh peas, having been unconscious before it appeared on a silver salver how hungry he had been. He felt cared for again.

"It's almost cool enough to have a fire tonight," Lady Jane said. "I'd like to stay in and be lumps here on the couch, and read. What do you say to that?"

"I say yes, of course. I wish it could be *Cranford*, but it must be blue books, I'm afraid."

"I'll call the footman to light it."

As she left he wandered into the dim dining room, restless. His eyes alighted on a watercolor of the London skyline. It had replaced that Paris painting, which was in a guest room now—it had made him feel uneasy, despite how he had liked it in France. In the skyline was St. Paul's, and Westminster Abbey, and there, just above a middling of roofs, the Palace of Westminster: Parliament.

He had been pulled in so many directions during the fortnight since his honeymoon ended. There were Toto and Thomas McConnell, there was Jane's distance, there was the case, there was first his disenchantment with Parliament and then the galvanizing realization of the public danger cholera presented, and beyond all that the hundred meetings to attend and duties to discharge. It had been impossibly fraught. Now his life clarified before him. Parliament was where he belonged. Everything would be all right with Jane, and he would do his work there. Seeing the Queen, hearing her order them to execute the business of the people, standing among lords, bishops, cabinet ministers, in the mix of power and possibility . . . here he was. It was time to work.

This new resolve lasted until the next morning. The pledge lingered with him—he meant it—but when Dallington came to see if he wanted to visit Freddie Clarke's boxing club, he couldn't decline the offer.

chapter twenty-eight

In the trip to Kensington, where the boxing club was situated along an old work road, Lenox described his day. To his initial disappointment and subsequent amusement Dallington could barely keep his eyes open.

The building itself was a large converted storehouse; as they entered, the instant tang of sweat and blood filled their nostrils, despite the draft of air among the high rafters.

"Hardly the back room of a tavern, is it?" murmured Lenox. "I had always heard these contests took place there."

"Those colored lads in the far ring are giving each other a walloping, aren't they?"

"It seems there's betting on it."

There were four rings spread around the room, and perhaps two dozen people in and around them. Fifteen of these were crowded around the match Dallington had mentioned; two were in a different ring, gently sparring with each other as they received technical advice. Close to the door several men were exercising on mats. An old, white-haired man, who was supervising, stopped when he spotted the detectives. He came over to them.

"Help you?"

"How do you do? My name is Charles Lenox, and this is John Dallington. We hoped to speak to somebody about Frederick Clarke."

"Freddie? Decent fighter. Shame what they did him."

"You knew him, then?"

"I'm the trainer. I know all the young gentlemen. The one you want to talk to is there, the one in the blue suit." He pointed out a tall, slightly paunched fellow with black hair who was watching the match. "He's the secretary of the club."

"Could you get him?"

"I wouldn't recommend it until the fight is over. He and Mr. Sharp-Fletcher have a pound on the bout." He turned to watch. "The bigger lad, Castle, ain't got much science—but what a brute! The smaller one doesn't have a chance. Poor Mr. Sharp-Fletcher is going to lose his money, what can scarcely afford to."

"I know them both," muttered Dallington, after the trainer had gone.

"The bettors?"

"Yes, they're wellborn lads. Sharp-Fletcher was sent down from Brasenose. The other one is called . . . I can't remember."

"Neither of them is a footman, I daresay."

"Unless they've changed professions, no. And I hardly think Sharp's mother would like it. Her father was a marquess."

"These pugilists move in pretty rarefied circles."

They walked idly about the club, waiting for the match to end, glancing over occasionally to see whether there was a winner. To their surprise, after they had heard the trainer's opinion, it was the smaller fighter who knocked the larger one out. More science, perhaps. Lenox saw Sharp-Fletcher grab his money excitedly from the hand of a third party and count it to make sure it was all true. The two boxers, exhausted, staggered to the corners and had water from their bottle-men. The winning gamblers went to the corner of the smaller boxer to congratulate him, while the losing fighter sat alone.

Soon they found the secretary of the club. "Sir?" Lenox said.

"Yes?"

"I'd like a word, if I might. The trainer pointed you out to us. We're looking into Freddie Clarke's death."

The black-haired man clicked his tongue. "Terrible thing, that. Have you found out who killed him? Wait a moment—Dallington?"

"Yes, it is. I'm afraid I've forgotten your name."

"Willard North. We met at Abigail MacNeice's aunt's house, several months since."

"That's it—I knew we'd met."

"You're a detective, then?"

"After a fashion. An amateur—it's rather a hobby of mine."

North snorted. "Well—to each his own."

Nodding slightly at the bloodied fighters, Dallington said, "Indeed."

North didn't notice. "I'm afraid I can't help you —about Clarke, I mean. He was a damned good fighter."

"Was he a member of the club, or a fighter for hire like these men?" asked Lenox.

"A member, of course."

"Wouldn't that have been expensive?"

North shrugged. "It depends for whom you mean."

"For a footman?"

"For a footman—well, of course. It's a pound to join and ten shillings a year after that. Why do you ask about a footman?"

North didn't know what Freddie Clarke did. The lad had been putting on a show—or at any rate hadn't volunteered his profession. Obviously the money from under the door financed the lie.

"How much do you pay these men—the colored fighters?" asked Dallington.

"A sovereign each."

"Is that all?"

"They're grateful for it, I can promise you. The winner usually gets tipped a shilling here and there. No doubt that rat Sharp-Fletcher is buying the littler one champagne and truffles with my money."

"Can you tell us anything else about Clarke?"

"I wouldn't have thought so. He always stood a round in the bar after we trained—there's a bar through that door," he added, pointing to the back of the gym. "I once saw him near Green Park, and he rushed away as if he hadn't seen me right back, which I found galling."

"What was he wearing?"

"What a strange question. A suit of clothes, of course."

Footman's clothes, it would seem from Clarke's reaction. But people see what they expect to.

"Did he have much money to splash around?" asked Dallington.

"Some, of course. Yes, I would have said more than most. He gave us to understand that he had quite a rich father."

"How?"

"Oh, something like 'Drink on the pater?'—he would say that when he offered to buy us a round and hold up a pound note."

"Was anyone here close with him?"

"Besides me? Our vice president, Gilbert, was pretty pally with Clarke, but he's been up in the country for three months."

"Not Eustace Gilbert, from Merton?" asked Lenox. "He took a boxing blue at Oxford while I was there."

"That's the one."

It was to all appearances a club entirely for gentlemen. Lenox asked, "How does one go about joining the club? Is there a system of reference?"

"Oh—we know our own crowd, don't we, John? If anyone fancies a bit of exercise he comes and sees us. We rent this space quite cheaply, and our trainer, Franklin, finds all the equipment cheaply and manages the place. In all it pays for itself with our big matches. The dues go toward our bar and clubhouse."

"So how did Clarke get in?"

"I don't remember. May have been through

Gilbert—they used to have drinks together. Gilbert thought him very dapper."

The suit. Show up in a well-cut suit at Claridge's bar, with the right accent, and you could generally fall in with the proper crowd. Had Clarke been a talented mimic? What had been the aim of all this?

"You can't remember anything else?" asked Dallington.

"No," said North. Then he turned and called loudly to the rest of the people in the room, "These men are here for whoever killed Freddie!"

There was a low chuckle at this. "It was me!" called out a joking voice.

Then, to the perfect astonishment of everyone there, a short man with light hair separated from the group and sprinted for the door as fast as he could. By the time Lenox and Dallington had reached the door he was gone.

chapter twenty-nine

"Who was that?" shouted Dallington at the crowd of people who all stood together now, mute and stunned. Lenox, who had run down the street to see which way the man had turned—a futile attempt—returned.

There was a long silence.

"I've never seen him before in my life," said Willard North at last. "Have any of you lads?"

There were murmurs in the negative and much headshaking. Lenox couldn't tell if they were protecting one of their own or if their mystification was genuine.

But then another voice chimed in.

"I know him. Fella who sometimes comes to see me fight." It was the losing boxer, the large one without much science. He spoke in the accent of the West Indies, but with a disconcerting cockney tinge mixed into it. "Butcher. I know because he bring me a steak if my eye is swelled up."

Dallington and Lenox looked at each other: a butcher. The piece of evidence incriminating Collingwood had been a butcher's apron.

"Where is his shop? Where does he live?"

The big man shrugged. "Don't know."

"Did you catch his name?"

"He told me, but I can't remember it." He looked exhausted and took a gulp of water. "S'all I know."

"Thank you."

Out on the pavement Lenox and Dallington both started to speak at once. "You first," said the older man.

"I was only going to say—this man, this butcher, may have come with Clarke."

"It could be," said Lenox thoughtfully, "but what about his disguise? Would Frederick Clarke the 'gentleman's son' want to introduce a butcher as his particular friend?"

"You're right."

"Did you get a good look at the man?"

"I didn't, unfortunately."

"Nor did I," said Lenox. "Still, I think I could choose him from a group of three if I had to. The next step is to go to all the butchers' shops around the alley. I'll do that."

"What if he's hiding?"

"We'll see."

"And what shall I do?"

"It's time we split up, I think. I have two tasks in mind for you: First, you can see whether you do any better with Fowler than I have. He may have imagined some slight against him from me, or some condescension. Otherwise I can't explain his behavior."

"Second?"

"We haven't spoken to Mrs. Clarke since Collingwood was arrested."

Dallington whistled sharply between two fingers. A cab started to pull up to them, its horse an old plodder. "Anything else?"

"I don't think so."

"Fowler—Mrs. Clarke—excellent." He swung up a leg into the taxi and soon was on his way.

Lenox soon was on his way, too, back to

Curzon Street. In truth he had always disliked butcher shops; it might perhaps have been because his family had never on either side been great hunters, or because Lenox House, while it had a working farm on its land, was set at a distance from its own barns. He went into the first butcher's that he saw near Ludo's house, and there were the familiar sights—two deer, their eyes glassed, skinned and slung up on the wall. A jar of pigs' hooves, being slowly cured on the countertop. The tidiness of the red-checked curtains and the large roll of wax paper in counterpoint to the bloody hunks of cow and pig everywhere. He could eat what came from these carcasses readily enough, but he didn't care to look at them.

"Does another gentleman work here?" Lenox asked the man behind the counter, who looked about 150 years old and could no more have attacked Ludo Starling than he could have swum the Channel.

"My son," answered the man.

"Is he here?"

"He's in York for the week, which he's visiting his wife's parents there."

"I see—thank you."

Then it occurred to Lenox that he might easily ask Ludo who the family butcher was—perhaps that would be the man.

He knocked at the front door, and as Elizabeth

Starling opened it he remembered that of course their butler was gone.

"Hello, Charles," she said. "I would have had the housemaid open the door for you, but she's busy in the kitchen, I'm afraid. At any rate Ludo is out."

"Perhaps you can answer my question, in that case."

"Oh?"

"Do you know what butcher Collingwood employed?"

With a deep, sorrowful sigh, she said, "Does your meddling reach no end? Would you not leave us to our lives? Our footman is dead—our butler in prison—my husband attacked—and still you annoy us with your impertinences! Have you heard nothing of the honor which may shortly be bestowed upon my husband, and the very real danger of losing it by indiscretion?" Again she sighed. "I'm not a hard-worded woman, you know. It pains me to be so vehement. Please forgive me."

Lenox felt unchivalrous. "I'm exceedingly sorry," he said. "Your son Paul—whom I met accidentally—was insistent that Mr. Collingwood must be innocent."

"Paul's no longer here."

"Excuse me? Where has he gone? To Cambridge, so early?"

"He has gone to Africa for a year, it pains

me to say. Downing College insisted upon a year's deferral because he was so inebriated at the visitors' weekend."

"My goodness."

"He left this morning."

"So quickly!"

"I have a cousin very well placed within a large shipping concern. Paul will make his fortune and be at a perfectly normal age to enter Cambridge as a fresher; since of course the Starling money will go to Alfred, it will do Paul good to have a foundation when eventually he begins in the world."

This was frankly specious; to have gone into business before Cambridge was unheard of. Her anger had seemed to subside, however, so Lenox ventured another question. "Are you sure you cannot tell me who does your butchery, which shop?"

"I don't know that information, no. Good day, Mr. Lenox."

As he walked away, what surprised him most was how instantly Paul was gone. Lenox had seen him two days ago. Elizabeth Starling had by Ludo's own account been a doting, even smothering parent, sorrowful to see her children leave for university, much less the other side of the world. What on earth was happening in that family?

"Psst! Chappie!"

Lenox whirled around. He was some four

houses down the block now. He saw that it was Tiberius Starling, the old uncle. The cat was in his arms.

"Hello," said Lenox.

"It's Schott and Son. That's our butcher. He's up a couple of streets, green building. Always leaves too much fat on, if you ask me, the blighter. Try that on your stomach when you're as old as I am."

"Thank you—thanks extremely."

Tiberius swatted an invisible fly and said grumpily, "I don't know what in damnation is happening. That Collingwood was as decent a chap as I ever met."

"So people seem to believe."

"Eh? Say it again, I'm a bit deaf."

"I'd heard the same, I said!"

"Ah, yes." He grew conspiratorial. "One more thing."

"Oh?"

"Look up as you pass by our house again."

"Up?"

"Just look up! There's something worth seeing."

He hustled away, slipping through a side door of the house (which was set ten feet apart from its neighbor). Lenox waited a few beats to let Tiberius get indoors.

As he passed the house he did look up, and there *was* something worth seeing. Pressed against the glass of a fourth-floor window was Paul's unhappy face.

chapter thirty

His mind swarming with doubts and possibilities, Lenox decided to seek relief. He knew that perhaps he should worry about the butcher flying from London; on the other hand, the butcher would probably have known that nobody in the boxing club could identify him by name. There was perhaps little to gain from haste. In any event it was nearly time for lunch, and he hadn't seen for several days any of the (now expanded) McConnell clan.

Arriving at the vast Bond Street house, he fancied he could see a change in it already; there were flowerboxes along the windows, fresh coats of bright white paint on the shutters, and on the knocker of the front door a small pink muffler, knitted from wool. The sign of a successful birth. It all looked dazzlingly merry.

Shreve, the funereal but excellent butler who had been Toto's father's wedding present, opened the door. He was a dour, unsmiling fellow, and so it surprised Lenox greatly that now he not only was fighting down a grin but holding a stuffed bear.

"Ah!" he said, discomposed. "Excuse me, sir, I

expected Mr. McConnell. Please, follow me through to the drawing room, Mr. Lenox."

In the drawing room was Toto, from the look of her as fizzy and full of spirit as she had been in former times. Lying on a blanket on the ground was George, still plump, still red, dressed in a fetching pale blue gown. From the infant's face Lenox could see that she had been crying.

"Why on earth would you take her bear, Shreve, you beast?" said Toto happily. "Charles, tell him."

"It wasn't sporting of you, was it?" asked Lenox, smiling.

"It was a grave oversight, madam. I apologize."

Then, apparently not thinking it dignified to get on the floor and wave the bear in George's face before company, he handed the toy to Toto and withdrew with a bow.

"What a stuffed shirt he is! Before you came he was saying all the silly things we say to George now without a modicum of shame."

"How is she?"

Toto stood up and gave Lenox a squeeze on his forearm. "You wouldn't believe how clever she is—really, you can't imagine. Just think, she knows her name!" She followed this remarkable news by attempting to prove it, calling, "George, George!" over and over again until the baby seemed to tilt her head in their direction. "See!" said Toto triumphantly.

"Remarkable! I know many a grown woman who hasn't learned that trick."

"I know you're teasing me, but I'll let it pass because I'm so happy. Do you know, I never realized that all babies have blue eyes! Did you know that?"

"I didn't. Does Thomas have some scientific reason to explain it?"

"Speaking of people who don't recognize their names—his eyes don't leave her face when he's in the room. He won't get on the floor as I will, or give her a thousand kisses as I do, but lor! How he loves the little speck."

"I say, I know it's rude of me, but could I bother you for a bite of food? It would help me admire her better—I'm famished."

"Oh, yes! In fact, you know, Nurse should take her away; we mustn't agitate the poor thing with too much attention, she says. So I can join you in lunch."

"Is Thomas here?"

"I forced him to leave the house. He's at his club, looking through a newspaper. I doubt he's actually reading, though—just worrying that I've burned the house down in his absence, I imagine, and boasting to anyone he meets as if there weren't thousands of children born every day, some of them in the middle of fields. Here, find me that bell—there it is—that will get Shreve in."

Her happiness was infectious. "You look awfully well," he said.

"Thank you, Charles. All credit for that must go to Jane. She saw me through all the difficult bits."

"I'm glad."

Shreve came in, and Toto asked for food. "Will a beefsteak do for you, Charles?"

"Splendidly."

"Let's have that, and some potatoes and carrots —and for my part all I have a taste for is bubble and squeak." This was a cabbage and potato dish. "We need something to drink, too, don't we. Whatever's at hand in the cellar for Mr. Lenox, please."

"Very good, madam," said Shreve and retreated.

There was a footstep in the hall and a muffled exchange of words between Shreve and another gentleman—and of course it was McConnell.

"There's the child!" he said. George wriggled happily on the ground. "Lenox, have you seen anything so fine?"

"Indeed not," he said. A faint pain passed through him; he wondered again whether he would ever experience McConnell's happiness.

"I asked Shreve to give me a bit of lunch, too."

Now Lenox looked at the doctor in earnest, and it startled him. If there had been a change in the house—in Toto, even in Shreve—it was nothing to the complete change in Thomas McConnell. Where before he had been sallow, jaundiced, and aged beyond his years by anxiety and idleness, now he seemed a man with vigor and purpose: pink, upright, with brightened eyes and a twitching mouth that constantly threatened to burst open into a smile.

"Did you tell Lenox that she knows her name?"

"Oh, yes, he's seen the entire rotation of tricks. Now where is that nurse? I won't be a minute —excuse me."

At lunch there was only one topic of conversation—George—until Lenox felt at last that just perhaps he had heard enough about his god-child's hundred charms.

"Won't you stay to see her after her nap?" asked McConnell when Lenox said he had to go. Toto was checking in on her.

"If only I could, but there's a stack of blue books I have to read through. We sit in Parliament this afternoon, of course."

"How could I forget—the opening! We're quite wrapped up here in the baby. How was it? Did you see the Queen?"

"I did indeed; it was a splendid show. You would have loved it."

"I wouldn't have been anywhere but here— now come, say good-bye to Toto, and be sure to tell her how highly you esteem your god-daughter."

He did indeed have to be at Parliament soon, and as was customary he wanted to spend the few hours before the session milling in the lobby, meeting people and speaking with them. It was a familiar way to plan among the backbenchers.

Still, he couldn't resist stopping by the butcher's shop, Schott and Son. Curiously—and perhaps tellingly—it was shuttered and closed.

Back at home on Hampden Lane, Lenox sat in his study reading those blue books (the ones particularly relevant to the Queen's Speech, which was still being debated in the Commons). Lady Jane was out, and had been since breakfast according to Kirk. Lenox had spoken that morning with Graham, who was at the House speaking to the appropriate people's political secretaries about water and cholera.

Just as Lenox was preparing to leave there was a knock on the door. Kirk brought in Dallington.

"There you are—I worried I might not catch you," said the younger man. He smiled. "It's dashed inconvenient for you to be in Parliament. You ought to have a bit of consideration."

"I'm leaving now—my carriage should be ready. Kirk?"

"It is standing in front of the house, sir."

"Would you come along, Dallington?"

"With pleasure."

Once they were seated, Lenox took out a blue

book. "Tell me what you found today; then, rude though it is, I must read."

"The mother wasn't in, and neither was Fowler. I spent a few hours skulking around that boxing club."

Lenox smacked his head. "How can I not have told you? I found the butcher's shop. Tiberius Starling, of all people, was the one who told me." Lenox went on and talked through the whole day, catching his apprentice up.

"Remarkable—but there's something else."

"Yes?"

"It's—it's unexpected news."

"I'll manage."

"Collingwood has confessed to killing Freddie Clarke."

chapter thirty-one

The news would have to wait. That was Lenox's first thought. He had to be down at the House. In the meanwhile Dallington could go speak to Collingwood.

"Where did you hear it?"

"Jenny Rogers heard first and left a note at my club."

"Did she give you any other details?"

"No."

"You say he confessed to killing Clarke—what about stabbing Ludo?"

"I assumed that went along with it."

Lenox was silent, thinking, for a moment. "Who knows. Incidentally, they're sending your admirer—Paul—out of the country for a year. Just like that."

"How did you hear of this?"

Lenox recounted the story of his afternoon: Elizabeth Starling's fearfulness, Tiberius's surreptitious aid, Paul's forlorn face in the window. "Why lie to me? What could she possibly gain by that?" He looked up at the clock on the wall. "I should be at the House already," he said. "Will you give me a lift in a taxi down there? That way we can speak a little longer. Just give me a moment to gather my things."

As they rode down toward Parliament, Dallington suggested an idea. "What if Paul Starling killed Freddie Clarke?"

"What evidence is there of that?"

"No evidence, to speak of, but it would explain why he's leaving the country."

"So he also attacked his own father and framed Collingwood, whom he passionately defended to me? I don't think so. On top of that his spirits were awfully high at our dinner there, weren't they? He hardly seemed to have something so great on his conscience as murder."

"Not all men have consciences," retorted Dallington.

"I don't believe it. Still, you're quite right to interrogate the decision by Ludo and Elizabeth. Here's a thought—what if Paul knows something about the murder?"

"To protect Collingwood?"

"Or indeed to protect Ludo. Has anyone's behavior through this entire mess been stranger?"

"He would hardly give his own father to the police."

"You may be right there."

"Besides, as always," said Dallington, "there's the question of the attack on Ludo. What are we to believe: that Ludo killed Freddie Clarke and then was attacked by random chance in the same alleyway?"

Lenox, with a defeated sigh, looked out through the window. "What do we know?" he said at length. "We know that Paul Collingwood, a butler, killed a footman working under him—possibly to protect his own job. We know that subsequently someone, perhaps Collingwood, attacked Ludo Starling—but for reasons that are dark to us. The problem is there's no internal logic to any of these actions. Clarke saw Collingwood nick a few coins, and that's why he's dead? And then *why* attack Ludo?"

"Perhaps it's the work of a madman, and we're looking at it all wrong."

"Maybe, maybe . . ."

"Here we are."

"You'll go speak with Collingwood?" said Lenox.

"Directly. Good luck in there," he added, nodding to the Members' Entrance.

Lenox stepped out of the cab. It was turning into a wet, cold day, and the falling rain managed to shiver into his collar before he got inside.

Once there, he saw the milling mass of Members he had expected. Before he entered the fray he decided to go up a back staircase to his office and find Graham, to discover what his progress had been on the water issue.

His tiny, drafty office was open, and entering he saw that Frabbs was at one of the two clerk's desks, his tie loosened and his face cheery.

"Lenox, my dear sir!" he said, lurching up from his seat. "Shake my hand, you old stiff!"

"Excuse me?" said Lenox incredulously.

Just at that moment Graham darted out of the inner office. "Hello, sir," he said. "Unfortunately I stood the young gentleman a glass of wine for lunch—in celebration, as it were—and he seems still to be feeling the effects."

Frabbs grinned and appeared to wobble on his feet.

"We'll spare him a flogging, then," said Lenox. "Graham, come into my office for a moment, will you?"

"Of course, sir. I was just putting the new blue books on your desk."

It was dim, the small mullioned window all but lightless; even on a sunny day it wasn't very bright. "Is he doing well?" asked Lenox.

"He's only fifteen, sir, and as a result is somewhat inexperienced as a clerk. But I can attest that he's extremely quick-witted, a fast learner."

"Well; as long as you don't give him any more wine we'll keep him on, then. Really I wanted to hear about your work here."

Graham looked grave. "Unfortunately there seems to be very little sentiment in favor of the idea of a new water system in East London, sir. Nearly all of the numerous people I've spoken to on the subject pointed to the great planning and expense that went into Mr. Bazalgette's new system."

"What about the flaw in it, though? The risk of a new cholera epidemic?"

"To a man they have responded with the observation that the new coverage of London is an improvement, and that further changes would be both costly and difficult to win support for on the floor of the House."

Lenox laughed bitterly. "In short, I arrive here too late."

"For this issue, sir, I fear that may be true."

"Did nobody grasp the gravity of our position? One case of cholera in Bethnal Green and people in Piccadilly could be dead tomorrow!"

"Some think that possibility remote, and if I may speak openly, I agree. Houses in the more affluent sections of London are well enough ventilated, and the new water system is well designed enough, that West London would likely be safe."

"Then what about the poor souls on the other side of the city!"

Graham looked troubled but offered nothing except "I'm sorry to have failed, sir."

Lenox moved over to the window and put his palm against its glass, cool from the rain. "It's not your fault." He turned. "Did nobody agree to approach the leadership with me?"

"Your brother, Mr. Lenox. And—well—" Graham looked doubtful. "Mr. Blanchett expressed some interest in the idea."

"Just my brother, then."

"Yes, sir."

Blanchett was the House eccentric, a mining baron who thought England should be a strict monarchy and therefore refused to vote. He belonged to no party and supported only ideas that would prove the government's past foolishness. It was a bad sign that he liked Lenox's idea.

"I'm going to go down, then," said Lenox. "I know a hundred men in this building. One or two of them must listen, mustn't they?"

"Yes, sir," said Graham loyally, though Lenox could see he didn't believe it at all.

Downstairs Lenox didn't speak to any of those hundred men; instead he found his brother, who was only there, rather than in the back rooms with the cabinet, preparing for the debate, because he wanted to see Charles on his first true day in Parliament.

"There you are," said Sir Edmund. "Why do you look as if you swallowed a fly?"

"Graham says there's no hope."

"The water supply? No—no, I wouldn't have thought so. You must wait, Charles. Wait a year or two, until you have more friends and allies here. Or, though I don't like to say it, wait until there's a bit of cholera about and people are walking through Hyde Park with handkerchiefs over their noses again."

"You were right all along—I know that, now."

"Come, let's go into the chamber. The session will begin soon. You must start planning your first speech, at least."

chapter thirty-two

Lenox didn't get home until past two in the morning, only about half an hour after the session had finished. To his surprise and pleasure, he found Lady Jane waiting up for him.

"My wife," he said, and smiled at her with tired eyes.

She stood up and without speaking gave him a fierce hug, clutching him tightly to her, face buried in his chest. When she looked up at him it was with tears in her eyes. "Since we returned from our honeymoon everything has been . . . wrong." Gesturing at the hallways she said, "Even our houses don't feel right together yet."

"I think perhaps it takes time, Jane. We're not used to being married yet. On the Continent it was all somehow unreal—somehow child's play. Now we're back to real life."

"It was bad timing, Toto and Thomas having their baby."

"What do you mean?" he asked. She was still clutching him, her face just visible in the half-light of the hallway. The house was quiet.

"I don't know what I mean," she said. She started to cry again. "I'm so sorry, Charles."

"I love you," he murmured.

"I love you more than all the world."

"Here—cheer up," he said. "Come and sit with me. We'll have a cup of hot chocolate."

"We can't get the servants up."

"You forget that I had to fend for myself once upon a time. There was Graham, of course, but I warmed up the odd cup of tea. At Oxford I once even made sandwiches for a young woman I liked."

With mock suspicion, Lady Jane said, "Who is she, the harlot?"

"She wasn't a harlot, of course. It was you."

She looked confused and then laughed with recognition. "That's right, I did visit you. Those were delicious sandwiches. I remember thinking you must have had a good scout, with salmon and every nice thing to offer me. Well—hot chocolate is just what I'd like."

Like disobedient children they crept down the stairs to the basement, which held the servants' quarters and the oversized, still-warm double kitchen of both their houses. With just a candle to light the way between them, whispering, they went and lit the stove. Jane burrowed through the cabinets until she found a few bars of chocolate, brought back from Paris, and then looked in the iced crate below the cabinets to find the last of the day's milk.

Meanwhile Lenox, taking a key from his

pocket, opened the silver cabinet and took out that strange hybrid pot, with a short spout and a long wooden handle sticking out of its side (never its back), that it was customary to serve chocolate in. He poured the milk into a saucepan, and then they slowly melted the chocolate bars into it, one by one, until it was rich, dark, and fragrant. At the last he dropped a pinch of salt into the mixture and swirled it in.

"Isn't this wonderful?" she whispered. "I forgot what it was like to sneak around—I used to be a terrible little thief as a child."

"So did we all, I imagine. My father was in a fearful temper once when he couldn't have cold steak and kidney pudding for breakfast, the day after we had it for lunch. I went down and ate it all. I was punished, though—I felt sick for two days, glutton that I was."

"You devil!" She kissed him happily on the cheek.

When the chocolate was ready Lenox carefully poured it from the saucepan on the stovetop into the silver pot. Jane took two teacups down from the hutch by the stove, then two saucers, and, still laughing, they stepped quietly upstairs and back into the study.

Nothing, they both said after they had finished off the whole pot, had ever tasted better.

As he fell asleep a little while later, Lenox realized that for the first time in too long he felt content. Gradually he began to think about his day—his afternoon in Parliament, his morning at the boxing club, Collingwood's confession, all in the drifting, cloudy way of half-consciousness.

What was missing, he knew, was a clear motive for Collingwood to kill Freddie Clarke. Would such an apparently genial soul—loved by Paul, Alfred, and Tiberius Starling—commit murder over a few coins? No. But then what could the real motive be?

The next morning he woke up and, just like that, he had it.

He jumped out of bed and dressed hurriedly, not bothering to shave or comb his hair. Soon he was at Dallington's flat—a particularly eligible set of rooms in Belgravia. Lenox had never been there. There was only one servant, who looked at Lenox suspiciously.

"Lord Dallington often sleeps well beyond—"

"Get him. I'll answer for it."

In the event it took Dallington half an hour to appear in a candy-striped dressing gown, and even then he was groggy. He grabbed at a cup of coffee his valet offered him as if it were the elixir of immortality, and until half the cup was gone he held out a hand to prevent Lenox speaking.

"Well," he said at last, "what in all of fiery hell could it be, to get me up so early?"

"Did you visit Collingwood?"

"I did. They wouldn't let me in."

"You have to bribe the guard. Didn't you see? Well, never mind that—yesterday, you remember, you suggested that Paul Starling killed Freddie Clarke, didn't you?"

"Yes, and you dismissed the idea."

"I was wrong. Listen: Collingwood has only confessed *to protect Paul Starling*."

Dallington looked skeptical. "Paul Starling killed Freddie Clarke?"

"I'm less sure of that, but I feel certain that Collingwood believes he did. Do you remember when Paul's name came up at our meeting with him?"

Slowly, Dallington nodded. "I think I do. He said Paul didn't have a key to the larder."

"I remember his phrasing because I found it awkward at the time . . . he said, 'He wasn't involved.' I was too focused on the green butcher's apron and knife to notice but I think you'll agree it was an odd thing to say."

Dallington, awake now, nodded. "So he's facing the gallows to protect one of the family he serves. Bricker, my man, won't even press my suits."

"I don't think he's facing the gallows. I think he'll wait until Paul is out of the country, then tell the truth."

"What good does that do Paul, then? He can't come back to Cambridge."

"No, but he'll be safe from hanging."

"I'm confused—do you believe Paul Starling murdered Freddie Clarke or not?"

Lenox grimaced. "I don't know. All I know is that it's what Collingwood believes. I want to go visit him again."

In Lenox's carriage, which had been waiting outside, both men gazed through a window, lost in thought. At last Dallington said, "And Parliament—how has that been?"

"Do you know that saying about answered prayers? No—but it's wonderful, in its way. It's just harder than I imagined it would be."

"Personally I wouldn't go into that House for love or money. Every man you meet a stuffed shirt or a bore, or one of those chaps at university who look down on fun. You know the kind—half vicar, half self-righteous scholarship student. If you have a glass of punch in front of them they start to tremble." Dallington suddenly looked more ruminative. "Do you think you'll continue to do this? To take cases?"

He sighed. "I don't know. It's too difficult to balance them, and I can't help but wonder whether perhaps my ability in each pursuit has suffered for the other."

Dallington's face, which was usually on the verge of a smile, now looked concerned. "More than just losing a teacher, I worry at London losing you. Many men can sit in a room and talk nonsense, as they seem to do in Parliament, but fewer can go to a prison and phlegmatically sit with a confessed murderer."

Lenox's own face, which he turned again to the window, showed that it was a point he had considered himself.

chapter thirty-three

Money changed hands, there was a brief wait, and then they were led into the same room. What was different in it was Collingwood.

The butler looked as if his insides had been hollowed out. Whether this was because of some emotion—guilt? sorrow for Paul?—or because the full terror of his situation had alighted on his mind, it was impossible to tell. But something was affecting him powerfully.

"Sunshine," he said to them dully. "That's welcome enough."

Lenox glanced up at the small, high window in the room. It was brighter today. "Your cell is dark?"

"What did you want from me, gentlemen?"

Dallington and Lenox exchanged a look. "Just the truth," said Lenox. "I understand you confessed to killing Freddie Clarke?"

"Yes."

"You were lying before, then, when first we visited you?"

"Yes."

Dallington looked at him critically. "You were remarkably full of conviction, my dear man. I daresay you could make a living on the stage. The deceiver's parts—Aaron the Moor, say, or Iago. When this is all over, I mean."

"When this is all over?" Collingwood coughed out an astringent chuckle at the thought.

"Mr. Collingwood, I came to ask you one question: Did you confess to protect Paul Starling?"

Collingwood could say what he wanted next, but his face gave him away entirely. "No—no—bizarre thought—" he stammered out, barely suppressing his shock.

"Did you attack Ludo Starling to shift the blame onto yourself, the suspicion? I can think of no other reason why you might have done it."

"The God's honest truth is I don't know anything about the butcher's apron or the knife. I was drinking a cup of tea and reading the newspaper when that happened, Mr. Lenox."

"I believe you," said Lenox.

"And Paul?" asked Dallington.

"May I return to my cell now?"

"Your cell! Certainly not."

"Then I shall be silent."

"Like Iago indeed," said Lenox. "In that case, let me tell you a story—a drama, if you will. In the days after Frederick Clarke's death, you had no idea who had killed him."

"I did it, for God's sake!"

"You didn't; my dear fellow, you really didn't. You had no reason to."

"I did," he said tiredly.

"To continue—only *after* you had been arrested did you realize—or were you told?—that Paul Starling was guilty. In order to protect him, you confessed. When he's overseas, you'll tell the truth and, you hope, go free."

"I don't see why they would believe you, though," murmured Dallington.

"That's true; you may swing either way," said Lenox.

Collingwood's face, so mobile during their conversation, transformed now into a mask of fear. "I can't hang."

"Confessions are valuable in Scotland Yard," said Lenox. "They don't question a confession there. My young friend and I have that luxury, however—we may question what we please. Tell me, then: Are you protecting Paul Starling?"

At last Collingwood relented. "Yes," he said and then went on, in a desperate tone, "Oh, please! He's only a boy! You can't send him to hang! He'll be out of the country soon—gone from England forever—he has time to change!"

"You have admirable loyalty," said Dallington. " 'How well in thee appears the constant service of the antique world,' and all that. You must love the Starlings."

"You can have the Starling family, all of them —but I've known Paul since he was an infant. He might as well have been my own child, for all the time we spent together."

"Then did you attack Mr. Starling?" asked Lenox.

"I've no reason to lie—I didn't. I told you before, I was having tea and reading the news-paper when you and Mr. Starling came back into the house."

In that bare room, one of its walls darkened by damp, Lenox suddenly felt something strange: a new grief for Frederick Clarke, that extended soon into grief for Collingwood and his irreparably compromised life. Wherever he went he would remember these days in jail, and his loss of faith in Paul Starling—accompanied by no matching loss of love.

"How did you find out that Paul was guilty?"

Collingwood sighed. "I didn't suspect him at the beginning. It was when I came to jail. Mrs. Starling visited me, two days ago. She said Paul had confessed to killing Clarke, and that he was being sent abroad forever."

"Did she tell you why Paul killed Clarke?"

"No."

"Yet she persuaded you to confess?"

"She said Grayson Fowler was beginning to put the clues together, and that it was only a matter of time before he discovered the truth."

"So if you offered the police a false trail—"

"Yes, a confession, which I could then retract—"

"You could save him from the hangman," finished Lenox.

"It was foolish," said Dallington.

Agitated, Collingwood said, "Remember, again, I dandled the boy on my knee when he was still spitting up his milk, Mr. Lenox, and I was myself only a tiny boy in first livery. He's a decade younger than I am and always looked up to me—always asked me to play games, to show him things. Until he went off to school, finally. But I could understand!" he went on hastily. "To be among the sons of nobility, princes from Bavaria, every such thing—I could understand his not having time for me anymore! It didn't mean I stopped regarding him as my own family."

There was a dead silence in the room.

Lenox broke it, in the end. "There are mysteries remaining in all this." He thought of the butcher, of Ludo Starling's lies. "Still, you have my backing, if that counts for anything during your trial, or before that when the police build their case. I believe you to be innocent. As for Paul—I'm not as convinced as you are that he's guilty. If he is, however, I cannot promise to protect him."

Collingwood was past caring. His soliloquy about Paul and his fresh confession, of innocence, had taken the last of his energy. "Can I go now, please?"

"Yes," said Lenox. "Thank you for speaking with us."

Outside of the prison Lenox and Dallington were standing on the pavement, waiting for Lenox's carriage to round the block and pick them up, when they saw Ludo Starling. He was smoking a short, fat cigar, a hand in one pocket, seemingly idle.

"Starling!" called out Lenox. To Dallington he whispered, "Don't mention anything Collingwood told us."

Ludo turned to see them, and his face fell. "Oh, hullo," he said. "I suppose you've been to see my butler?"

"Yes, we have."

"It's damned . . . I wish you wouldn't have done it. Elizabeth and I have both asked you over and over to step out of our family's business. What will it take, money? Let me pay your standard fee, and we shall be done with each other."

"Money doesn't interest me."

"Fowler has everything in hand. Collingwood has confessed, for the love of Christ."

"That's true."

"Will you stop?"

"There are one or two small things I wish to learn the truth about before I do," said Lenox.

"Damn it, you're a Member of Parliament! It's a disgrace!"

"Because you're angry I'll let that pass, but don't say it again."

Ludo waved an angry hand at him. "We're at an end, by God." He paused to regain some measure of composure. "I'll be pleased to deal with you in the House, or see you socially— but as for this business, there will be no more relationship between us."

"A final question, then?"

"Well?"

"Who does your butchering?"

Starling reddened and walked inside the prison without another word, throwing his cigarette angrily to the ground as he went.

Dallington looked at Lenox. "You know who his butcher is."

"I wanted to see his reaction."

"Is it so mysterious? He wants to protect his son from you. Just like Collingwood."

chapter thirty-four

Dallington was perhaps right, but too many loose threads remained for Lenox to feel happy. Why had the butcher run out of the boxing club? Was he from Schott and Son? And above all: If Paul *had* killed Frederick Clarke, then first, what was his motive, and second, who had attacked Ludo? For Paul and his mother had been in Cambridge then. Though the idea of him being asked to defer entry must have been a lie, the trip wasn't.

Lenox explained this all in the carriage, which he directed to Schott and Son. "Will you come along with me?" he asked Dallington. "I can drop you at home."

"Oh, I'll come. I'm as curious as you are. Actually I feel stupid—all the facts before us and no solution, no rhyme and reason to any of the blasted thing."

A dry laugh from Lenox. "If you dislike that feeling, you should leave the profession before it's too late."

Unfortunately Schott and Son was closed again. It was strange, of course, for a prominent butcher in the heart of Mayfair to close on consecutive days without any explanation.

"There's a wine shop I know next door," said Dallington. "Trask's. We could ask about our butcher there."

"Perfect."

They went inside the shop, which was so honeycombed with wine bottles—on the walls, in great cases down the middle of the floor—that it was hard to move to and fro. A tall, thin, gray-haired gentleman, evidently with poor eyesight because he had thick glasses perched on the end of a thin nose, approached them.

Only when he was very close indeed did he exclaim, "Lord John Dallington! It has been far, far too long."

Dallington, smiling ruefully, and participating gingerly in the shopkeeper's vigorous handshake, said, "Only a week, I think."

"I remember when you were here every day! Will it be another case of champagne? Or did you like that Bordeaux we ordered for you in August? Too heavy a wine for such weather, I said, but you had it; and liked it, I fancy, for it's a hard wine not to like."

"I'm after information, actually," said Dallington.

"Oh?" said Trask, crestfallen.

"Well—why not send me another crate of champagne."

"Excellent! I'll have the boy take it over this

afternoon. Let me find my book, here . . ." He pulled a ledger off a nearby crate of wine and made a note in it.

"Do you know anything of the butcher next door?"

"Schott?"

"And son," added Lenox.

"It's *only* the son," said Trask. "Old Mr. Schott died four years ago, and his son runs the place with a cousin now."

"Do you know where he's been the past two days?" asked Dallington.

"No, and it's quite unusual. When Schott is sick his cousin is usually there, at least, or the other way round sometimes. They don't often close."

"You haven't heard anything else?"

"No. Shall I tell you if I do?"

"Please—that would be wonderful."

"May I ask why you gentlemen want to know?"

"To settle a bet," said Dallington.

"Not the first time I've done that—do you remember, sir, coming in with the stopwatch to see whether you or your young friend could drink a bottle of wine in under ten minutes? An exciting day, that was."

"Yes, yes," said Dallington hurriedly, "well—thank you—I'll expect that champagne. Good-bye!"

Outside again they walked in silence for thirty seconds, Lenox smiling inwardly.

Dallington stopped and with an irritable grimace said, "Well? They know me at the wine store, as no doubt you'll have observed."

"Did you drink it all? In under ten minutes?"

"Oh, bother it," said Dallington and stepped into the carriage. "If you have time, let's go see Clarke's mother again."

She was still at the Tilton Hotel in Hammersmith; unfortunately she was now in a bad way. With the passing of time her stern resolve to stay until her child's murderer was found had changed into a mother's grieving dissolution. She smelled of gin, and wept twice in their presence.

"Have you spoken to any of Frederick's friends?" asked Lenox.

"No, no—the poor boy!"

"Did he mention a friend—a butcher?"

"A butcher? He never would have associated with that kind—the poor boy!"

And so forth.

"Don't feel guilty," Dallington told her just before they left. "It's not your fault."

"He needed someone. A real father would have protected him," she said. "That's what he needed—he should have had a real father. Ludovic—Mr. Starling—he could have been that, when I entrusted my poor Freddie with him. Or at least a friend. It's not right to leave a boy alone in a city like this. I should have been here

—I should have come down from Cambridge more often . . ."

And fresh tears.

When they finally managed to elicit her opinion on Collingwood's confession, all she could say was that it shouldn't have happened —that *someone* should have protected her only son.

The two detectives left dispirited. They had tried to give her some solace by speaking in euphemism about death and afterlife, but she would receive none.

"I must go home now," said Lenox.

"What can I do?"

"You could try Fowler again."

"Very well." Dallington smiled. "And thanks for waking me up, even though it seemed like a cruel thing to do at the time."

When he arrived back in Hampden Lane, starving and feeling just marginally more intelligent about the whole messy Starling question, the house looked somehow brighter to him. Its matched and yet strangely mismatched facade, only partially a house still—it needed to be lived in longer—finally gave him a feeling of contentment.

Inside, all was in confusion. Footmen were moving furniture to and fro, the door to the servants' quarters downstairs was swung wide open into the front hall, and over it all Kirk was presiding, harassed.

"Are we being evicted?" asked Lenox.

"No, sir, not to my understanding."

"It was a joke—a poor one, I'm afraid. What's the row?"

"I see now, sir—very good—ha, ha. If your question refers to the activity in the house, this is the standard preparation for one of Lady Lenox's Tuesday evening parties."

That explained it. "Does she always go to such lengths?"

From the front stairway Lady Jane's voice called out, "Charles, are you there? Leave Kirk alone, the poor dear has a great deal to do."

"There you are," said Lenox, finding her as she trotted back up the stairs. "Can't you stop to say hello?"

"I wish I could! But I want this evening to be memorable—your first days in Parliament, you know!"

"I forgot all about it. Will there be any dratted soul I can talk to there?" said Lenox moodily.

"Oh, yes, you and Edmund can sit in the corner and grumble together while the adults make conversation."

She turned as she reached their bedroom, and her warm smile showed she was teasing; a perfunctory kiss and she had gone to her changing room. "Toto may come!" she called as she walked.

Lenox, who was nearly hit by a passing bookcase, beat a rapid retreat to his study. On the desk there was a stack of blue books that needed his attention. Leaning back in his chair, his feet propped up on the ledge of the tall window that looked over Hampden Lane, he picked one up. "Railroad and Waterway Taxation," it was called. There was a note in Graham's surprisingly messy, quick script (he was so fastidious in other ways) that read, *Many important men are interested in this subject. Please study carefully.*

With a sigh Lenox turned to the first page and started to read.

chapter thirty-five

Kirk might not have known all of Lenox's idiosyncrasies, but there were few like him in London for a party. When at eight o'clock that evening Lenox went into the rose-colored drawing-ing room (now quite large after the joining-up of the houses, though Jane had done well to create several small sitting areas within it), he saw three long tables piled close with food and drink. On one was the hot food, a nod toward incipient autumn: roast fowl with watercress, jugged hare, steak and oyster sauce. On the next was cold food, appropriate for the summer that was now passing out of existence: cold salmon, dressed crab, and a great bowl of salad. Finally, on the third table were drinks. There was champagne, of course, and a drink made of champagne and cold sherbet, which many of the women liked if the room became overhot. There was wine in plentiful quantities besides, and for the gentlemen spirits. At the center of the table was the party's true heart, an enormous silver punch bowl filled to the brim with orange (or peach?) colored naval punch.

Footmen stood behind each table, ready to serve. What was considered charming about Jane's Tuesdays—and even by some inappropriate —was their informality. All around the room were card tables and sideboards where people could set their plates, but beyond that there was no central dining table. It was rather like being with family for breakfast on the morning after a great party; everyone with a bit of something on a plate, milling through the room and chatting. Tonight there would be thirty people or so, half of them who might be deemed friends, the other half who would more properly be called personages.

"You're home, sir," said a voice behind Lenox, who was asking for a glass of punch.

"Ah—Graham. I just got back."

He had just rushed home from Parliament and

changed. The immemorial practice of the House was to convene in midafternoon and go late into the night; on the face of it an impractical schedule, until one remembered that there was a great deal of work done in the morning and early afternoon to prepare for the later assembly. In fact the morning work was perhaps more important, and now that they were just finished debating the Queen's Speech the House would be only lightly populated for the rest of the evening.

"I wanted to remind you before I retire, sir, to pay special attention to Percy Field, the Prime Minister's personal secretary."

"Surely you'll be coming?" said Lenox. "You're invited, you know."

Suddenly there was a pained look on Graham's face, and Lenox realized that to be a guest where just weeks before he had been a butler would be too awkward, too abrupt—even too painful. "I fear not, sir. At any rate, your attention, or perhaps Lady Lenox's, would be far more significant than mine."

There was a ring at the bell, and Graham bowed very slightly, a habit of his former profession that still hadn't left him, and withdrew.

"Who the hell wants to be first?" muttered Lenox to nobody in particular, setting down his punch to greet whoever it was. He heard Lady Jane's quick footsteps on the stairs and smiled, imagining her sentiments—similar to his own—on early arrivals to a party.

Presently Kirk came down the hallway with someone who was in fact a welcome guest: Edmund.

"Oh, hurrah," said Lady Jane. "I worried it was someone I would have to speak to. I'll be down again shortly."

"I call that a greeting!" Edmund laughed, and as she went out he said, "Well—if I'm not somebody one must speak to, I'll sit in the corner and have my punch alone."

"Thank goodness you've come—I don't want to talk to the Archbishop of Winchester. How are Molly and the boys?"

"Molly sends me letters from the country—from the house—that I don't mind telling you make me weep with frustration to be in this city all the time. I haven't been on a horse in two weeks, Charles. Two weeks!"

They had both grown up in Lenox House, Edmund's seat now, as the baronet, and Charles spent most of his holidays there. "Any word on the Ruxton farm? Is the son taking it over?"

"No, he's selling out to open a chemist's shop in town. It's a relief—both of them, father and son, have been devilish. Rest in peace," Edmund added obscurely.

The farms on the land were a source of income for Edmund—Charles had been left money outright, through their mother—and he had to deal frequently with discontented tenants. "What will you do with the land?"

"Southey, on the next parcel of land over, wants to expand. I'll give him a fair rent to take the Ruxton land—about ten acres, I think—because he doesn't need the house on them. A hellish little house, you remember."

"Oh, yes. Mother used to go sit and teach the Ruxton children how to read, though she never got any thanks for it."

Edmund snorted. "Well, hopefully the son can read well enough, or his new shop will poison half the people we know."

"What about the boys?"

A glow came into Edmund's face. "Teddy is owed a lashing for having candy at church, but I shan't give it to him. Church is boring enough as a child without candy—oh, the door!"

Soon the party was crowded with incoming guests, Lady Jane greeting them, Kirk taking whole double armfuls of shawls and coats here and there, the punch bowl quickly shallowing down. There were small groups forming around the archbishop and around an extremely amusing man named Griggs, a clubman and a wastrel who nonetheless was held to be the most enjoyable conversationalist in London. Edmund and Lenox, deep in their own conversation, broke off when two very important Members came in from the House, looking extremely gratified to redeem their first invitations; this was always an exclusive event, not generally overpolitical in its composition.

Percy Field came in, Lenox noticed, tall, thin, and austere, and soon experienced the same gratification. For a while, fifteen seconds or so, he stood uncomfortably in the doorway. Just as Lenox was going to greet him, however, the Duchess of Marchmain beat him to it. In truth she was more of a cohost than Charles was at these events.

"Can I find you a drink?" she said to Field, as he was stammering out an introduction.

He was both pleased and nonplussed by this sudden intimacy with nobility ("Why—Duchess —no—I couldn't—ah—yes—punch would be lovely") and his stern visage, with its rather pompous chin, flushed with the excitement of met expectations. Lenox smiled.

Edmund came over, mouth full. "This is quite nice, actually. Have you tried the crab?"

"Not yet. Generally I wait until the party's over to eat—there's so much food left Jane has it for days."

"By the way, that case—Ludo Starling. Is it true the butler did it?"

"Keep it quiet, but I don't think so." Lenox lowered his voice to a whisper. "In fact there's some suspicion that it was Ludo's son Paul, though I'm not convinced of that either."

Edmund's eyes grew wide. "His son! Never!"

Charles nodded. "We'll see—at any rate it wasn't the butler. Be grateful you only have to fret about candy in church."

Edmund shook his head. "I don't envy the boy anyway, having Starling for a father—he loves cards and drinking, and no chance of much attention when you compete with those."

Lenox froze. Something had slotted into place in his brain, but he couldn't quite see what it was.

"Charles?"

"Just a minute—I need—excuse me." With a look of deep distraction Lenox left his brother, then left the sitting room altogether, with its gay hum of conversation, and ran into his silent study.

There was rain tapping on the windows, and for ten minutes Lenox stood in front of them, gazing at the wet, shining stones of Hampden Lane and thinking.

Edmund's comment about Ludo Starling's faults as a father had raised some possibility in his mind.

Suddenly he remembered what Mrs. Clarke had said that morning.

He needed someone. A real father would have protected him. That's what he needed—he should have had a real father. Ludovic—Mr. Starling—

he could have been that, when I entrusted my poor Freddie with him.

Just as that thought jumped into his brain, another one followed on its heels: the ring. The Starling ring, with *LS* and *FC* engraved inside of it.

A real father would have protected him.

Ludo Starling was Frederick Clarke's father.

chapter thirty-six

A whole cloud of associations and small incidents had sent forth this lightning bolt. They were separately inconclusive but together powerful. Foremost in Lenox's mind was the ring.

It was exactly the kind of ring that Lenox's father had given Edmund long ago, when he turned twenty-one. Each ring had an element of its family's crest embossed on it—a griffin for the Starlings, and for the Lenoxes a lion. Each was meant to be worn on the smallest finger of the left hand, but rarely came out of a locked case. Engraved inside Lenox's father's ring had been his initials, and now there were Edmund's opposite it; inside Starling's old ring were *LS* and *FC,* for Ludovic Starling and Frederick Clarke. Father and son.

That wasn't all, though; something ineffable in Mrs. Clarke's tone told Lenox he was right. Pacing for some time along the length of his library, the din of the party for background noise, he at last stood still and then threw himself onto the sofa. What had it been? A sense of betrayal, perhaps, or anger at Ludo. She didn't *suspect* Ludo—he was an old love—but she blamed him.

And she had called him Ludovic! She had quickly checked herself, but she had unmistakably mentioned him by his first name.

Then, in the dark workings of his mind, he remembered another fact. She had come from Cambridge, and Ludo had once lived in Cambridge—at Downing, where Alfred was a student now. They were roughly the same age, Mrs. Clarke and Ludo Starling, and she—she was still quite striking. Not beautiful or soft or even very feminine, like Elizabeth Starling, but a woman with whom a gentleman of a certain kind could undoubtedly fall in love.

She still had no husband, Clarke being perhaps a fiction invented as she went off and had the child on her own somewhere private, with Ludo's money. What had she done? Sent her fictional husband off with the army and had him fictionally killed?

Lenox smacked his head—Ludo's money. "Of course," he muttered.

There hadn't been any uncle's inheritance.

What kind of London housemaid had an uncle rich enough to see her retire upon his death? She had bought her pub with Starling money, and raised Clarke with Starling money, too. It all made so much sense.

Dallington was due to come to the party but hadn't arrived yet when Lenox retreated to his library. Now he went down the hallway, back toward the lively noise, to see if he could find his apprentice.

"There you are," said Lady Jane, face smiling but voice steely. "Where have you been?"

"I'm sorry—truly I'm sorry. I lost track of time. Is Dallington here?"

"You're not leaving, are you? You can't, Charles."

"No—no, I shan't. There he is. I see him. His mother is wiping something from his chin and he's pushing her hand away—look."

His mind racing with possibilities, Lenox went over and coughed softly behind Dallington's back.

"Oh! There you are," said the young man. Dressed as discriminatingly as ever, a fragrant white carnation pinned in his buttonhole, he turned to face Lenox and smiled. "It's the worst party I ever went to, if I can be candid."

Lenox forgot the case for a moment and frowned. "Oh?"

"Too many people I want to speak to, and I

can't imagine it will run into breakfast; I'll be sorely disappointed when I leave that I didn't get to speak to this one or that. There's an art to parties—there must be boring people, too, so we don't feel too regretful when we leave."

Lenox laughed. "A finely paid compliment. Listen, though—about the case."

Dallington's eyes narrowed with interest. "Yes? Shall we go somewhere quieter?"

"We can't, sadly—Jane—well, we can't. But I've figured something strange, I think. Freddie Clarke was Ludo Starling's natural son."

"He was a bastard!" whispered Dallington, deeply moved. The look of astonishment on his face was gratifying. "How on earth do you reckon that?"

Lenox told Dallington quickly how this epiphany had come about. "I don't swear by it," he said last of all, "but I feel in my mind that it must be right. It would explain so much."

Dallington, lost in thought, had stopped listening, but now he looked up. "I say—at the boxing club, do you remember what Willard North said?"

"Which part?"

"About—"

Lady Jane cut in then. "Charles, the Chancellor of the Exchequer is here. It's just what I hoped for. I invited Mary to have lunch with me next week, and mentioned specially to her that I was having a Tuesday that would be very political in character, and that she should come—and bring her husband."

The Conservative party was in at the moment —Lenox hoped not for long—and that meant that the chancellor standing in his doorway was Benjamin Disraeli. He was a tall, severe, intelligent-looking gentleman, with deep-set eyes that seemed almost predatory. He had risen to become the first or second man in his party (the Earl of Derby, though Prime Minister, was considered less brilliant in political circles) despite the considerable disadvantage of having been born Jewish. Some considered him an opportunist—his wife, Mary, was the widow of Wyndham Lewis and a very rich woman—but Lenox suspected the attribution of avarice was due perhaps in part to his ancestors' religion.

More importantly to Lenox, he was the only man in Parliament who had balanced politics with a second career. Throughout the past decades, if less so of late, he had published a series of celebrated novels. This dual purpose made Lenox feel an affinity for the man despite their different parties; both of them had to balance two lives, two worlds.

Beyond all that, it was a tremendous thing to have him in the house. It meant that Lenox was a serious participant in the grand game of London politics, someone on the move. Disraeli wasn't any longer a very sociable fellow; his visit here would be on people's lips the next morning.

"That's a thing to celebrate," Lenox said. "With your skills of persuasion you should be in Parliament yourself, Jane."

She smiled and walked back toward the chancellor's wife.

Lenox made to follow her but stopped and said, "Quickly, Dallington—before I go—in a few words, say what you meant to say about the boxing club."

"Only that I remembered something else. Do you recall that North said Clarke was always hinting that he had a rich father? 'Drinks on father,' or something like that? It fits with your theory."

"I'd forgotten—you're quite right. We'll piece the rest together in a moment, but I must go speak to Disraeli."

"Wait—the butcher—Paul—where do they fit into any of this?"

"I don't know yet," said Lenox, turning away.

As he crossed the room he crossed, too, between his professions and tried to shed the details of the case from his whirling mind. It was hard. Ludo Starling had a great deal to hide, evidently. What besides a natural son?

In Charles's absence Edmund had greeted the Chancellor of the Exchequer, the man who might be reasonably called the second man in government and the man who ultimately would control the funds for any project Lenox ever hoped to pursue to completion.

That wasn't the subject this evening, though, nor even politics. "How do you do, Mr. Disraeli?" said Lenox.

"Fairly; fairly. I could do with fresh air. London feels stifling."

"You ought to come hunting at Lenox House," said Sir Edmund. "We can find you a pony, and as for fresh air—well, we won't bill you for it."

"You'll see my brother's truer self there," added Lenox, smiling. "His talents are wasted in the House, I realize when we hunt together."

"His talents are not wasted in the House—he has been a positive inconvenience—but I see it was meant to be humorous. Edmund, thank you kindly. I might well accept your offer if my secretary deems it possible. As for you, Mr. Lenox, may I say welcome to the House?"

"Have you any advice? What mistakes did you make upon your arrival?"

He let out a barking, humorless laugh. "Mistakes? In that day it wasn't within a young Member's purview to make mistakes. He voted with his party unfailingly, never agitated on behalf of a particular issue, and waited to mature into his position."

Lenox felt like a chided schoolboy. "I see."

"Still, you'll do well if you're at all like your

brother," he said. "By the way, Mr. Lenox, is that punch I see? I would quite like a glass of punch — yes, I think I'll have one. No, no need to fetch it for me. Please, stay here and speak to your guests."

Lenox watched him for the rest of the night, occasionally returning to him to say another courteous word or two, and by the end of the evening the old man's demeanor had softened. Still, he smiled only once: when Toto came in, accepting congratulations from everyone and chattering as rapidly as an auctioneer. For all his seriousness Disraeli was known as a man who loved a pretty young lady.

Many hours later, when the last guests had gone and the tables in the sitting room were empty, with only a low pond of punch left at the bottom of the bowl, Lenox, Edmund, and Dallington were sitting in Lenox's library, smoking cigars.

Edmund and Lenox talked of the chancellor first, and the very great honor of his visit, and then all three spoke appreciatively of Lady Jane's turn at the piano.

"I wonder what Ludo Starling is doing at the moment," said Dallington at a lapse in their talk. "I'd pay a shilling or two to read his mind, the devilish sod."

"Why?" asked Edmund. "It was the son, wasn't it?" Seeing his brother's smile, he said, "Am I behind the times? I always am in these things."

"Yes—or a bit, anyway. We think that the footman, Freddie Clarke, may have been Ludo Starling's natural child."

Edmund blew out a low whistle, shocked. "Who told you?"

"Nobody," said Charles and recapitulated the series of small facts that had led him to the idea.

Dallington chimed in when he was done. "Something else. Do you remember how he hovered around the hallway when we looked at Clarke's room? Guilty, I thought at the time —as if he couldn't come in, for whatever reason."

"Then, too, his reaction to the ring was singularly strange," said Lenox.

"How?" asked Edmund.

"He didn't recognize it at first. If he had, I would have believed more readily that Freddie Clarke stole it, although the act of his engraving his own initials on it would still have been a mystery to me. I think perhaps Ludo gave it to Clarke's mother many years ago."

"Just the sort of foolish gesture Ludo Starling would make to a maid," added Edmund.

"It may even have been that they were in love. At any rate, I don't think he had seen it for some time."

"Freddie Clarke was proud of it," said Dallington thoughtfully. "It was polished, well engraved, kept in a safe spot."

"The one memento he had of his father," said Edmund.

They talked it over for a while longer, but soon enough their cigars had burned down to stubs, and both Edmund and Dallington left, taking a taxi together away from Hampden Lane. After he had seen them off, Lenox went upstairs to have the real postmortem for the party, with Jane.

chapter thirty-seven

The next morning was a break from it all, politics and murders and secret sons. It was George McConnell's christening.

A few days before, the cards had been sent out: small white ones with the child's full name engraved in the center in gray, and in the lower left-hand corner, per custom, the birth date. On the reverse was the name and address of a church—St. Martin's—and a date and time.

"A bit early, isn't it?" asked Lenox when Lady Jane told him about the note. "As I recall the christening is usually a month or so after the birth. It's scarcely been a week."

"She wants visitors," was all Lady Jane said in reply, with a slight, affectionate eye roll. Except for the very closest friends and family, a new mother couldn't receive social calls until after her baby's christening. "You know Toto has never thought much about convention, either."

"Have you decided what you think we should do for the child? As godparents? We'll have to give her something now if it's already the christening."

"She'll have enough money—I don't think we need to make an investment on her behalf." This was a common enough present. "I would like to give her something special, though, besides the silver porringer I already gave Toto."

"What sort of thing would you call special, my dear? The horn of a unicorn? The headdress of a Red Indian?"

She laughed. "Nothing that exotic, now—though for my birthday I may permit you to give me a phoenix's feather. What would you say to a little pony for her?"

"A pony? Shouldn't it outgrow her?"

"We would give her a newborn foal when she turned four, say—then it might be broken in time for her to ride at six or so."

"I call it a handsome idea."

So the present was decided, and on the appointed day, at the appointed time, they arrived at the church prepared to fill their more serious role as godparents.

It was one of the small alabaster white churches

of the eighteenth century, with a single high spire and a brick parish house next door. Between them was a small circular garden, ringed with a path of white gravel. The whole picture was almost rural, and its simplicity seemed fitting to this simple occasion, with the whiteness of the church, too, recalling the child's purity.

"Do you remember all of your lines?" asked Lenox as they walked up the steps of the church. They were fifteen minutes earlier than the invitation said, because they had to speak briefly with the clergyman.

"Lines!" said Lady Jane, turning to him with alarm. "What have I missed?" He laughed. "Ah —I see you're teasing me. Well, it's not very gentleman-like of you, is all I can say."

A few stray parishioners were in the pews of the church, but otherwise it was empty. It had a remarkably open, airy feel, with high clear windows—no stained glass—flooding light inward. Along the transept stood long tables of ferns and Easter lilies—from a hothouse of course, for it was September—and at the crossing, where the four sides of the church met, was a large, round baptismal font, made of silver and with crosses worked into it.

The clergyman was a bishop—Toto's father had asked him to be present as a personal favor —and when Lenox saw him he remembered the man spoke with a terrible lisp.

"Mr. Lenoxth!" he called as they approached. "Thith ith truly a joyouth day!"

"Indeed it is, my lord," said Lenox and bowed his head. "Are Thomas and Toto here?"

The bishop nodded. "You know your roleth?"

"I think we do," said Lady Jane. "Will you tell us once more?"

They heard their roles, and soon the church started to fill up. Lenox stood to the right of the font, Lady Jane to the left, and though they nodded to anyone who caught their eye neither moved, save once: when the grandparents arrived, and came into the first pews. Toto's mother was a formidable, large old woman, but her father was something else, tiny, with pure white hair and a jolly face; it was clear that his daughter's shine came from him. McConnell's parents were stout Scots, both red from long hours outdoors, the father very dignified and the mother positively monumental, with a whole fox for a stole. Both wore the McConnell plaid, gray, green, and white, he in the form of a kilt, she in her hat.

There was a loud din of conversation until suddenly the bishop, now in his vestments, appeared at the font between Lenox and Lady Jane. Lenox found himself suddenly nervous, in the new quiet, and with the sun directly on him rather warm. It felt like a solemn moment, to be sure, but more than that he realized now for the first time that to be a godfather meant more

270

than a present now and then—that it was of importance to God, and in God's eyes.

Without speaking, the bishop gestured for the child to be brought forth. Toto, looking radiant, held her, with McConnell behind her. They took their places beside the bishop (with Lenox and Lady Jane now on the outside of them), who began to speak.

"Almighty God, who by our baptithm into the death and rethurrection thy Thon Jethuth Chritht dotht turn uth from the old life of thin: Grant that we, being reborn to a new life in him, may live in righteouthneth and holineth all our dayth; through the thame Thy Thon Jethuth Chritht our Lord, who liveth and reigneth with thee and the Holy Thpirit, one God, now and for ever. Amen."

As he spoke he ladled water over the child's head with his hand and anointed her with oil. To Lenox's pride, he found, she didn't cry. She looked wonderful, too, not at all red anymore. Her dress, a long, flowing white sort of gown, perhaps three times longer than her whole body, was one Toto had worked on throughout her pregnancy, the object of great anxiety and effort and time; there was also a satin bonnet, white of course, and a profoundly embroidered—indeed, beautiful—ruff at the neck.

"Who ith the thponthor of thith child?" cried out the bishop.

Here was their moment. Lenox and Lady Jane stepped forward and silently bowed.

"Very good. And what ith her name?"

"Grace Georgianna McConnell," said McConnell loudly, then handed the bishop a slip of paper with the name clearly spelled out, as had been customary since a powerful couple had long ago found themselves at home after a baptism with a wrongly named child.

Then (also as was customary) Toto placed George in Lady Jane's arms, where she stayed while the ceremony finished with a short speech from the bishop.

Lenox's eyes flitted over to Jane quite often, and once as he looked he saw that she was in a state of high emotion. Tears swelled in her eyes and began to fall, singly and doubly down her cheeks and onto her brown dress. Lenox handed her a handkerchief, and she pressed it to her mouth without taking her gaze away from the child tucked safely in the crook of her right arm. Toto saw it and started to cry, too. McConnell caught Lenox's glance and smiled.

The moment the bishop said the final words of his blessing, soft conversations started all over the church, soon rising to quite normal speaking-voice levels and finally into something of a racket. Lady Jane returned the baby to her mother, and the three members of the new family vanished into their private room.

"That was lovely," said Lenox to Lady Jane after she had hugged Toto good-bye and he had shaken McConnell's hand.

She slid her arm through his and leaned her head against his shoulder, her face still wet. "It was beautiful," she said in a barely audible voice. "I've never seen anything so beautiful."

"I thought Toto would start giving the blessing herself, she looked so excited."

Jane hiccupped with laughter. "It's true. She was quite calm at first, but I saw her get caught up. How lucky she is, Charles!" As she said these last words the laughter left her face and she looked up at him, bereft.

He looked back at her, his eyes slightly narrowed, trying to read her expression. Instead of saying anything he squeezed her hand and hoped it would be reassuring enough.

Just then someone with so little tact that he couldn't see he was interrupting a private moment, a gentleman named Timothy Macgrath, approached Lenox and said, "Jolly good show, wasn't it!" and they were all thrown into the general conversation that rattled on as people began to file into the street.

Meeting on the steps of the church, Lenox and Dallington consulted quickly.

"Will you go visit Fowler before the party?" asked Lenox.

"Of course. I never saw him, did I?"

"Ask him about Clarke's father, who he was and why he's gone. Maybe that will tell us something."

"Shall I ask him about Frederick being Ludo's son?"

"I don't think so. Not yet. Use your judgment— if you feel he's willing to commiserate with you, then share all the information you like."

They were only a couple of short blocks away from the butcher's, Schott and Son. Lenox couldn't resist checking in to see if he was there; he told Lady Jane, who was deep in conversation with the Duchess of Marchmain and didn't have much present need of him, that he felt like a stroll.

It was still warm, and as he walked he loosened his tie. Some thought about children, elusive and dim, went through his mind more than once, but it was unclear even to himself what he wanted—for himself, for Lady Jane, for their life together.

He was so lost in thought that he overshot the butcher's by a block and had to turn back.

Someone was in. The white tile of the shop's interior gleamed brightly, and behind a row of beef sides that hung from the beams someone moved. Lenox couldn't see a face, but then realized what he *could* see was perhaps even more interesting.

It was a green butcher's apron.

chapter thirty-eight

Lenox wavered. He didn't want to miss his chance to speak with Schott, but he didn't want to stand in a tight space with a man who had thirty knives nearby, and knew how to use them.

Impulsively he crossed the street and opened the door.

As soon as the smell hit him he knew it had been a mistake. From twenty feet he could admire a butcher's shop, its sanitary white, its reddish pink slabs of beef cut so tidily. Close up, though, it nauseated him. If it was browned in a red wine sauce there was nothing he preferred to a steak, but seeing it before it had reached that stage was less pleasant.

The man in the green butcher's apron had been in the back, but at the sound of the bell attached to the door he popped up to the front. To Lenox's disappointment, it wasn't the gentleman from the boxing club.

"Mr. Schott?" he said.

"Yes? What can I get you?" The butcher was a short, tough lump of a man, bald and round-headed, with a belt of fat and arms that looked powerful from the heavy work of lifting and chopping. He looked at Lenox without suspicion. The detective put his age at about forty.

"I was wondering why you'd been closed the past few days."

"I suppose a man can keep his own hours in his own shop, can't he?"

"Certainly, yes."

"Will that be all?"

"In fact I was hoping to speak to your cousin."

Schott looked aggrieved. "Why on earth would you wish to do that? If it's a cut of lamb you want, I've sold a fair few more than he has—only four or five thousand, I admit, but experience must count for something, mustn't it?"

Lenox almost laughed. "It's a fair point. But it wasn't a question of butchery that I hoped to discuss with him. It's about Ludo Starling. Or Frederick Clarke, really."

Even as he said the second name Lenox heard something ominous: a lock turning behind him. He whirled around and saw the man from the boxing club, a cleaver in his hand, a key going into his pocket.

He looked back to Schott, who had his arms crossed and a dead-eyed look on his face.

True, visceral terror gripped at Lenox's heart. There was no way out if these men wished to harm him. How stupid not to have waited until someone could come with him. Or at least to have told someone where he was going!

"Hello," he managed to say in what he hoped was a mild voice.

"Well?" said the man from the boxing club. "I'm the cousin. What do you wish to say?"

"May I hear your name, sir? Mine is Charles Lenox; I'm an amateur detective and a Member of Parliament." There. Let them know that if they killed him they were killing someone of note, someone who would be avenged.

"A Member of Parliament?" said Schott.

"Yes, for Stirrington."

"Where's that?"

"Durham."

"What are you doing in London, then?" asked Schott's cousin. Lenox noticed that he was young, perhaps only twenty.

"Parliament is here, of course," said Schott in an exasperated tone.

"Your name?" asked Lenox again.

"Mine? Runcible—William Runcible."

"May I ask you why you ran out of the Kensington Boxing Club that way?"

Schott spoke up. "He was scared. He did something stupid, and he was scared of being found out. Now he has been, the fool."

"What did you do?" asked Lenox.

Runcible seemed to grip his cleaver tighter. "I'm not going to jail," he said.

"Why don't you tell me what happened? Did you kill Freddie Clarke?"

To Lenox's surprise, Runcible smiled at the suggestion. "Never. Of course not. Freddie was my mate. Came every Tuesday and Friday for the meat. It was him that told me about the boxing club."

"You were friends there? I thought he associated with some pretty high gentlemen."

Runcible frowned. "Well—not friends, least-ways not there. He was taking their money, and they wouldn't have bet him if they knew he was a servant, he always said. He invited me to watch, but we never talked while we was there."

"How was he taking their money?"

"Betting, I suppose. I never asked."

"If you didn't kill him, why did you run out of the club?"

Schott spoke up. "Show him the paper. It ain't worth the trouble—staying closed, losing business, worrying about the police."

To Lenox's enormous relief Runcible nodded, put down the cleaver, and started to root around in the pockets of his green apron with both hands. At last he withdrew a soiled piece of paper, folded many times over, and presented it triumphantly to Lenox. Better still, he didn't pick up the cleaver again.

Lenox smoothed it out and read aloud. Based on the spelling, the penmanship, and the slightly incoherent grammar, Lenox decided that it had been written by Runcible himself.

I, Loodovick Starling, confess I paid Wm. Runcible two pounds to stab him in the leg in Curzen Street Alley.

Ludo had scrawled a hasty signature at the bottom of the page.

Lenox read it to himself again, totally puzzled, and said, "What is this?"

"What does it look like?" Runcible asked indignantly.

To Lenox's unhappy surprise he picked up the cleaver again.

"Is it real? You stabbed Ludo?"

"It was me."

"The young idiot," added Schott.

"He paid me!" said Runcible to his cousin, in a tone that suggested they had discussed the subject before.

"Wait—wait," said Lenox. "Why did he ask you to do this?"

Runcible shrugged. "I don't rightly know. He came to me after hours and said, 'You, William Runcible, I need you to do me something. I'll give you two pounds.' 'What is it?' I said. 'Stab me in the leg. Make it bloody but not too painful. And make sure the damn knife is clean!' 'Show me the two pounds,' I says—"

Lenox interrupted to ask when Ludo had signed the paper.

"Just before I went over I got to thinking about my risk—my *legal* risk—so I made up this

279

dockiment for Mr. Starling to sign. He was angry, but it was all arranged, like, and he wanted to go through with it."

Lenox felt entirely befuddled. The signature looked real, and the story was—well, was it plausible?

More importantly, how stupid could Ludo Starling be? Of all the men in London willing to stab him for two pounds, why oh why choose his family butcher? He must have been desperate.

"Did he ask for anything else, besides you stabbing him?" asked Lenox.

Runcible frowned. "Like what?"

Schott, as if he had given up on his cousin, was starting to pulverize a piece of veal. Lenox saw this as welcome further proof that they didn't intend to slaughter him.

"Anything." He didn't want to lead the young man on. "To give him something, to . . ."

"You mean the apron! He asked me for the apron, the mask, and the knife when it was done."

That settled it. The boy was telling the truth. "It's the stupidest thing I ever heard of anyone doing, Mr. Runcible," said Lenox.

Suddenly he remembered that day. Lenox had come to visit Ludo, who had been extremely cordial but then disappeared for twenty minutes, rather mysteriously, before returning full of apologies. *That* must have been when he struck his deal with Runcible. How strange. It was one small puzzle solved, anyhow.

Runcible looked dangerous and hefted the cleaver in his hand.

"That's what I told him," muttered Schott and gave the veal an especially vicious pound.

"I fear I must tell the police."

Both men looked up, and again Lenox felt real terror, his heart thrumming in his chest.

"The police? He wanted me to do it," said Runcible, brow darkened ominously. "That can't be a crime."

"Perhaps you're right," said Lenox nervously.

"Don't placate us."

"Very well, then. I think it can be a crime, and it makes you a suspect in Clarke's murder."

"I didn't do that," said Runcible.

"It was Collingwood, wasn't it?" asked Schott. He had stopped tenderizing the veal, and his arms were crossed.

"I don't believe you did," Lenox said to Runcible, a roundabout answer, "but why did you run out of the boxing club?"

"I panicked," said Runcible. "I figgered Mr. Starling's getting stabbed—paying me to do it— was connected. Now the question is who you think you're going to tell."

"Don't do anything foolish, William."

"Going to prison would be foolish."

Suddenly there was a sharp rap at the window. Lenox, terrified, jumped at the noise.

"The door is locked!" called a woman's voice. "Let me in!"

Runcible looked at his uncle and then, reluctantly, put down the cleaver and unlocked it. The detective's body flooded with relief.

"How can I help you?" he said to the young woman. Lenox turned and saw she was with a man.

"You can't! I want to see him!" She pointed to Lenox.

He looked again. "Clara?" he said with surprise. "Clara Woodward?"

The girl looked indelibly beautiful, rosy with happiness. "You dear man," she said, "I'm going to give you a kiss on the cheek."

Lenox stammered something as she made good on her word. "Thank you," he managed to come up with at last, blushing, "but whatever for?"

The young man at her side, who looked equally happy, said, "They're finally letting us get married, and it's down to you and your wife, sir. Pardon my rudeness—I'm Harold Webb."

"I'm very pleased to meet you, Mr. Webb." They shook hands. "More pleased than you know."

"Isn't it the most wonderful thing?" said Clara.

"I saw you through the window and had to tell you. The way you spoke to my aunt at our dinner in Paris—it brought her to my side of things, and after that it was simple to convince my parents. Harold proposed to me yesterday. You dear, dear man!" she said again and stood on her tiptoes to kiss him again on the cheek.

In another mood Lenox might have found this comical, but only now was his heart slowing down. "I'm delighted for you," he said.

"In eight months' time," said Harold, who was a tall, well-built lad, with friendly eyes. "Clara has said more than once that she hopes you'll come."

"It was the best luck running into you," said Clara, her eyes sparkling.

"Indeed," he murmured. "It would be my pleasure to come to your wedding," he added and bowed slightly, smiling, "and Jane will be so pleased."

"Excellent. Now let's leave him to his shopping, Harold. Good-bye! We'll send you your invitation soon!"

The three men were left alone again, too quickly for Lenox to say he would leave with the young couple. There was a crucial difference, however, which was that Lenox was closest to the—now unlocked—door. More importantly, perhaps, the mood of anger and tension had deflated.

"Listen, Runcible," he said. "Starling shouldn't have gotten you into this mess. I'll not tell the police if I think I can avoid it."

The young butcher looked at him suspiciously. "Oh? How do I know?"

"You have my word."

Now Runcible sighed. "All right. Thank you, Mr. Lenox." It was strange to see him almost deferential, gentle, after his earlier anger. He would be a dangerous boxer, in the right mood. "Can I have my dockiment back, though?"

Lenox looked down and saw that he was still holding the piece of paper. "Here it is," he said, handing it over, "and please, be smarter in the future."

"Stupidest thing I ever heard of," repeated Schott and went back to his veal as Lenox left the shop.

chapter thirty-nine

On the street Lenox breathed freely for the first time since he had laid eyes on the figure in the shop. Being near Ludo as he was stabbed (Gratefully! Imagine!) had given him a certain squeamishness about blood.

There was always a breakfast or luncheon after

a christening. Thomas and Toto had planned a particularly grand one, with lunch served at three o'clock and dancing in the early evening. A select group had been invited to dine, and a larger number to dance, eat sherbets, and gossip about each other.

Lenox tried to recompose himself as he arrived at the house only ten minutes after he had been held at knifepoint, and found that he had an appetite. McConnell was at the door, greeting people, and Toto was seated in the drawing room, a few friends scattered around her for protection, all young and pretty. She motioned him over.

"Charles, you dear, how are you? Didn't you think George performed admirably? I can't tell whether I would mind if she ran off and became an actress on the Parisian stage. She has the talent, to be sure—but the life they lead you! Of course she would be popular, but the impudent men that an actress attracts . . . and of course it would be too low for words, though I don't mind that . . . no, I think she shall marry a Prime Minister. Yes. That's more suitable."

"Where is she?" asked Lenox.

"With her nurse. She's not coming to the party, though she may sneak down for a moment. Look out for a woman with a face like a tombstone and see if she's holding a baby. If she is, the baby's George."

Lenox laughed. "Can I get you anything? A glass of water?"

"No, thank you."

"Are you sure? It's better to drink."

"Everyone has been inundating me with glasses of water, I promise you. Now go, sit! I want to eat soon."

Lenox knew that it was to be a "white" meal, a tradition in Toto's family every Sunday, but especially observed on days of baptism. All the food would be white, and the tablecloth and candles, too. But he hadn't realized the imagination that would go into it all.

To begin with, for each person there was a glass of champagne and a white-robed chocolate with *G* written in cream-colored cursive on it. Then there was an oyster, potato, and cauliflower soup, warm but not steaming, and perhaps made with white wine, because it felt very light. After that was a lovely piece of haddock, dressed in a sauce of celery and butter, and then *suprême de volailles*, white chicken in cream sauce, stuffed with (hidden) mushrooms and served with pure white potatoes, sliced thin and steamed. With these two courses was a crisp, fresh Sauterne; with the next was light sherry, fresh out of the cask according to the butler who served it alongside small plates of wafers and two sorts of white cheese.

Dessert, however, was where Lenox found

himself most impressed: a meringue, then a light-as-air piece of sponge cake with the browned crusts removed, and on top of that a perfect mountain of whipped cream.

As a final touch there was another chocolate, again robed in white, again with a cursive *G* written on it, and coffee. Coffee was the mystery they all spoke about ("They'll overcream it," Lady Jane predicted confidently), but when it arrived it surprised them all; floating above the black coffee was a thin white disc of crystallized sugar. They broke out into spontaneous applause at that, and Toto blushed.

"It was my father's thought," she said, and her father reddened slightly, too, then looked very serious and said, "Oh, no, quite a frivolous idea," and hastily drank off a great gulp of his wine.

After the food there were speeches. McConnell's father addressed them in a deep voice, with his son sinking into a chair like a young child at his father's table; he spoke about Scottish traditions, the Scottish countryside, and even Scottish food with tremendous veneration, and concluded by saying, in a loud voice, "To our Highland granddaughter! May she live a full, happy life!" This drew overwhelming applause from seven or eight McConnell relatives and polite clapping from the rest of the party.

Then Toto's father stood up. "I shall be very brief," he said. "This is the happiest day of my life." He sat down, quite emotional, and earned truly overwhelming applause, along with shouts of "Hear, hear!" Lenox felt goose pimples on his arms; he knew how dearly, more dearly than anyone, the man loved Toto, and how pained he had been by her unhappiness over the years.

Finally there was the bishop, who blessed the meal, called the day "joyouth indeed!" and sat down with the beaming face of a man who has done the work of God and, in the way of business, drunk six or seven glasses of good wine on a warm afternoon.

When the lunch was finished the women and men retired to separate rooms, the women to sewing and gossip, the men to cigars and gossip. As it neared six o'clock some people, particularly the older ones, left, and others started for the ballroom, where guests were beginning to congregate. McConnell was at the threshold there, promising Toto would come down soon. It was a large, very high-ceilinged room, which was usually full of his sporting equipment but had been emptied out and varnished for the occasion. Along one wall were tables with punch and sherbet on them, and waiters with trays of the same now circulated among the guests.

"McConnell," said Lenox when he came in, with Lady Jane. "We've barely had a chance to speak."

"This sort of thing is never for friends, is it?

Friends you see on any old night—this is for cousins and acquaintances, I think." He smiled. "Still, would the two of you drink a glass of champagne with me?"

"With all my heart," said Lady Jane.

McConnell stopped a servant and sent him to fetch three glasses. "To Grace's godparents!" he said when they arrived, and held up his own champagne.

"And to her father!" added Lenox.

Out of the corner of his eye he saw a figure enter the room; he turned and recognized Dallington. "Will you excuse me, both of you?" he said and walked off.

"Lenox!" said Dallington when he spotted the older man walking toward him. "I don't mind telling you that it's five hundred degrees out there—really, I wouldn't be surprised if some natives set up a colony on the banks of the Thames. There—a glass of champagne, that will cool me." He swiped one from a passing tray.

"How was Fowler?"

"Bloody-minded old bastard."

With a reproving twist of his eyebrows, Lenox said, "This is a baptismal party, you know."

"True enough, and more to the point there's a real bastard involved, isn't there? I don't want to confuse us." Dallington grinned. "Well—call him an old fool, then."

"Did you even speak?"

"Oh, we spoke. He asked if I had lost my mind, interfering with Scotland Yard."

"And you said?"

"That I wasn't interfering. I asked him if he knew about Frederick Clarke's relationship with Ludo Starling—their secret—and he said yes and slammed the door in my face."

"I wonder if he does know."

"But not before saying 'Tell Lenox not to darken my door again, either.' I thought that was pleasant."

"I've news as well. The butcher."

"Oh?"

"For a moment I thought he meant to skin me alive, but it turned out better than that." Lenox laughed ruefully. "Though it's all even more puzzling than it was before."

He told Dallington the story in detail, speaking in a low voice so as not to be overheard. With increasing astonishment the younger man listened, but at last felt compelled to break in.

"Charles, this can mean only one thing!"

"What?" asked Lenox.

"That Ludo Starling killed Clarke!"

chapter forty

Lenox's eyes shifted across the room, checking to see if anybody had heard the outburst. In fact someone was nearby, a pretty, rather large girl of twenty named Miranda Murray, red-haired and pale-cheeked. She was one of McConnell's cousins, distantly. Toto disliked her for being humorless, but Thomas loved her dearly for her intelligence and pride. Dallington had cause to feel more strongly than any of them, because for a brief while they had been engaged. The end of the engagement, some years before, had been the talk of London, and in truth it was he who had jilted her. Quite unreasonably he hated her for it, in particular because she tried to be friends with him, putting a brave face on things.

Approaching them, though, she must have seen something closed in their visages, and veered away as she was about to reach them.

Dallington turned back to Lenox and in a lower voice said again, "Ludo must have killed Frederick Clarke. He needed an alibi from the butcher."

"I wish it were as simple as that."

"Why isn't it?"

"Ludo has flaws, but do you think he would kill his own son? And more perplexing still, come to me within an hour or two of it happening?"

"Why not? What better to make him seem guiltless than to come to you and ask for help? I remember how he acted when we were inside Freddie's room, as if he had a guilty conscience."

Lenox sighed. "I don't know."

Dallington paused. "I discovered something else, too."

"What?"

"I hope you don't think I overstepped my duty. I went to see Collingwood." He went on in a rush. "I felt he might need a visitor—some company. I should have asked you, I daresay, but it occurred to me while I was on the other side of London—and it was useful, as I say."

Lenox allowed himself the fleeting thought that perhaps Dallington was ready to work independently. "I think it was an excellent idea. What did he say?"

"He knew about the money."

"That's wonderful! What did he say?"

"Starling was slipping him the money."

"Ludo Starling? Was slipping Frederick Clarke money?"

"His son."

"Everything comes back to Ludo—the money, the stabbing," muttered Lenox, almost to himself. "I wonder whether it was he who hid the apron

292

and the knife, too . . . but can he have been the murderer?" He fell silent and stared intently at the floor, his mind far away from the party.

"Lenox?" said Dallington quietly.

"Sorry—quite sorry. Did he have a story to tell, Collingwood?"

"Indeed he did, and I don't mind adding that he lives in mortal terror of the gallows. His trial will begin in a week. I told him we would do our best for him."

"Of course."

"He didn't want to talk about the money at first, but I could see he knew something, and I tried to pull it out of him gently."

"What was the story?"

"His bedroom was close to the door of the servants' quarters, the one you walk a few steps down from the street to reach. It was the biggest room and always belonged to the butler. According to Collingwood he heard someone stumbling down the steps one night."

"Starling?"

"He didn't know. An envelope slid under the door, and he opened it to check what it was."

"Even though it had Clarke's name on it."

Dallington grimaced. "He wasn't proud to tell me that. He didn't steal anything—or so he said. At any rate, he didn't twig what was happening then, but the next time it happened he heard Starling coming in upstairs."

"Interesting."

"Nobody else was out of the house—it couldn't have been anyone but Starling. Then the *third* time he had confirmation, saw him through the window."

"I had hoped the trail of money would lead somewhere more conclusive," said Lenox. "Instead it must draw our focus even tighter on Ludo, I suppose."

"Another interesting thing—all three times, he bragged to Collingwood afterward about winning at cards the night before."

"But Ludo's rich. He could have given Frederick Clarke money whenever he wanted. Or for that matter, stopped him working as a footman!"

Dallington laughed. "Apparently not. Elizabeth Starling keeps the family's finances under tight control, Collingwood said. There was gossip in the servants' quarters that Ludo owed more than a few men money for cards, and only paid when he won."

Lenox pondered this. At last, when he spoke, it was methodically, with determined logic of thought. "Here's a simple enough story," he said. "Clarke was tired of having so little money—wanted to be recognized as a gentleman's son, which his mother had raised him in the knowledge that he was—and threatened to tell Ludo's family. Ludo killed him to stop that.

It's all the more plausible because he's so concerned about the title he may get."

The young man laughed. "Not that mine has done me any good. But Charles, think—if the simplest story makes such sense, mustn't it be correct? Hasn't Ludo been behaving strangely all along?"

"It makes sense, I know. Except it doesn't sit right with me. Look at the facts. Ludo was Frederick Clarke's father—I think his giving the boy money only confirms what we thought on that subject—yet he allowed Clarke to work as his servant and pretended to me barely to know his name. He had ambivalent feelings, not angry ones. For God's sake, he took him into his house, at least in some fashion! Yet you say he murdered him? His own son? It doesn't sit right with me," he repeated.

"But having himself stabbed by Schott's cousin makes it seem conclusive to me," said Dallington. "Not to mention framing Collingwood! And for that matter, implicating his other son, Paul! These are the actions of a man with something to hide."

Lenox shook his head. "Maybe. Maybe Ludo Starling killed Frederick Clarke. There's something we're missing, though. I feel sure of it. Ludo is no mastermind, and I've never known him to be violent."

"Well, what shall we do, then?"

Dallington looked unhappy. Lenox knew the feeling—to feel so sure, and not understand why other people didn't, too.

"We start over. First of all I think we ought to confirm with Mrs. Clarke what we suspect about her son's paternity. I'm meant to be in Parliament tomorrow, but I'll see her early in the morning, out at the Tilton."

"Then?"

"Then we need to sit down and speak with Ludo, and ask him to describe exactly what his relationship with Frederick Clarke is. I don't think Inspector Fowler has done it, or is likely to, and we can't let Collingwood rot in jail."

"It may not work."

Lenox looked grim. "It will if we keep trying. The truth wants to come out."

They had been in a dark corner of the ballroom for so long that Lenox had forgotten there was dancing and merriment nearby. He only recognized it as noise, until a female voice called out to him.

"You must be the two dullest men in London!"

They turned and saw that it was Miranda Murray speaking.

"You don't want to get caught between us, then. Perhaps you should dance," Dallington said.

It was abominably rude.

Miranda, who looked wounded, tried a smile. "Perhaps you're right!" she said.

"Might it be a dance with me, then?" asked Lenox. "I'm not much account, but of course the eyes in the room will be on you." He held out a hand.

Gratefully she took it and followed him onto the dance floor. "Thank you," she said as a new song started.

"Now tell me," said Lenox, smiling mischievously, "do you think that baby looks more like Thomas or Toto?"

"You must know my answer," she said. "I think Grace favors my cousin, of course. No doubt Toto's cousins think as I do but in reverse. But look at the child's strong chin! She's a McConnell."

"If you can keep a confidence, I think as you do. Of course I would never dream of saying it to either of them. She would be put out, and he would become terribly vain."

She laughed gaily and turned with him toward the center of the room.

chapter forty-one

Lenox awoke the next morning bleary-eyed. It wasn't so much that he had had three or four drinks but that they were spread over so many hours. In his younger days he would have woken the next morning and taken his scull onto the river to refresh himself, but it was his fortieth year now, and it took him longer to feel quite normal again.

Still, he dragged himself downstairs early and over a strong pot of tea devoured five blue books, none of them riveting but all, according to Graham's carelessly penned notes, quite important. The sole moment of amusement that any of them afforded him was when a piece of paper dropped out of a blue book on education and he discovered that it was a self-portrait by Frabbs—that is, a self-portrait of how Frabbs wished he might look, which was nineteen years old, much more muscular, and with a rather dashing mustache. It was signed *Gordon Frabbs* in a deep, swooping hand.

"Graham!" he called out when he had finished his reading. It was nearly ten o'clock.

"Yes, sir?" said the political secretary when he appeared a moment later.

"I'm going to attend to the Starling case this morning—no, there's no use looking stern, I tell you—but I want to be at the House promptly. Is it important to be there at the beginning?"

"I rather think so, sir. There will be an address on India by Mr. Gladstone, much anticipated, and he could use the benefit of your support on the benches."

"Shouting 'Hear, hear,' and that sort of thing?"

"Yes, sir."

Lenox sighed. "I only feel half part of the Parliament, Graham. I should have known about Gladstone's speech. You told me, if I recall—but my mind has been elsewhere."

"If I may speak freely, sir, I think it has."

A look of anger quickly muted into resignation passed over Lenox's face. "It's not what I expected, I suppose. Not as easy, or revolutionary, as what I expected."

"No, sir."

"Well," he said and stood up. "Thank you."

Graham bowed. "Sir."

When he was alone again Lenox's mind traversed once more the details of the public water system, alighting on both its strengths and flaws. He was pacing his study when there was a ring on the doorbell. Dallington.

They rode together in a cab to Hammersmith, with the foul-mouthed driver cursing everyone who stood in their way. For much of the time they didn't speak; Lenox had a blue book and Dallington a copy of *Punch*, and they read in the two corners of the carriage.

When they were close to Hammersmith Dallington looked at him. "How would you like to speak to her? Shall we come right out and ask who Clarke's father was?"

Lenox was silent for a moment. "You mustn't always look to me, if you intend to learn anything for yourself," he said. "Perhaps I've been too domineering an instructor. Would you like to speak to her yourself?"

The younger man looked surprised. "If you like," he said. "I've no wish to jeopardize our chance of hearing the truth."

"You've sat with me often enough as I spoke to people, and stuck in your oar once or twice. Be gentle, I think—she seems quite fragile—and more importantly, when she looks like she's wanting to speak, for heaven's sake don't say anything."

"Well—excellent, then."

They waited for her in a cluster of armchairs in a private corner. Lenox ordered tea and sandwiches. When she arrived to meet them she looked terrible, wracked by grief. She declined food and let a cup of tea sit untouched on the table before them all.

"I fear I cannot help any of you," she said. "Not Mr. Fowler, nor you, Mr. Lenox. What am I meant to believe? That Mr. Collingwood killed my son?"

"What do you think?" asked Dallington.

She turned her eyes on him. "If I had an opinion I would be a great deal less unhappy, young man," she said. "And don't think I don't remember you, at my pub—breaking glasses—carousing—inviting loose women into the bar. Sent down from Trinity College, weren't you? Lord John Dallington! Out of respect for Mr. Lenox—a man in Parliament, no less—I've held my tongue, but I don't want you asking me what my *opinion* might be. I want help!"

He blushed furiously and stammered out something less than cogent. It was true that Cambridge had expelled him, not so long ago. "Younger days—terribly sorry—new leaf—broken glasses a terrible expense—please allow me—" and so forth.

"Your scout, Mr. Baring, paid for the broken glasses. Your tab as well. He took it from the pocket money your father sent him instead of you. You ought to be ashamed for it, too."

"I am," said Dallington in a low voice.

Lenox, who had at first been inclined to smile when Mrs. Clarke began her rebuke, saw how gravely affected the young lord was and stepped in. "I'm sorry we can't help you," he said. "I wish we could."

"Yes—well." Momentarily her fragility was

covered up by something hard and angry.

"We had a question, actually. That might help."

"About Frederick?"

"After a fashion."

"What is it, Mr. Lenox?"

It was Dallington who spoke. "Who is his father?"

"Frederick Clarke Sr. Of course."

With a gentle frown, he said, "Is that—is it quite true? Might his real father be Ludovic Starling?"

She first looked taken aback, then crumpled into tears. It was a moment before any of them spoke again, and as Lenox had advised, Dallington stayed quiet. It was she who broke the silence.

"Yes . . . but I can't believe he told you."

"He d—"

Lenox interrupted Dallington. "How did it happen?" he asked.

Crying again, she said, "Oh, when I was a pretty little fool in Cambridge. He was a student at Downing, where I was a maid."

"There was no uncle, was there?" asked Lenox. "The money for the pub?"

"No. It was his money. Ludovic's."

Lenox remembered her calling him Ludovic the last time they spoke, a little too intimately. "Why did you go to work for him?"

"We were still—I thought we were still in

love. I said he had to let me work there, or I would tell his new wife."

"It must have been a miserable time," said Lenox.

"Miserable?" She let out a sob. "How can you say that when Freddie came out of it all? Dear, wonderful Freddie?"

"And when you were—with child?"

"I was six months pregnant when I moved to London, and only stayed for about two months. It was a terrible ordeal to watch him build a new life without me, but I blackmailed him into letting me stay. I was always very cordial to Elizabeth, and she gave Freddie a job straight away when I asked. In the end Ludovic gave me the money I bought the pub with and sent me to the seaside, where a nurse looked after me. After I had the child I thought perhaps he would wish to speak to me, but he never did, and in my pride—in my foolishness—I decided I hated him. Though I love him still, God curse me for it!"

There was a long break in the conversation, as she cried and cried. The wound was still fresh, it was obvious, or had perhaps been reopened by her son's death.

"There was a ring," Dallington ventured at last. "A signet ring, with Ludo's initials in it."

Haltingly, she said, "He gave it to me—he—" She began to sob again.

"Then you gave it to Frederick?"

"Yes. When he was fourteen I sat him down at our kitchen table and told him the truth. From then on there was nothing in his head but the Starling family. Just like his mother—a pair of fools."

"No."

"A pair of fools."

"So is that why Frederick went to work for Ludo's family?" asked Lenox.

"Yes. I begged him not to, but he wanted to be close to his father."

"Did his father acknowledge him?"

"Yes. Freddie told me they were getting more and more friendly. Freddie said he would end up a gentleman one day."

"No wonder Ludo has seemed so agitated," said Lenox.

Dallington merely raised his eyebrows; apparently he still considered Ludo the primary suspect. Lenox wasn't quite as sure.

Something else, though, made sense: the intellectual reading, the philosophy and great literature; the tailored suits and shoes; the aristocratic boxing club, where he spent money freely; and the ring, most of all having his own initials engraved on the Starling ring. Frederick Clarke was setting himself up, in his own mind, as a gentleman. Raised in a pub, but apparently of some natural gifts, he had decided to emulate his father. *Freddie said he would end up a gentleman one day.*

It reached a tender spot in Lenox's heart, this idea of Freddie Clarke, the footman, striving to be so much more than himself—striving to be like a father who would never fully own him, indeed who would likely never fully love him.

"There was something else, too."

"What?"

"Something even worse, for poor Ludo—for poor Freddie," she said, sniffling into her handkerchief.

"Poor Ludo?" said Dallington with disdain.

"What is it?" asked Lenox.

"We—" She couldn't go on, and for a tantalizing moment it seemed as if she were going to silence herself.

Then suddenly Lenox saw what it must be. "You and Ludovic Starling were married, weren't you?"

She nodded and burst into further tears. "Yes. That's it. That was when he gave me the ring! As a wedding ring. I thought his family would kill him when they heard, and they began to put an end to it quickly enough. Pretty soon after that they forced him to marry Elizabeth, though I know for a fact he didn't love her, and in our little chapel in Cambridge!" A wracking sob went through her body, as if she could only now see just how much she had lost. "An arranged marriage."

Lenox put a hand on her arm. "It will be all right," he said.

"Why is that worse? What am I missing?" said Dallington.

"When is Frederick's birthday?" asked Lenox of Mrs. Clarke by way of response to the question.

She looked at him, and he saw the truth.

chapter forty-two

Lenox thanked Mrs. Clarke, promised to visit her again soon, and dragged Dallington out to the front of the hotel, where they picked up a new cab.

"Where in damnation are we going?" asked Dallington as they climbed in. "Don't you have to be at Parliament soon?"

"I have an hour. We have to go see Ludo Starling."

"Why?"

"To confront him. For the first time I think he may be guilty."

"Finally!" Dallington exhaled. "What convinced you?"

Lenox smiled. "Let me have my little game—come and talk to Ludo with me."

As they rode through the streets from

Hammersmith to Mayfair, the buildings going past in a transition from shabby to genteel to pristine, Lenox tried to read his blue book, but there was no point. Nothing, not even Parliament, could match the excitement of the chase.

In a part of himself, though, he understood that this must be an ending. He would pass more cases on to Dallington now, and if Dallington needed help or advice Lenox would provide it, but only as a secondary figure. Cases of particular interest, or brought to him by those with a deep personal claim on him, would be the only ones he undertook to solve.

As they approached Curzon Street, Dallington leaned through his window to look up at the Starling house.

"Look—he's just leaving!" Dallington said.

"Probably on his way to Parliament. There, driver, leave us here!" called Lenox, rapping the top of the brougham with his fist. "Dallington, will you pay the man?"

"Yes—I'll be behind you."

Lenox stepped out of the cab and walked briskly down the street. "Ludo!" he called out.

He had begun to understand in the past few weeks how a tax collector must feel. Ludo's face, expectant as he turned, fell into a look of disappointment.

"Oh. Hullo. Walking down to Parliament? Come along, I suppose—yes, come along. Same party, after all," he said, with a forlorn shrug.

"I'm going there in a moment, yes, but I came here to speak to you. I'm glad I've caught you."

"What is it?"

"It's about Frederick Clarke."

"Oh, for heaven's—"

"Or more precisely, I should say, about your son Alfred."

Ludo's puffy pink face looked startled. "Alfred? What on earth could you want to know about him?"

"Only one thing—his birthday."

Dallington came up to them now, and with that distraction Ludo managed to compose his features. "You, too?" he said. "Would you like to know the date of my wedding anniversary? Or old Tiberius's saint's day?"

"I'm as much in the dark as you are," said Dallington. "What did you ask him, Charles?"

"Only his son's birthday."

"Paul?" asked Dallington doubtfully, perhaps suspecting that Lenox had returned to his quick departure for the colonies as a key point. "Why would it matter?"

"No. Alfred."

"It's taking a good deal of restraint not to snub you, Charles," said Ludo. "Why should I submit to this intolerable invasion of my life? I've repeatedly asked you to leave the case to Grayson Fowler and Scotland Yard, and yet here you are for the fourth or fifth time, asking impertinently for help I've no desire to give you! I'm due in Parliament soon, and I would take it kindly if I could walk alone." He turned away.

"Is Mrs. Starling home?"

"Yes—but she won't want to speak to you, either!"

He began to walk away. Lenox waited a beat before he said, "Alfred—he's almost a year younger than Frederick Clarke, isn't he?"

Ludo turned back, white with either anger or surprise. It was hard to tell which. "I don't see your point, and I don't care to."

"If you did get a title, it would have descended to Freddie Clarke."

Dallington, suddenly comprehending all, whistled lowly.

The reaction of Ludo was much more pronounced. He gaped at them for a moment, then started to speak, then stopped, and finally just stood there, flabbergasted. "What do you mean?" he said at last.

"Freddie Clarke was your son, wasn't he?"

"What—what possible—"

"Worse still, you were married to his mother. He was legitimate. Not a bastard. My question is this: How could you have let your own son work as a footman for three years, and in your house? What sort of man would tolerate such a circumstance?"

Staggered but determined to extricate himself

from the situation, Ludo said, "I will take my leave now."

"We'll speak to Elizabeth, then," said Lenox quietly. He had grown more certain in his own mind that Ludo was the murderer.

"She's not home!"

"You said she was."

He came back toward them in short, furious strides. "I was wrong! Now leave my family the hell alone!"

"You couldn't bear the thought of depriving Alfred of his lordship, or of the Starling land up north. The Starling money is entailed, I believe? A system I never liked much, I confess. I doubt you would enjoy living out your days in the knowledge that a youthful indiscretion you made twenty years ago meant your two sons were disinherited."

"You're a liar! Leave them alone!"

But the truth was plain on Ludo's face; Lenox had hit home.

The detective smiled faintly. "The real shame in it all is that Freddie Clarke would have made an admirable gentleman. He read philosophy, he boxed. He was quite plainly intelligent. Well liked."

"It's nothing to me what he was—he was a footman."

"And Collingwood—for shame, Ludo. An innocent man. Who really did this deed?"

Ludo looked for the first time as if he were on the verge of confessing. The people going by on the pavement jostled him closer to Lenox, and a confidential look appeared on his face.

Just as he was about to speak, however, something entirely unexpected happened.

The position of the three men on the pavement was such that Dallington and Ludo were facing Lenox, and suddenly they both saw something he didn't.

"Lenox!" cried Dallington.

He knew somebody was behind him, and with a quick step backward he saved his own life. (He had always found stepping *into* the attacker the most successful gambit, unbalancing the other person—a boxing lesson Freddie Clarke might have known.) Something extremely heavy and blunt grazed the side of his face painfully, tearing at his skin.

Even as he turned he saw from the corner of his eye Ludo, stock still, eyes wide with astonishment, and Dallington, springing forward to help him.

He felt a heavy blow on the side of his head. His last thought was to wonder where the person had come from so quickly, and then he forgot the living world.

chapter forty-three

When he came to he was for a moment quite dreamy, but then the nature of the situation returned to his mind and he sprang away with all his might from whoever was grasping him.

"Lenox! Lenox! It's only me!"

As he blinked his eyesight back, he saw that the person holding him had been Dallington, who had supported him to Starling's front steps.

"Who was it?" Lenox asked in a hoarse voice, his head still spinning.

"We couldn't see—he wore a mask, whoever it was. He ran off as soon as he had fetched you that last smack on the head. The coward. I caught you as you lost consciousness."

"And Ludo?"

"He tried to catch the attacker, and now he's off to find a constable."

"Or pay the person his fee," said Lenox. He felt a throb in his head. Groaning, he let his body go slack, as it wanted to, on the step. "Just get a cab, will you? I want to lie down."

"Of course."

On the short ride home Dallington only spoke

once—to ask whether Lenox believed that Ludo knew the attack was coming.

Lenox shook his head. "He didn't know we were coming to see him."

"He could have set the person after you nevertheless, and told him to attack you when you were in Ludo's presence. Another alibi!"

Lenox shrugged. "It could be."

In fact part of him wondered whether it was William Runcible, still afraid of jail and no longer pacified by Lenox's promise in the butcher shop. Still, wouldn't he have used a knife, or a cleaver?

At home there was a flurry of activity when it was discovered that he had been attacked. Kirk sent for the police, Dallington went to fetch McConnell, and two or three maids hovered anxiously around the door, waiting to see if he needed anything. As for Lenox, he lay on the couch with a wet, cold towel over his eyes, the lights all dimmed. He wanted to see Lady Jane.

When she arrived he felt comforted. She spared just a moment to come and put a hand on his forehead, then became a whirlwind of businesslike commands. She ejected the maids (who were having a very exciting day, it must be admitted) from the threshold of the room, and asked one of them to return with a basin of water and a cloth to clean the wound, though

Lenox had already assayed the job. Then she called Kirk into the room and berated him for not returning with the police, who were on their way, before instructing him to find a doctor in case McConnell wasn't in.

He was in, however; he arrived not fifteen minutes later. "What happened?" he asked Lenox.

"Some thuggish chap tried to hit me with a brick."

McConnell smiled. "He succeeded admirably."

"Don't make jokes," warned Lady Jane, her face tense with anxiety. "Look at his head, will you?"

McConnell spent the next few minutes gently cleaning the jagged wound on Lenox's forehead (a third cleaning), prodding around its edges, and asking Lenox what hurt and what didn't. At last he offered a verdict. "It looks painful, but you'll be all right, I think."

"You think?" said Lady Jane, alarmed.

"I should be clearer—you *will* be all right. The only thing that worries me is whether you might not have some dizziness and light-headedness in the next few weeks. If that happens you'll need bed rest—"

"He'll have that anyway."

"You'll need bed rest," McConnell said again, "and minimal activity. But you aren't in any danger of long-term consequences, thank the Lord."

He then took from his battered leather medical bag a length of cloth and set about making Lenox a very dramatic bandage for his head.

"There," he said when he was done, "now you look like you were in a war, or at least a duel. Walk down Pall Mall on a busy afternoon and it will get all over town that you did some heroic deed."

Lenox laughed and thanked McConnell, who left, in a hurry to get back to George. Dallington had stayed in the room, at Lenox's request, but now he left, too.

"Shall we discuss the—" Lenox had said, turning to the lad.

"No, we shall not," Lady Jane had answered firmly. "John, come back tomorrow if you like."

When at last they were alone—Lenox feeling much more human, a cup of tea from one of the (again hovering) maids in hand—the pretense of anger and hardness fell away from Lady Jane.

"Oh, Charles! How many more times will I have to worry this way?" was all she said. She hugged him close to her.

McConnell had joked about the attack reaching other ears, but he wasn't far wrong. In the past when Lenox had been harmed in the line of duty he had never read of it in the evening papers, but now he was a Member of Parliament. After the police had come and gone, offering very little hope to the victim that they might catch his attacker, the newspapers arrived. It was only a small item on two of the front pages, doubtless placed there close to the hour the papers went to press, but it reminded Lenox that he had responsibilities to people other than himself now—and even beyond Jane.

By suppertime he could stand up and move about, and after eating a light bowl of soup in his dressing gown, he went to bed.

In the morning he had a splitting headache and a thousand questions about the case. But he had slept well, and he felt ready for the fight again.

Graham was the second person he saw, after Jane had brought him his coffee and asked how he felt.

"May I inquire after your health, sir?" asked Graham.

"I'm a bit thumped, of course—but no permanent damage."

"The police have no idea who might have attacked you?"

"None."

"But you feel quite well?"

"Oh! Yes, not bad."

Graham coughed discreetly. "In that case might I ask you to discuss parliamentary matters?"

"Of course."

Lenox came away from the conversation with a stack of fresh blue books (he hated the sight of the things by now) and spent the morning reading them. McConnell stopped in to change his bandage, and Lady Jane brought a pillow or a sandwich or something else useful every half hour, but otherwise he was alone.

He tried—really tried—not to think about Ludo Starling or Frederick Clarke. There was Dallington who could look into it all now.

Nevertheless, as the hands on the clock seemed to slow to a halt and his eyes grew dry from all that unrewarding prose, the questions he had woken up with returned in greater force.

Why had he been attacked? Was it a message, or a true attempt on his life? Did the attacker know that Dallington had the same information Lenox did?

Most importantly, *had* Ludo been involved?

It was a relief when at noon or so Dallington arrived. He brought with him a few magazines full of crime stories.

"It's what I always read when I'm sick. Somehow having a fever makes them even more exciting."

Lenox laughed. "Thank you. But what about the real thing?"

"Starling? I spent the morning on it. Something occurred to me."

"Oh?"

"The method of attack—it was the same as killed Freddie Clarke."

Lenox inhaled sharply. Of course it was. How

could he have missed it? "Good Lord, you're right. That must mean it was an attempt—a real attempt—to murder me."

Dallington nodded gravely. "I think so, yes. Or else Ludo wanted again to transfer the blame away from himself. After all, a similar attack rather conveniently removes suspicion from someone we both saw didn't do it."

"And less conveniently away from Collingwood."

"Precisely. In any event, I checked the alley."

"Yes?"

"There was a different chunk of brick missing from it."

"The same weapon."

"Exactly."

Lenox was still holding a blue book on corruption in the Indian army; he tossed it aside lightly, brooding on the new information.

Suddenly something occurred to him, and he stood up.

"What is it?" asked Dallington.

"I've thought of something. We need to go see Inspector Fowler."

chapter forty-four

Lenox had a wide enough acquaintance scattered through Scotland Yard that he could still walk through the building unchallenged. Several people eyed his bandage curiously, nodding cautious hellos to him, while others stopped to make some small joke about the Member of Parliament returning to his less reputable (or more reputable?) old haunt. Dallington, however, was stopped at a front desk, so Lenox went to see Fowler alone.

The door to his office was ajar. Lenox braced himself for a stream of vitriol before he knocked, and got about what he expected.

"Mr. Fowler?" he said, knocking the door and pushing it open.

"Mr. Lenox," said Fowler with dangerous calm.

"I'm afraid it's about the Starling case. We must speak about it."

Fowler reddened. "I would ask you kindly not to tell me what I must do, sir!"

"I—"

"Really, this infernal and constant intrusion into official matters of the Yard cannot stand a moment longer! Good Lord, Mr. Lenox, do you have no sense of boundary? Of decorum? Of—"

"Decorum?"

"Yes, decorum!" He stood up behind his desk and began to cross the room with a menacing air. "You would do well to learn it, rather than presuming upon our past contact to make a nuisance of yourself."

Then, rather quietly, Lenox said something that stopped him in his tracks. "I know you're being bought off."

The transformation in Fowler was extraordinary. He tried to bear up under the truth of the accusation for a moment, but it wasn't possible. As he spoke initially a domineering, imposing man, he now drew inward, seemed to get smaller, looked tired and, most of all, old. Lenox was right. The burst of insight had come, funnily enough, from that unreadable blue book—the one on corruption.

"Of course not," he muttered.

"The truth is in your face, Mr. Fowler—and I can think of no reason on earth why you would behave toward me as you have, when our relationship has always been cordial."

"Paid? Don't talk foolery."

"Yes—by Ludo Starling, to look the other way."

"No!"

"About a day after the murder, I would hazard. I'm here in part to speak to someone about it."

The dam broke. "You can't do that!" cried Fowler.

"Oh?" said Lenox coldly. "I understand that you were going to let an innocent man go to trial, Jack Collingwood—testify against him—perhaps even send him to hang. That I do understand."

"No! It's not true, I swear on Christ's name. For God's sake, shut the door, come in, come in."

Lenox entered the office, reluctant to be alone with Fowler but certain the man had information. "He paid you, then? Ludo Starling?"

"Yes."

Lenox had resisted heretofore believing that Ludo was the killer. Based both on the man's mien (his rather hapless, debauched life was nonetheless lived without cruelty to others) and the facts (it was his son, for God's sake), it had never seemed like the likeliest truth. Now the final barriers to his credulity fell away. *How unknowable man is,* he thought.

"I can't believe you accepted money from him."

"You don't know the circumstances, Lenox." The inspector sat back in his large oak chair, underneath a certificate praising his work from the Lord Mayor of London, and lit a small cigar. While it was clenched in his teeth he reached into a low drawer of his desk, pulled a bottle of whisky out, and poured two tots of it into a pair of dingy glasses. "Here you are," he said, his voice weak. "Have a drink with me at least."

"What circumstances?" asked Lenox.

Fowler smiled a bittersweet smile and took a puff on his cigar. "We're very different men, you and I," he said. "It's all very well for you to take the high ground on a subject like money, knowing full well that in the normal run of life it would never come up between us. But do you know what my father did?"

"What?"

"He was a pure collector." Lenox grimaced unintentionally, and Fowler laughed. "Not so nice, is it? No, it wasn't then."

Lenox knew of pure collectors; they had formed part of his reading on cholera. They were men—very poor men—who scavenged for dog and human waste, which they then sold to farms. It took extremely long workdays in extremely unpleasant places to make a living at it.

"I don't understand the connection of that to Ludo Starling," said Lenox.

"No; you wouldn't. While I was using tea leaves four times to get all the flavor of them, living in a house that smelled of—well, why mince words? It smelled of shit! Yes, you can make all the unpleasant faces you want, but while I was living there you were in your father's house, looked after by nannies, eating off of silver, learning about what your old ancestors did at, at Agincourt . . . no, we're very different, you and I."

Lenox felt on uncertain ground now. This was a tender spot for him. Money was the great unexamined area of his conscience, in a way. "But you took bribery, Grayson, and you have a job now. You're not a pure collector. That was your father."

The look on Fowler's face was contemptuous. "You know about it, do you? Did you know that I have nine brothers and sisters, and that of us all I'm the only one with a decent job? That I've given them nearly every cent I earned to keep them in food and clothes, to try to educate their children, and that four of them have died anyway, of that blasted cholera? You have a brother, I know. Can you imagine burying him, Mr. Lenox?"

"No."

"I have my house, Mr. Lenox—a modest enough affair, but it took me ten years to buy it. Beyond that, nothing except my next wage packet from the Yard . . . and last year I found out that I'm getting too old to stay on here."

"What?"

"There'll be my pension, but that's only enough for tea and toast. So yes, I've taken a few pounds here and there. Always in cases when I thought I knew better than the law. Can you judge me for it?"

The answer was that he couldn't. No. It was possible of course that Fowler was spinning a story for him, playing for sympathy, but something final and confessional in the man's air convinced Lenox it was all true.

"Well, but what about Collingwood?" asked Lenox with a struggle.

"He would have been free next week."

"Why next week?"

But Fowler was in his own world. He stood up and looked through the window, which was flung with a few raindrops. "Do you know when I joined the Yard?" he said. "It was the best thing that ever happened to me."

"When?"

"1829. I was one of the first peelers. Fifteen years of age, but I looked eighteen. Thirty-eight years ago, it was."

Lenox nearly gasped. In 1829 Sir Robert Peel— one of the great politicians of the last century, famed for the greatest maiden speech ever given in Parliament—had founded the modern police force. He started with a thousand constables, the peelers. Over time they had taken as a nickname not his last but his first name: They were bobbies. To have been among the first rank was an honor, and Fowler was surely one of the few dozen who remained alive.

"I never knew that," said Lenox and could hear the awe in his own voice.

Proudly, Fowler nodded. "I always drink to Sir Bobby," he said and nodded toward a dusty pencil portrait of Peel as a young man that Lenox had missed before. "I met him four times. Once he asked if I had heard who won the fourth race at Goodwood. That was the only time we said anything other than hello."

Lenox smiled despite himself. "You said—"

"Can you imagine what that meant to me? My brothers and sisters worked the worst jobs— dipping matches or out with my father—and so had I. It was on a lark that I applied to be a peeler. I had always had good marks, when they could afford to keep me in school, but to be *selected*, Mr. Lenox—to be *chosen*—can you understand that? Birth selected you; I had to wait fifteen years. And then, the greatest day of my life, when I was plucked from the constables and allowed to train as an inspector! Can you imagine the honor, to a boy like me?"

"Yes," murmured Lenox.

Fowler, who had been at the window, now faced Lenox. "I've given this work every ounce of my being. You know that."

"I thought I did."

"I cannot apologize for accepting money. I needed it, not for myself alone, and after thirty-eight years the Yard is going to turn me away. That—no, that I could not brook."

Lenox didn't know what he should do with this information, but he knew what he would do. Nothing, as long as Fowler pointed him toward the truth. His own conscience wasn't strong enough.

"Listen," he said rather desperately. "You said Collingwood would be out of Newgate next week. Why?"

Fowler waved a dismissive hand. "Paul Starling will be out of the country by then," he said and drained his drink.

chapter forty-five

"Just a moment—Paul Starling?"

Fowler looked at him. "You didn't know?"

"I assumed it was Ludo."

"Why did you think Paul was being sent away on such short notice?"

Lenox looked stunned. "I know Collingwood took the blame because he wanted to protect Paul, but it didn't add up for me. What can the motive have been?"

Fowler shrugged. "I don't know. Mr. Starling saw it all happen, apparently. He laid out the facts before me, and I decided that a young man's life could still have value."

This inflamed Lenox. "What about Frederick Clarke's life? That didn't have value?"

Fowler sighed. "I didn't say it was easy to look

in the glass every morning as I shave, but I've explained to you why I did it already."

"There's a mother sitting in a hotel in Hammersmith right now, crying her eyes out."

"Would it really have helped her to know that Paul Starling was in prison? Between his father's connections and his youth he wouldn't have swung for it, I don't think."

"Leave all that aside—how does Ludo being stabbed fit into this theory?"

"I don't know. Perhaps it was a way to pin the blame on Collingwood."

"My God!" said Lenox. "Don't you see that the stabbing suits *Ludo* perfectly as an alibi, not his son? Did you even bother to find out that Ludo was Frederick Clarke's father?"

Fowler blanched. "His what?"

Lenox was in no mood for explanation. "There's every chance Ludo killed the boy and blamed Paul to keep them all safe."

"There's—no, it was Paul! The mother knew about it, too—she came here weeping, begging me for lenience!"

Lenox chuckled grimly. "I see now why Ludo came to me, at least. I never quite understood that. He must have wanted someone to bribe, and thought he would test the waters with both of us. My reaction was less civil than yours, apparently."

"I assure you Paul—"

"How did you intend to get Jack Collingwood out of Newgate, can I ask?"

"Telling them the truth! Ludo said he would come forward and confess that he had seen his son do it."

"You believed him? The stupidity, man—my God."

Fowler looked horrified. "But he swore—"

"To a man who had accepted a bribe from him! What pressure could you have exerted on him, may I ask? No—I must be off."

Lenox stood up, and his head, which had felt quite under his control as he sat, gave a twinge and started to throb like a heartbeat. Nevertheless he just managed to turn to the door.

"Wait! Lenox!" cried Fowler, standing up, too. "What about me?"

"You?" Lenox paused, and remembered the story about Fowler in the peelers. "Do you have enough money now?"

He nodded slightly. "I suppose."

Lenox saw that there had been other times—perhaps many—when Fowler had taken money. Perhaps it had begun nobly, but it had turned into base greed. "Are you quite rich?"

"No!"

"The Gauss imbroglio—I wondered at the time that you couldn't solve it." This was the murder of a diplomat from whom quite secret papers had been taken the year before.

Fowler tilted his head in miserable assent. "It was the cousin."

"Gauss's? Ah—I see. He sold them to a foreign government and cut you in on the proceeds. Yes. Well, Grayson, if you retire this week I can leave it alone. I've known you to do good work, after all."

Fowler cringed with gratitude. "Instantly— straight away. Reasons of health—easiest thing in the world."

Without responding, Lenox turned and left.

Out in the street it had started to rain hard, gray in the sky, with wind gusting the raindrops every which way. Nonetheless Dallington was stood there, waiting, and Lenox felt a wave of respect and admiration for him.

"We may have to swim out!" called the young lord.

"There are usually cabs at Brown's Hotel—let's walk there."

Eventually they reached Hampden Lane, a little wetter than they had ever been before. Lenox tipped the driver handsomely, and they dashed inside.

Dallington had heard about the meeting with Fowler on the drive there, and they had only intended to regroup before going to the Starling house. But Lady Jane was waiting at the door and insisted Lenox rest for an hour or two.

After arguing only halfheartedly—for his head

did hurt—Lenox said, "Will you see what you can find out about Paul?"

"Find what out?" asked Dallington.

"Whether he's left the country. If he hasn't, you might try to sneak a word with him."

"I'm sure he's under lock and key."

There were fuller reports in the morning newspapers about the attack on Lenox, and as he rested he cast a critical eye over them, looking to see whether any marked the connection with Ludo. In fact the only bystander named was Dallington, and the comments from Scotland Yard were diffident. It would be out of the news tomorrow.

What did it mean, he wondered? Had it been foolish to leave the house today? Was the attack even related to the Starling case? Or was it another alibi Ludo had created for himself, in the vein of the butcher's attack?

His head ached, and he prodded the bandage above the wound gingerly, looking for the spot that hurt. Tossing the newspaper to one side, he picked up a fresh blue book. He was in the back sitting room, a small, quiet chamber where they often read in the evenings, stretched out on a sofa. The small fireplace nearby was burning bright orange, keeping out the cold of the rain.

The blue book was, for a change, absorbing. It was about perhaps the most significant political issue of the day, Irish home rule. On the first day of 1801 Parliament had passed a bill absorbing Ireland into Great Britain, and ever since then there had been bitter, occasionally violent opposition by the majority of the Irish people. Lenox had always been of two minds on the subject; the Irish would be independent sooner or later, it seemed clear, but in the meanwhile it was perhaps to the benefit of both nations that they be joined.

There were those within his party who would have perceived this as a treacherous viewpoint —who regarded home rule as absolutely and unquestionably a right of the Irish—and as he read on he realized that his opinions, which he had always thought so carefully formed, were based on ideas rather than facts. The book taught him a great deal he hadn't known, and troubled his mind on whether his more vociferous friends weren't correct.

Some time after he had begun reading, Lady Jane brought him a plate of sliced oranges.

"Your brother has been by twice," she said, sitting by him as he ate. "He was very worried."

"You told him I was doing well?"

"I did. He said he would come by later in the day, and asked when you thought you could come back to Parliament."

"The home rule debate will be interesting." Lenox frowned. "Although I want to see this case through, at the least."

She looked at him with a mix of sympathy and concern. "Which is more important to you?"

He thought about it and then gave an honest answer. "I don't know."

chapter forty-six

It was time to go confront Ludo once and for all, he decided. The die was cast. He would wait for Dallington—it was the case in which the lad had had the most involvement, and it was his due to be there at the end—and then go. Whether the murderer was Paul or, as he now suspected, Ludo himself (but why?), the truth would have to come out soon.

When Dallington arrived back some hours later he looked tired. "I've been all over this blasted city," he said, "without finding a trace of Paul Starling."

"No? Perhaps he really did leave from Norfolk, as Elizabeth said. I didn't think it possible."

"No, I don't think he did. He was booked into a first-class berth on a ship called the *Bruce*, which carries indentured servants from Trinidad to other colonies and ends here. It makes port in three cities along the way."

"Has it left?"

"It has—yesterday—but I couldn't establish whether he was on it." Dallington, who had been in the doorway, strode over and mixed himself a rum with tonic water. "The chap who books passengers on the *Bruce* gets paid when the ship leaves, and apparently he drinks himself half to death every time. I didn't have the heart to visit forty different taverns in the Dials, so I came back."

"Nobody else might have seen him?"

"They *might* have, quite easily. Whether they did or not—well, it's a busy dock, of course, and none of them were impressed by my vague questions about Paul Starling."

Lenox nodded. "Thank you for trying," he said. "It was well done to find out that he was booked on the *Bruce*."

"I daresay he's on board, having a whale of a time playing cards with these poor indentured fellows," said Dallington. "But where does that leave us?"

Lenox stood up and, despite a wave of light-headedness, said, "At the end. We must go and confront Ludo."

Dallington looked impressed. "Fair enough. Let me finish my drink and we'll go. Won't he be at Parliament, though?"

"We're not sitting tonight—tomorrow is the great debate about home rule."

It was dark out, the days shortening, and still

there was a threat of drizzle in the air. Lenox, impatient, didn't bother waiting the fifteen minutes for his own horses to be rubbed down and his carriage to be readied, and instead hailed a cab. The drive was a short one.

They arrived at the Starling mansion in time to hear Elizabeth Starling's usually gentle voice saying, "Now polish it again!"

"Yes, ma'am," came the tearful reply.

Dallington reddened and clicked his tongue indignantly—the girl was Jenny Rogers, as they could both hear.

It wasn't Elizabeth who answered, however; they heard her footsteps (or someone else's) walking briskly away from the entrance after they had knocked.

It was Tiberius Starling who opened the door for them. "No damn butler," he said moodily.

"That will be fixed soon enough," answered Lenox with a broad smile. Then he noticed a fresh red welt on the old uncle's cheek.

He didn't say anything, of course—manners forbore it—but Tiberius must have seen his glance. With the occasionally excessive frankness and confidentiality of old gentlemen, he leaned into them and said, "That devil woman did it. Threw a book at me, one I had left lying on the table. She's in a fearful temper. About Paul, I expect."

"I'm extremely sorry to hear it," said Lenox.

"Come in—Ludo's at his desk."

Elizabeth Starling was indeed in a fearful temper. It was no wonder, of course. Her son was gone, in all likelihood off to the colonies, and either the boy or his father was a murderer.

Ludo's face again fell when he saw who his visitors were, and he started to say what he had before. "A damn intrusion" was his greeting to them, "a nuisance of the first order and—"

Lenox interrupted him. "I had an interesting discussion with Inspector Fowler. About your friendship."

Ludo, nonplussed, stopped talking for a few seconds. "Oh?" he said at last, in an attempt to be brazen. "At least he's competent enough to be employed as an inspector. A pair of bumbling amateurs, you two."

Lenox shook his head gently. "It's no good, Ludo."

"What do you mean?"

"We know far more than we did—enough, I should say."

"What do you mean?" he said again. He was seated at his desk still, not having risen to greet them, and Lenox could see the stress in his visage—of lying, of guilt, of sleepless nights.

"You've reached an agreement with an inspector of Scotland Yard. You paid him money in order to conceal a crime. Both of you will appear before the bench for it. Your trial will be in the House of Lords, yes"—this was customary for all members of Parliament and the nobility—"though I don't know that it will matter. What sickens me is that you've let Jack Collingwood sit in Newgate Prison, wondering whether he'll be hanged by the neck until he's dead."

"No!"

"Even though he's an innocent man."

"How do you—how do you think you know this?" asked Ludo.

"It's no use bluffing. Between this and Frederick Clarke's true identity—as your son—I thought it was time to consult with Scotland Yard. Because we're acquaintances I wanted to give you the chance to confess first."

At last now Ludo broke down. "I didn't kill the boy," he said. "I gave him money, for heaven's sake! I looked after him! We were—well, friends, you might say! I only paid Fowler because I was trying to protect someone I love."

"Was it—"

Lenox silenced Dallington's question with a look. It was always best to let them ramble on.

"You must believe me, Charles." A pleading look came into his eyes. "You must. I didn't kill him. I wouldn't have, never."

Very gently, still not wanting to intrude upon the confession, Lenox said, "Paul? Did you want to protect Paul?"

"Paul's gone," was all Ludo said.

"He isn't," bluffed Dallington. "I checked at the docks."

Ludo shook his head. "He's gone. Collingwood can come out of jail."

"I checked the docks!"

Lenox quietly said, "He's in Wiltshire, isn't he. Starling Hall. I imagine Elizabeth couldn't bear to see him go overseas."

Ludo nodded just perceptibly. "Yes."

"Ludo inherited it last year," said Lenox to Dallington. "It's empty, other than staff, of course. I imagine Paul could stay well concealed there for some time."

It was all clear enough. Paul Starling had killed Frederick Clarke. Since that awful moment Ludo had scrambled to protect his younger son, shifting the blame to anyone he could, paying out money to whomever he could.

There were two things Lenox didn't understand, still. The first was motive. It had seemed so clear: Ludo killed Clarke because the sudden appearance of a bastard son would have destroyed his plans for a title to pass on to Alfred—perhaps for a title at all. Paul, though—what did Paul care? Whether Frederick Clarke or Alfred Starling was next in line surely was irrelevant to the youngest son, wasn't it?

The second point was even more puzzling: Who had attacked him, Charles Lenox? The plan to steal Paul away to Starling Hall had already been set in motion. Had Ludo wanted to clear his own name, too?

"Who attacked me?" Lenox asked. "Were you trying to give yourself an alibi? But no," he said to himself, "that doesn't make sense. You already had an alibi from the butcher attack."

"I didn't know anybody was going to attack you," said Ludo mournfully. He sank back into his chair and put his face in his hands. "There's so much I would take back if I could—I should never have protected—"

There was a sound outside the door, a "shush!" in a woman's voice.

And suddenly Lenox put it all together, what had been invisible for so long. It wasn't Paul Starling who had killed Freddie Clarke. He was innocent.

I only paid Fowler because I was trying to protect someone I love.

The wound on Tiberius's face, and a dozen other details.

It was Elizabeth Starling who had attacked Lenox.

It was she who had killed Frederick Clarke.

chapter forty-seven

A dozen things crowded Lenox's mind: Elizabeth's occasional temper, which he had seen over the past weeks, Ludo's seemingly inexplicable tangle of actions, her ironclad alibi for the butcher stabbing, when she had been in Cambridge. Her intense devotion to her sons, and her sometimes scorn for Ludo; it would have killed her to know that his title went to a footman, of all people, another woman's son, rather than her Alfred. Her soft, gentle exterior, her quiet manner—he saw now that they concealed a character that was dreadful and dark, capable of evil things.

He thought back to the day of the murder. She had come into the alley. Why? At the time she had said she wanted to see if the constable was hungry or thirsty, but now this seemed unlikely. It was much likelier she would have sent a servant out. Did she want to move the brick? Conceal some other clue?

And the attack on Lenox: She had been standing at the door to see Ludo away, no doubt, and heard him come. When she learned the secret was out, eavesdropping on the conversation in the street, she must have flown into a rage.

There was the note! In Frederick Clarke's room, the note asking him when his birthday was. She must have found out that he was Ludo's legitimate son, and wanted to know exactly how old the lad was.

These ideas flooded his brain, one tripping on the heels of another, but he didn't have time to articulate any of them.

Ludo had stood up. "What!" he called. "They know about Fowler. They know about poor Freddie."

Elizabeth Starling flung the door open, her face transfigured by rage, and screamed, "Shut up, you fool!"

Dallington, who was still in the dark, looked taken aback, but for Lenox it was the final nail in the coffin.

"You killed Clarke, didn't you?" he asked very softly.

The three other people in the room froze, but he walked to Ludo's desk and rapped it with his knuckles, eyes cast down, brow furrowed, thinking it through.

"It makes sense to me now. Poor Ludo isn't a violent type. He's happy with a game of cards and a glass of brandy. But you—you're a plotter."

She was bright red. "You've always been a small man, Lenox. Get out of my house."

"I don't think I shall. What happened? When did Ludo tell you? Or was it Freddie who told you? Yes—I suspect that's right." He started pacing up and down the room. "Freddie wanted to be acknowledged as Ludo's son and heir, the heir to any Starling title, the heir to Starling Hall. In the heat of the moment—or did you do it coolly?—I can't decide—at any rate, you pried a brick from the ground and waited at the bend in the alley, where you knew he passed often enough."

"No!"

"Then you did it. Smiled to his face and struck a blow on the back of his head as he walked away. I shouldn't have been fooled by your gentle manners, I see now."

"Lenox, what are you saying?" asked Dallington, appalled. "A woman—a gentle-woman—to have killed—"

Ludo interrupted. "It's true," he muttered, almost involuntarily.

"*Ludovic!*" screamed Elizabeth Starling, her fists tightly clenched and trembling.

"I hate this," he said. "Because of you—to have been stabbed—our son cast out of our home—our faithful butler—my son! Freddie was my son!" He descended into incoherence now, muttering single words that formed a loose narrative in his own mind.

Lenox saw that the spell of her personality,

her willpower, had been broken when the secret came out.

"Why did you cover for her? Why agree to be stabbed?"

"She's my wife," was all he managed to stammer out. "But this folly has to end, Eliza."

As Lenox turned to see Elizabeth Starling's reaction, two things happened: He heard a sound behind him, and Dallington shouted "Lenox!"

She was attacking him again. She had picked up a good-sized gold clock and had it above her head.

Dallington, who had jumped to his feet, was too late. Fortunately Lenox had managed to spring around her strike and grasp her from behind. She struggled mightily against his grip, but soon she let the clock go and fell in a heap into an armchair, sobbing without restraint.

Lenox, his heart pounding, felt the bandage on his head. Ludo and Dallington were standing beside him, looking shocked.

"I think we must call the police constable," said Lenox, "but perhaps a doctor would be better first." He picked up the bell and rang for the maid, whom he directed to fetch both.

It was strange to be in that quintessentially English room, with its hunting prints, its lines of leather-bound books, its fireplace, its old portraits along the wall, and to imagine all the violence that it had borne. Both Ludo's careless life—marrying a maid, having a child with her, and later accepting him in as a footman (the madness!)—and more importantly Elizabeth Starling's raging anger, her dark heart.

As she sobbed, dispossessed now beyond a doubt of whatever life she had made for herself, he almost felt pity for her. Then he remembered the other mother, the one in a hotel in Hammersmith, slowly coming apart at the seams.

"Come, Ludo," he said. "You shall have a drink. This will all be over soon. I'm sorry you had to endure it."

Ludo looked at Lenox, tears in his puffy, dissipated eyes. "My own son" was all he said. "The insanity of it."

"What happened?" asked Dallington. "You wanted the blame to fall on Paul?"

"No!" It wasn't Ludo but Elizabeth who spoke, between sobs, from the chair. Despite her anguish she couldn't stand to see her son's name fouled. "He saw it. He saw me. Then when the trial was close he refused to let Collingwood stay in jail any longer."

"And you—you let Collingwood believe Paul was a murderer? Your son?"

"Why do you think I'm crying, you halfwit?" she said. "Because of Paul. I don't care whether Freddie Clarke burns in hell. Or his father, for that matter."

"But I helped you!" said Ludo, shocked again.

"You—you told me we had to protect ourselves! Our family!"

"I'm not going to say another word," Elizabeth answered.

In its dimensions it was more like a Greek tragedy than anything he had ever come across in his career: the striving bastard (who turned out not to be a bastard at all), educating himself, seeking the approval of a diffident father; the mad wife; the incidental victims; the double-crossing and lies. Dallington was glassy-eyed. There was none of the satisfaction that usually comes at the end of a case.

In due course the doctor arrived, and so the wheels of bureaucracy began their slow revolutions. He gave her a sedative; she was docile enough but, true to her promise, didn't speak. After him the police came, and then more police—the inspector, Rudd, was extremely troubled, needless to say—and soon she was taken away.

Rudd stayed behind, a bluff, genial, stupid man with a great red nose, the sort who would be the most popular man at his local public house. He was one of the two or three men who had risen after the death of Inspector Exeter.

"What do you reckon, Mr. Lenox?" he said. "Can she really have done it?"

"She admitted as much."

He shook his head as if he didn't like that

much. "And attacked you! Lady Macbeth ain't in it!"

"She ain't," agreed Dallington, still awestruck. Then a thought occurred to him. "I daresay Collingwood will be relieved."

"Mightily," said Lenox.

"Ah, you've put your finger on the thing, young man—is he innocent? Was he not complicit? What about the green butcher's apron?"

Both Dallington and Lenox turned uneasy eyes on Ludo, who was sitting in the corner alone, a devastated man; everything in his mien said he hadn't realized the extent of his wife's evil.

"He certainly wasn't involved," said Lenox, "unless he agreed to go to Newgate to protect the Starlings."

There was a tremendous commotion at the door just then, and two constables with their hands full of a fifty-year-old woman staggered back into the room.

"Where is she! I'll kill her!" cried Frederick's mother. "Where is that devil woman?" Her wild gaze alighted on Ludo. "Oh, Luddy!" she cried and in two or three steps fell on him.

To Lenox's surprise he returned the embrace, and tears seemed to escape his eyes, too. "I'm so sorry," Ludo said, patting her on the back. "Our poor son. He was such a lovely boy."

In that instant Lenox wondered whether Ludo had loved her all along.

chapter forty-eight

The next day Lenox resumed his place in the House of Commons. He was determined to make a go of it; the brief spark of excitement that the cholera problem had given him was fresh in his mind still, and he realized that to last in Parliament you had to be one of two sorts of people. You could be the dogged, workaday type (there had been plenty of Prime Ministers and Chancellors of the Exchequer who belonged to this category, and it was by no means lesser), and spend long hours in study and work. Or you could be the sort who felt strongly the inciting passion of ideas, and work to bend other men to your will.

He had no chance of being the first kind. It wasn't in his makeup. But he could be the second kind, he hoped.

In the meanwhile it was Graham who filled the first role. As the days passed after the case had concluded and Lenox spent more and more time in his office, he found out that Graham had inexhaustible reserves of energy to devote even to the minutest issues. He was a wonderful taskmaster to Frabbs, both cajoling him into better work and teaching him how the work was to be done.

Lenox ran into Percy Field one morning in the halls of Parliament, and Field stopped him to say thank you again for the invitation to Lady Jane's Tuesday.

"You're all over the papers," he said after they had exchanged "thank you" and "you're welcome." "Elizabeth Starling?"

"Poor Ludo—I wonder whether he'll return to the House, or if he's finished."

"He's back at Starling Hall, isn't he?"

"Yes."

He was there with Frederick Clarke's mother. Before he had left he had come to Hampden Lane, some three days after his wife's arrest, to apologize for the past weeks. As they sat in front of the fireplace, lit because the first frost of the autumn had been in the gardens and parks of the city that morning, Lenox studied the other man. His face was pained and older than before. He had taken the glass of claret Lenox offered but, in a way that was very unlike himself, didn't touch it.

"Do you ever feel you've wasted your life?" he asked, an exceedingly, even inappropriately intimate question, but of course Lenox was prepared to make allowances for him.

"I daresay everyone feels that way once in a while."

Ludo smiled. "No—I see you don't know what I mean."

"Perhaps not."

"I'm taking Alfred to Starling Hall. Paul is there."

"How are they?"

"Alfred is bewildered—between you and me, he's rather a bewildered kind of soul—and Paul is angry. I think it will do them both good to get to Cambridge. They go next week."

"Have you seen Elizabeth?"

"No," he said shortly, "but Collingwood was in the house this morning. I poured my heart out to him." He laughed. "I don't think he forgave me. I wouldn't either."

"I can't imagine he would, no."

"There are no criminal charges to be laid against me." Ludo paused. "Tell me, will you turn Fowler in?"

"He and I have our own agreement."

"I wonder whether you would forgive me, Lenox."

"Certainly."

"Don't be hasty. She might have killed you, you know, on the street outside of our house. D'you know, I feel now as if it was all a dream —a bizarre dream."

"She was a strong-willed woman."

"That's like saying London is a biggish village," responded Ludo, with a flash of his old bantering ways.

"Could I ask you a question, Ludo? Was Derbyshire supposed to vouch for you? Is that why you didn't sign in?"

Ludo sighed. "Yes," he said. "That's right. If I had signed in, when I arrived it would have showed I wasn't at the club during the time Freddie was murdered. I was home, in fact."

Lenox nodded. "I woke up in the middle of the night and thought of it. After Elizabeth murdered Freddie, you went to the club to create an alibi for yourself. You must have tried to make people think you had already been there for many hours."

"Yes. I lost money to Derbyshire so he would remember I was there, and said as often as I could that I had been there most of the day. I hoped they all would misremember how long I had been there, and in the end I said to Derbyshire point-blank: 'Do you know how long I've been here? Ten hours. Time slips away, doesn't it?' It didn't do me any good, apparently."

There was a long pause. Both men's eyes turned away from each other, Ludo's to the fire, Lenox's outside to the street, where men with upturned collars trotted by, trying to get indoors as fast as possible.

"Could I ask you another question?" asked Lenox at length.

"Oh? What's that?" asked Ludo, startled from a reverie. "Of course."

"The title—was that only important to Elizabeth? That Alfred should inherit? Or that there should be a title at all?"

"You're a mind reader, I sometimes think. It was the subject that was just in my head." He settled back in his chair, a pensive look on his face. "You've heard of old Cheshire Starling, I assume?"

"Yes, of course."

"You've no idea what it's like to have as your first landed ancestor a common man—a blacksmith, no less. We could have owned three-quarters of Wiltshire and none of the families there would have cared about us. Oh, there were the merchants. To be sure we were above them, or the new generations. We had some status. We built churches.

"But a blacksmith! My father brooded about it every day of his life. When I did something wrong I was the son of a whore and a smith to him. When we were snubbed by the Duke of Argyllshire it was 'Back to the hammer and tongs.' It was the worst terror to be taken out to the smithy and beaten by the blacksmith there."

Lenox didn't speak; Ludo, lost in reminiscence, didn't seem to mind.

"Elizabeth made it worse. Her father was a lord, yes, but only an Irish lord . . . I think we—what is it called when two people live inside the same dream together, Lenox?"

"I don't know."

"There must be a word for it." He waved a dismissive hand and stood up. "It's all history now, anyway. I'm taking Marie, too, with me. To the Hall. Marie Clarke. Perhaps she'll forgive me one day."

"I hope so."

Ludo gathered his cloak and hat. "There are second chances in life, after all. Aren't there?"

It had indeed been in the papers, and inevitably Lenox's name had, too. Elizabeth Starling likely wouldn't hang, but she would certainly be in prison for the rest of her life. Lenox had debated in his own mind whether to go visit her, and seek out more explanation, but in the end he decided that there wasn't anything else. He knew what there was to know.

Although there was a sour postscript from Percy Field, in the hallway.

"Tell me," Lenox said, "was Ludo close to receiving a title? In the New Year's Honors?"

Titles were in the hands of the Queen, of course, but more and more often she received recommendations from Field's superior, the Prime Minister. Field would almost certainly have seen the list.

He snorted. "Mr. Lenox, have you heard of a man of Ludovic Starling's age and position becoming a baron out of the blue? It was the purest fantasy. He agitated, to be sure, for it, but even to be knighted! Why—it was impossible."

"If you'll allow me to ask something rude, Mr. Field: Are you only saying so now, because of what happened last week?"

Field laughed. "I would tell you the truth if it were so, Mr. Lenox. You're a man who can keep his lips sealed. It was a fantasy, nothing more and nothing less."

chapter forty-nine

That was a heavy-hearted fall for Charles Lenox. As September passed into October and October into November, he felt weighed down by both the needless misery of the case and the slight, constant disappointment of Parliament not being the paradise he had wished it. This he came to terms with slowly, but surely; it was his duty. He referred two cases that came his way to Dallington, who solved the first and botched the second terribly. They were no longer daily companions, but they had taken to dining together two or three times a week. What they did during these meals was go over old cases, teasing through the clues, Lenox pushing his apprentice gently in the right direction, teaching him to think like a detective. Gradually Lenox discovered that they were the best parts of his week, these dinners—a visit to his old life. Still, when the third case came in early December, he turned it toward Dallington and, after the entreating visitor had gone, turned back to a new blue book.

It was around this time that he realized there had been a third unhappiness, too. His marriage. He and Lady Jane were best friends as ever, and they had a dozen different parties and balls they might have attended each week.

Yet he found he wanted something different. Each time he was with Toto, Thomas, and George, his heart ached with envy.

This blue period finally lifted one day in the first week of December. They had been at the McConnells' that night for supper, and the McConnells were returning the visit the next day, to trim Lady Jane and Lenox's Christmas tree. As they were riding home in the carriage, Lenox sensed that Lady Jane had come close to bringing up the subject of a child. At the last moment, however, she didn't.

He was in Parliament the next morning, meeting with a committee. There was no session in the evening, and he returned to their double-house on Hampden Lane hungry for lunch.

Instead of Kirk it was Jane herself who met him at the door.

"Will you guess where I've been this morning?" she asked.

"Where?" he said, giving her a kiss on her soft, pink cheek.

"Only to Kent!"

He hung up his cloak. "Have you really? Whatever for?"

"It was an hour each way—not far, really—but I found you a present."

"In Kent? Thank you, darling. You're lovely. May I open it after lunch? I'm famished."

He was headed toward his study, about to open the door, and she said, "You're going to open it this second."

He frowned, puzzled, until he twisted the door.

Two puppies, neither of them bigger than a loaf of bread, came bounding out of the room in a state of profound excitement.

One was dark, midnight black, and the other was a pure white gold. They were retrievers. Both of them had floppy ears and thick coats, and they tumbled over each other into Lenox's ankles, barking in happy voices at his arrival.

With an enormous smile on his face he bent down to them. "What are they?" he said.

"I would have thought a child could identify them as dogs—puppies."

"I mean—well, why?"

Then Lady Jane did something touching to him; she came and knelt by him, letting the puppies jump into her lap, and put an arm through his. "I'm not ready—not quite yet," she said. "Can we wait one more year?"

He looked at her, and love, love greater than himself, filled his heart. "Of course," he said.

"I thought perhaps we could practice on them."

"A capital notion, that. What shall we call them?"

"I want to call the black one Bear. She looks like a bear to me."

"And the white one?"

She laughed. "Well—he reminds me of a rabbit."

Lenox smiled. "Bear and Rabbit. It's settled."

As if they understood, Bear and Rabbit started to bark again, then chased each other around Lenox, first in one direction and then the other, occasionally felled by their new legs or stopping for a judicious sniff of shoe or rug. He loved them already.

It was later that afternoon that his blue period truly ended. He was sorting through old mail (and had just found Clara Woodward's wedding invitation) when Graham, who stayed long hours in Whitehall, came home unaccustomedly early. He drew up short when he saw Bear and Rabbit, remembered they weren't his responsibility, and then made an urgent petition for an immediate conference with Lenox.

"Whatever is it?"

Graham, usually so reserved, was flushed with enthusiasm. "It's your speech, sir. They want you to give your maiden speech."

"What?"

"The party leaders. They'd like you to speak in two days' time. During the afternoon session, sir, when all the press will be there! In time for the evening papers."

"A speech? In two days? Not now, Bear!" he said to the little black retriever, who was pawing at his shoe.

"Yes, sir."

Suddenly every nerve in Lenox's body began to tingle, and he felt his brain begin to race. And in the same moment he realized: This was the thrill he had wanted all along.

The next fifty hours was a period of ceaseless activity. Lenox, closeted in his study, skipped the blue books that accumulated on his desk and instead wrote feverishly. Graham would come into the room every half hour or so and take away a much crossed and scratched and corrected piece of paper, consult with Lenox about his intentions for this part of the speech, and then take it to Frabbs, who was stationed in the dining room, to make a fair copy for further revision.

(Frabbs was delighted. He had a grand table to himself and plenty of time to draw, and the dogs were constantly whining at his heel for him to get on the floor and roll about with them—which, it should be said, he very conscientiously did only after he had copied out a page and locked the door.)

The other presence in the house was Edmund. Though he was a necessity to his party, he resisted every appeal and skipped two straight days of Parliament in order to sit with his brother, converse when Charles felt he was stuck, and mull over ideas with him. They decided together, after a long conversation, that he shouldn't mention cholera—that he should save it. There would be time to come back to it. They took their meals together, down to the chocolate and brandy they each had at two in the morning the day before the speech.

The day.

It arrived far, far sooner than Lenox would have liked. He had committed his speech, which would take twenty minutes or thereabouts, to memory, and as he and Edmund walked down Whitehall he muttered the difficult bits of it to himself over and over, occasionally checking his notes—so that he looked very much like an aristocratic madman, roaming the streets of Mayfair with his minder.

"Have you any advice?" he asked Edmund as they came to the Members' Entrance.

"I've given you nothing but advice for these

last two days, Charles. I should have thought you had far too much of it from me."

"No, no—that was for the speech itself. I mean any advice about delivering the stupid thing."

"Ah—I see. You remember my maiden speech?"

"Oh, yes. I was in the spectators' gallery."

"I had this counsel from a sage old head, Wilson Randolph—been dead for fifteen years—and it worked well enough for me. He said that ten minutes before my speech I should have a glass of wine and a crust of bread to fortify me."

"Fair enough."

Edmund laughed. "After that, I'm afraid you're on your own."

The chamber seemed ten times more imposing than it ever had before, ten times more crowded, its range of faces ten times more judgmental, the Speaker of the House ten times more momentous, the gallery of reporters and spectators ten times more eager for a failure.

His heart in his stomach, Lenox sat through half a dozen parries back and forth, hearing not a word of them, going over in his head each line of his speech. There was the astute slash at the other party's policies on India, the witticism about the daily papers, the stirring (he hoped) final argument about colonial obligation. When it was ten to four he sneaked out of a side door, where Graham was waiting with a glass of wine and a piece of brown bread.

"Good luck, sir," said Graham, who looked as if he were bursting with pride.

"Thank you—the credit is yours. Unless I make a mess of it, of course, in which case you may blame me."

Lenox laughed, Graham frowned, and soon he had drunk off the wine and eaten the bread. He slipped back into the House.

A speech was concluding, and after it was done Lenox raised his leaden arm, his heart beating rapidly, as he knew he must.

"The Right Honorable Gentleman from Stirrington!" cried the Speaker.

Lenox rose, his legs insensate. For strength he chanced a look at his brother.

Edmund returned the gaze. He was a man with a pure, tender heart—less doubtful than his brother's, more open—and as Charles rose to speak, he felt conflicted. He knew that the excitement of the past two days was what his brother really loved, what he thrived on, and he was happy. In another part of his heart, however, he worried that Charles would never again be a detective—that he would live in this less happy profession he had found out of a sense of duty, occasionally excited as he was now but more often dispirited.

And Edmund worried about Charles and Jane.

Lenox himself, who knew perhaps a bit better, shifted his gaze from Edmund to Jane herself.

She was in the spectators' gallery, a gray dress on, the knuckles of her fists white with tension. She gave him a small smile, and to his surprise he realized that it calmed him.

From her he looked out into the chamber, and with a clear, confident voice, began to speak.

Center Point Publishing
600 Brooks Road • PO Box 1
Thorndike ME 04986-0001 USA

(207) 568-3717

US & Canada:
1 800 929-9108
www.centerpointlargeprint.com

CB 3/12

mL